THE SHOCK

(BOOK 1 IN THE AFTER SERIES)

By Scott Nicholson

Copyright ©2013 Scott Nicholson
Haunted Computer Books
ISBN: 978-1-62647-029-3

Haunted Computer Productions, Inc.
P.O. Box 135
Todd, NC 28684 USA

CHAPTER ONE

There were three of them.

She'd stopped naming them a week ago. It had been an amusing distraction for a while—and the Good Lord only knew, she needed distractions—but then they'd all started blending together, the Black-Eyed Susans, the Raisinheads and the Meat Throats.

Now, though, Rachel Wheeler couldn't resist looking through the grimy drugstore window as she waited, crouched in the litter of baby powder and cellophane.

Stumpy.

The one on the right, sitting on the sidewalk bench surrounded by a mountain of bulging plastic bags, was missing his left arm just below the elbow. The wound was swathed in a filthy towel strapped in place with duct tape, stained dark brown at its blunt end.

Stumpy was waiting for a bus that would never come. Rachel couldn't tell if he was a Zaphead. He might just be another of the schizophrenic homeless, one of the underclass that hadn't even noticed that the world had ended. Although gaunt, he didn't appear particularly motivated to kill, obsessed instead with swatting away the flies that swirled around his stump.

He was fifty feet away, and she could outrun him easy. All she had to do was run as if her life depended on it. It wouldn't be much of a challenge because her life had depended on it for days.

A hundred yards down the street, The Beard, the guy

staggering back and forth, was almost certainly a Zaphead. His expression was hidden by the unkempt hair, but he was hunched and his fists were clenched, rage curling around whatever strange energy burned inside of him.

Okay, Beard, you've solved my little dilemma of whether I should head south or head north.

The mountains were her destination, and they lay to the northwest, but she wasn't willing to risk The Beard.

The word "destination" sounded odd in her thoughts, because of the root "destiny." Such abstractions were laughable now, but laughter was the only weapon against the fear that sapped the strength from her legs. And she needed her legs.

Oh, yes, Lord, give me stumps for hands, but please don't mess with my legs.

In this scary new world, in this After, you had to run, dragging your guilt and fear and all the dark weight of Before.

Even if she'd wanted to head south, where not even hope was an option, Chain Guy had other ideas. He was moving through the smoky haze between a Volvo sedan cattycornered in the intersection and an abandoned police car, its doors flung open like the wings of a spastic, grounded bird as it perched with two wheels on the curb.

Chain Guy was dressed in a torn leather jacket, despite the late-August heat—and in Charlotte, the August heat grabbed your throat and scrubbed you with salt water—and he carried a knapsack. Clearly, he was one of the higher-functioning lunatics. The chain in his right hand trailed out on the asphalt behind him, its faint *clink* the sole soundtrack to a scene that had once featured rush-hour traffic.

She ducked lower in the drugstore window, clutching her backpack more closely. The pack was bulging, and she'd needed the dried foods she'd collected, but now, the comfort items felt more like indulgences that would slow her down and maybe get her killed.

Really, toilet paper and tampons, Ray-Ray? Why not grab some hemorrhoid cream and Viagra while you're at it? You can't beat these prices, so you might as well stock up.

She wondered if she should wait it out, to see whether The Beard and Chain Guy squared off. Maybe while they were busy, she could slip out and head down a perpendicular street. It was likely that one or two Zapheads would be on the prowl, but she didn't want to stay there until dark. The store's front door was smashed in, and other scavengers might show up for this unbeatable, once-in-a lifetime, going-out-of-business sale.

The sun was still high, but barely visible through the smoke that curled from the downtown high rises. She suspected a bonfire was raging in the football stadium, too — the wind carried the stench of charred meat.

Chain Guy wrapped loops of his weapon around his forearm until he had a four-foot length. He swung it back and forth, gradually picking up momentum until he was whipping the chain in a circle over his head. He was still about forty yards from The Beard, who still paced back and forth, apparently oblivious to the coming storm.

As the chain *whirred* like a slow helicopter blade, a dog bounded out from behind the police cruiser, snarling and yapping. He was a German shepherd — lean, dark and hungry. The dog made a beeline for Chain Guy, evidently smelling something he didn't like. But the dog must have sensed the reach of the chain, because he halted and lowered himself onto his forelegs, haunches reared as if poised to attack.

Get 'em, boy, Rachel silently cheered, thinking the distraction would give her an opening. She squeezed the straps of her pack, testing the weight and calculating how much it would hinder her speed.

The dog's lips peeled back as he growled. Chain Guy's expression didn't change. He spun the chain faster, almost daring the dog as he headed for The Beard. The shepherd danced forward a few feet and snapped, but Chain Guy kept walking, not breaking stride. The dog apparently didn't like being challenged, so he made a run for Chain Guy's ankles.

The chain lashed out of its orbit and descended with stunning speed, the blow so sudden that Rachel wasn't even sure she'd seen it. Then came the *thwack* as metal hit meat, the chain flaying the dog's rib cage. It emitted one garbled yelp of pain and collapsed. Chain Guy still wore that blank, businesslike expression as he brought the chain around for another blow. This one took out a leg and the shepherd crawled away like a broken spider.

The sickening attack reminded Rachel they weren't playing "Ring Around the Rosie" here. It was dog eat dog. And, they definitely weren't playing. If it came down to it, she'd rather Chain Guy eat the dog than eat her.

If Chain Guy looked to his left, he might have glimpsed her hiding behind the shards of glass in the storefront. Her curiosity was slightly more compelling than her fear, and every bit of information might mean the difference between survival and its opposite. She wasn't sure what the "opposite" was, but it was worse than death.

Chain Guy maintained his pace, but he let the chain slow again above his head. Stumpy hadn't moved from his bench, and The Beard still seemed intent on whatever crack in the asphalt had consumed his entire attention for the past minute.

Or Jesus. Jesus in the oil stain, the rainbow warrior, the light of wisdom.

Rachel bit her lip to keep from giggling. *Don't lose it. Only crazy people lose it, and you know what happens to crazy people.*

Something tumbled from the shelves behind her, near the prescription counter.

She hadn't checked the aisles after seeing the corpse of a child, although the place had seemed dead. But "dead" had a new meaning now.

She tensed, but didn't bolt, because the real threat of Chain Guy outweighed the imaginary threat spawned by a jar falling to the carpet. The Zapheads weren't known for subtlety, so there was zero chance of one of them creeping up on her. No, a Zaphead would roll forward like a Cadillac out of hell, fueled by the frenzy zapping and hissing in its brain.

Chain Guy was busy bearing down on The Beard, so she crawled to the left a few feet and peered around a display of Hallmark cards. A hand stretched out on the floor beside the prescription counter, the fingers twitching.

Could be a Zapper in the last throes of internal combustion.

The hand curled once, twice, and then she recognized it as a beckoning motion. A Zaphead wouldn't beckon. It would go for what it wanted, not lure you closer.

Somebody—a human—was down. And here came the litmus test of After: Did the old codes still apply? Did she still have to love her neighbor? Did she have to treat everyone as a child of God?

Maybe God wouldn't notice just this once. Maybe she could just sit right here near the door and then make a run for it, gasping prayers.

Better to ask for forgiveness than for permission, right?

However, forgiveness probably wasn't a question one wanted to ask of God. Not now, in the After. Rachel tried to look away, she really did, but the hand made another beckoning motion. It looked frail, the fingers knotty and thin. It was not the kind of hand that would wrap around your throat and drag you screaming into the darkness.

Outside, the chain clanked against the asphalt, as if Chain Guy was working out the kinks and getting ready for business.

The hand gave one final gesture, this time just the index finger, motioning *Closer, closer, closer* with an intensity that only silence could fully project.

Still, she resisted the impulse to help, the love-thy-neighbor credo that had been drummed into her from childhood, sitting bedside with her cancer-stricken mother, volunteering at the Humane Society, joining the Wellspring Fellowship's Happy Helpers, and taking counseling classes at UNC-Charlotte. Little Ray-Ray had been on track for a golden-rule life of selfless service. In the Before.

However, she'd been sidetracked.

She wasn't even sure there was a track anymore, because the train had jumped off into a dark, directionless territory.

Rachel looked away from the hand and eyed the door. She could probably get twenty yards down the sidewalk before Chain Guy broke his fixation and noticed her, and maybe that would buy her enough of a jump on him. Her legs were young and limber and strong, built by a cycling addiction. She could outrun him.

Probably.

"Huhhh…"

The wheeze came from behind the prescription counter. She jerked around her neck, and the hand now balled into a fist, as if tapping some last reserve of energy. The whisper came again, weak and broken.

"Huhhh…help…"

Goddamn you, God.

She checked on Chain Guy, still closing in on The Beard, who swayed in obsessed circles. Stumpy sat on the bench as if waiting to feed pigeons. It was just another busy weekday in downtown Charlotte.

Just another day in After.

"Help." The voice of the hand's owner gained volume, and she hissed a "Shhh" in response as she crawled down the aisle. The last thing she needed was for Zapheads to show up, pissed off that they hadn't been invited to the party.

She'd long ago—well, *days* ago, but it had seemed like years—decided that it was selfish to pray for survival and deliverance, but it was righteous to pray for the strength to help others. She'd also promised to live for Chelsea, to spend all the years that had been taken from her little sister—taken by Rachel.

But she couldn't think of that now, or she would become paralyzed, accepting her fate. *Deserving* death. Deserving it because each breath was a selfish act in a world where she had destroyed something beautiful.

As Rachel drew closer, a rank, sour odor assailed her. She'd smelled her share of corpses, with their heavy, sweet fecundity—decay had become so pervasive in After that only a truly sharp odor had a chance of piercing it. Whatever lay behind the counter had achieved that rare status.

The arm pulled itself into the gap and she crawled faster, chafing her knees even through the blue jeans she wore. Her backpack was off-balance, banging against her right hip, and she had to navigate an obstacle course of stuffed animals, jars of nutritional supplements, soft drinks, and other artifacts of a lost culture.

It was darker back here, removed from the sunlight, but not so dark that she had to dig out her flashlight. She wasn't sure she wanted a clear look, anyway, because the sour odor suggested something had turned inside-out.

"Help," the man's voice said again, and she answered, "Okay."

God, I'm trusting you here, and if you're leading me to a horrible, painful death, I swear I'll never speak to you again.

Then she reached the counter and felt concealed enough to rise into a crouch and duck-walk the final ten feet around the counter. The man was curled on his side in a fetal position, wearing a white coat that suggested he'd been the pharmacist on duty at some point, back when duty mattered and pulled a weekly paycheck. Resembling a lighter-skinned Gandhi, he was bald and old and wore rounded glasses with wire frames. A pool of vomit explained the stink, and the flies had already migrated from the child's corpse to check out this new taste sensation.

"You're...one of us," he said.

"Yeah," she said, wishing she could summon that caregiver confidence expounded upon in her counseling textbooks. "Are you hurt?"

He gave a pained smile, and a wet fleck of vomit appeared in the corner of his mouth. "I hurt just fine, thanks."

"Let me help you."

She reached to check the pulse in his neck, but he shook his head. "No, don't save me. For the sake of...all that is holy...let me die."

Great. So he wants me to play Dr. Kevorkian here. Too bad.

She touched his neck, and he didn't resist. His carotid pulse was a weak flutter. It was a wonder that he even had enough strength left to speak.

"Don't save me." His face curdled with an emotion somewhere between anger and defiance.

"Why did you ask for help, then?"

He rolled his eyes down to his other hand, the one that was curled into a fist around something. "I wasn't *asking* for help. I was *offering* it."

His reply startled her. He didn't look like he was in a

position to help anything but the maggots. His breathing grew shallower.

"How many are outside?" he asked.

"Two or three," she said. "I'm not sure about one of them."

He opened his hand, which held an orange prescription vial. "Nembutal," he said. "The easy way out."

So, *he* was the one playing Dr. Kevorkian. She'd seen Nembutal in the animal shelter, where it was used to end the suffering of sick pets. He let the vial roll from his hand and he gave it a weak nudge along the floor, toward her.

"Antiemetics, too," he said.

"Huh? What's that?"

"Don't want to vomit it out before it has a chance to work." His words were slurring now. "I should take the old sawbones advice...of 'Heal thyself'...to heart, huh?"

She wondered how many of them he'd swallowed. Probably far more than enough, if he knew his trade, and he had the look of experience. In a matter of such importance, he'd be dead certain about the dosage levels.

"I'm not ready to die," she said.

"None of us were," he wheezed. His eyelids fluttered.

She checked his pulse again, and she could barely detect the blood making its last sluggish rounds through his circulatory system. At any second, he'd fall unconscious, and then his brain would begin the slow process of turning off the lights until the party was over.

"Do you...want me to pray with you?" she said. She didn't want to ask if he was saved, because that seemed too judgmental for this most personal of moments.

"I'm...good," he said. He nudged the vial toward her. "Here. My final request."

His hand bore a wedding ring, and she wondered about

his wife. Had he "helped" her escape from After? Had he guided her into the next great uncertainty? Maybe he'd even tricked her, grinding the pills into powder and spiking her sweet iced tea.

Take it. May as well let him die feeling helpful.

"Thank you." She collected the vial and he grinned and closed his eyes. She slipped the vial into a side pouch of her backpack. A moist whistle came from his throat, and then he grew quiet.

Outside, in the street, Chain Guy bellowed in that inhuman manner that meant he was about to indulge in his Number One Priority, following his purpose, as did all beings under God's high heaven. Even Zapheads.

She sat with the suicidal pharmacist for another minute until his pulse stopped, and then crawled back to the front of the store.

CHAPTER TWO

Marvin the Martian is seriously underrated.

Campbell Grimes had always admired the faceless little Looney Tunes alien. Everybody loved Bugs Bunny. Bugs was a rabbit for all seasons, but just like Tweety Bird, Sylvester, and Porky, Bugs occasionally came up on the short end. Wile E. Coyote was admirable for his persistence and innovation, but that pencil-necked Road Runner always turned the tables.

Campbell despised the Road Runner, because the cartoon bird reminded him of Sonny Stanton, the Worthy Master of his Alpha Tau Omega chapter, back at the university. Stanton had a habit of sneaking up behind people and doing his nasally version of the Road Runner's *"meep meep."* What Campbell wouldn't have given for an Acme Asshole Eradicator, patent pending.

Whereas, Wile E. Coyote was a hopeless slave to his hunger, Marvin had a more refined sense of the universal order. To the faceless little ant-creature with the push-broom on top of his Roman helmet, destruction was merely an aesthetic choice.

Now, looking across the dead expanse of interstate and the hushed vehicles sprawled along it like a child's abandoned toys, Campbell figured it was a good time to borrow one of Marvin's taglines.

"Where's the *kaboom*?" he said, in a nasally cartoon voice.

"What?" Pete asked, barely listening.

"I would have expected more of a *kaboom*."

"A doomsday asteroid would have sold more tickets. The world ends not with a bang but a whimper, right?"

"You're an English major. You're really not going to be

worth much of a damn at this survival thing, are you?"

Pete took a swig of warm Busch beer and pushed dark curls of hair away from his face. "Hey, I'm here, but a lot of folks aren't. I'd say that gives me major points."

"Well," Campbell said. "You must have been wearing your tin-foil skullcap when the zap came."

Pete took another swig and hurled the empty can onto the grass median, where it bounced and came to rest in a sea of strewn clothes. "I'm not the one quoting Marvin the Martian, dude."

"Score."

Campbell booted down the ten-speed's kickstand and shook the dust from the sleeves of his leather jacket. They'd had their pick of the rack at Triad Cycles, and while Pete had gone for an off-road bike with knobby tires, Campbell had chosen a utility model with a wire basket. It even had a small "Made in America" tag wired to the basket. Pete had needled him by calling him "Cheesy Rider," but Campbell had a basket full of food and gear while Pete was stuck with whatever he could fit in his backpack.

Which was mostly beer at this point.

Campbell's body tingled from the vibration of the ride. They'd logged twenty miles in the last three hours, slowed by occasional traffic pile-ups that forced them to go off-road. They'd spent the night in an abandoned VW van in a campground, afraid to build a fire. It was their sixth day out of Chapel Hill, one week since everything had stopped, and they were no closer to understanding what the hell was going on.

No signs of intelligent life, Campbell thought in his Marvin the Martian voice. *Which isn't necessarily a bad thing. No, not at all.*

"Want to search any of these cars?" Pete asked, punctuating the query with a deep belch.

"My basket is full."

"Might find something fresh. A pistol, beef jerky, more beer."

"I already have a gun."

Pete pointed at the revolver jammed in Campbell's belt. "Aren't you ready for an upgrade?"

"It's enough." Campbell had gone with the .38 because he liked to see the chamber. He thought it would be easier to keep track of how many bullets he had left, in the event he ever actually had to use it. Pete had adopted a Glock and seemed to draw great satisfaction from the *clack* made by driving the clip home. The guns had been courtesy of an outdoor supply shop that had been picked over a little, but apparently the survivor count was so low that supply far exceeded demand.

"What if somebody's alive in one of those cars?" Pete asked.

"Unlikely." Campbell scanned the interstate more carefully, bothered by the thought.

"Could be somebody like us. One of the lucky ones."

"Damned if I'd call us 'lucky.'"

"Maybe we should have stayed at the university. If anybody can figure this thing out, it would be our good old home-team researchers."

"So what if they did?" Campbell grew annoyed, on the edge of anger, and he didn't like it. Because that's probably how *they* started out, when the wires melted and the brain circuitry zapped. When *they* started becoming *them.*

"Maybe they can come up with a vaccine or something."

"This isn't a goddamned case of the clap, Pete. And how are you going to get the crazies to cooperate? Blast them with your Explosive Space Modulator?"

"Jesus, dude, what crawled up your ass and pitched a

tent?"

"Sorry." Campbell punched the top of the sweaty helmet that rested between his legs. "The end of the world…I thought I could handle it."

Pete rolled his bike forward a few inches. "It's always easier in theory. Let's give that Lance truck a try."

The snack-food truck was parked on the shoulder parallel to the road, as if the driver had been prepared for the sudden loss of power. It was an older model, and Campbell suspected it had manual steering. Modern vehicles, dependent upon computers, had locked up or gone haywire. Hondas, Kias, and Fords were crashed or angled askew in the median. An SUV was upside down at the bottom of an embankment, doors hanging open. A twisted motorcycle straddled the guardrail, its occupant now a decaying lump of leather-encased flesh some twenty feet away.

"I don't know," Campbell said, feeling exposed and vulnerable. Or maybe it was the sight of at least a dozen corpses that caused his uneasiness.

"Chickenshit."

"We've got food. Maybe we should just keep pedaling."

"You still worried about roving bands of Zapheads? We don't have to fight over it. There's plenty for everybody."

Pete was letting the beer talk for him. He'd downed at least a six-pack so far today, and the autumn warmth wasn't sweating it out fast enough. Campbell understood his friend's escapism, but personally, he preferred the survival buzz.

"Those snack crackers are loaded with preservatives," he said. "They'll be around long after all of us are gone."

"*Har har*. Campbell made a funny." Pete dug into a side pouch of his backpack and brought out a pack of Marlboro Lights. "The Surgeon General has determined the end of the world is hazardous to your health."

"Don't make me use my Space Modulator on you."

Pete lit his cigarette and scanned the nearest vehicles. He exhaled a rising wreath of smoke and dismounted, then rolled his bike past a black Lexus with a personalized plate that said "SKIN-DR."

"Rich bitch," Pete said.

Campbell had a bad feeling about the car, maybe because of the way the windows looked a little steamy, despite the dry air. "Leave it."

"What are you so afraid of, dude?"

Afraid.

That was a good one. One minute he'd been playing Left 4 Dead on the Xbox, and the next he'd been sitting in his dark apartment, wondering if his stoner roomie had forgotten to pay the power bill again. He'd gone in Roy's bedroom and found him sprawled on the bed, glassy eyes fixed on the ceiling. Campbell hadn't dared touch him, because something had seemed *wrong* about him, and he grabbed his cell to dial 9-1-1, but his phone was as dead as Roy.

Then he'd gone outside and learned that Roy wasn't the only one…

"Check it out, bro," Campbell said, their little code for caution, a reminder that every decision had consequences. If nothing else, it was a cheap mockery of the notion of control.

Pete leaned his bike against the rear flank of the Lexus and went to the driver's side door. Giving one last look around, probably due to the lingering tug of Old World morals, Pete yanked the door open. He immediately cupped his hand over his mouth, the cigarette still perched between his fingers.

"Ugh," he said, his voice muffled. "Ripe one."

Campbell didn't bother looking. He was busy checking out the back seat, which was empty. "What did you expect?"

"I was hoping for Angelina Jolie in a see-through nightie."

"Pervert."

"I meant *alive*. I'm not that desperate…yet."

"You could have hooked up with the chubby chick back at that camp."

"Gypsy Rose? I'll take a corpse over that mess any day." Pete reached down beside the driver's seat and flipped a latch. The trunk popped open.

Campbell had never known anyone who could afford a Lexus, so he was a little curious about what the trunk might contain. Since the Big Zap had caught people with their pants down, sometimes literally, it offered a snapshot of human civilization in the early twenty-first century. A cultural anthropologist might have noted the widespread worship of plastic electronics and gasoline-powered engines, but Marvin the Martian would have summed it up as, "Well, back to the old drawing board."

The trunk of the Lexus was clean, carpeted, and empty, except for a leather briefcase. It featured a combination lock with a dial. Campbell gave the serrated metal wheels a few random turns, but the hasp stayed tight. He was about to close the trunk, realized there was no point, and heard a moist squishing in the car's interior.

He hoped Pete wasn't doing anything disgusting. His friend had gone through a brief desecration phase on the third day, placing corpses in humorous poses. In one memorable instance, he'd drawn a mustache and goatee on a little old lady who'd fallen down with her dead poodle's leash still wrapped around one frail wrist.

"Doomsday score," Pete said, lifting a purse.

"Charming. It matches your fashionable ensemble." In truth, the bright lime-green vinyl clashed horribly with Pete's plaid jacket and filthy red sweatpants.

Pete rummaged around in the purse and pulled out a

make-up kit. "Maybe I can rub this junk on my face and look like one of them."

"They look like one of us."

"No, they don't. They're redder around the eyes and their skin is pale."

"That's racist, dude."

Pete tossed the make-up kit to the pavement and continued scrounging. He came away with a wallet, an iPod, a spare set of keys, and a plastic package of tissues. He tapped futilely on the iPod's dark glass screen. "Dead like everything else."

"Good. I don't think I could endure your Lady Gaga marathon."

Pete hurled the iPod across the road, where it *dinked* off the side of a blue SUV. "What's in the briefcase?"

Campbell hefted it. "Heavy. Like papers."

"Or cocaine?"

"Yeah, right. All you think about is getting high."

Pete made a show of looking around. "You got anything better to do? Besides, I think those Zapheads kind of lowered the bar on moral inhibition."

"I don't give a damn about coke, but you got my curiosity up." About a hundred feet ahead, a plumbing van had coupled with a Toyota Prius in an obscene tangle of steel and plastic. Campbell could see the driver of the Prius slumped over the wheel, dark dots of dried blood stippling the windshield. The panel van had no windows in the rear, but Campbell was willing to bet it contained all sorts of tools, probably jumbled and scattered by the collision.

All he had to do was endure the smell of corpses for a moment, but that was getting easier by the day. The stench had become like a second skin, something worn instead of smelled. Carrboro had been the worst, in the immediate wake of the Big Zap, but even outside the city, death had sent its sweet musk into the sky as if to mark the territory it now ruled. And, in the absence of governments, law, and civilization, death was the only world order remaining.

Pete followed him to the van, still shucking items from the purse, calling out as he dropped them. "Hair clip…fingernail file…a little billfold with—"

Campbell looked back to see Pete stopped in the middle of the glittering asphalt, staring at the fold of vinyl in his hand. His friend's abrupt silence was amplified by the desolation around them.

"Family pictures, man," Pete whispered.

Campbell hadn't thought of his family all day. Dad Brian, a financial advisor, a guy you could toss a football and drink beers with, a solid Republican who'd vote "liberal" if he was mad at the stock market. Mom Mary, like most every Mary in the world, pretty, pleasant, and Catholic-loyal, although she'd made relief mission trips to eight different countries. Little brother Ted, or Turdfinger, as Campbell used to call him, back before Ted hit his growth spurt and could kick his butt.

The Grimes family lived on Lake James, in the North Carolina foothills, with the 3,000-square-foot Swiss-style house and little speedboat dock that was expected of people in Dad's circle. Campbell tried to picture the three of them out on the lake: Dad at the helm with his sun visor, shades, and tanned face, Mom perched loyally by the outboard motor and keeping an eye on Ted, who trailed behind them and cut his skis through the greenish-brown water.

But that other image—the one with them all slumped and rotting in front of the widescreen TV, flies dive-bombing their eyes—was the one that burned into his head.

"We'll get there, Pete," Campbell said, with a conviction he didn't feel.

Pete flapped the little photo album. "Yeah, and then what? Don't you think *her* family is sitting there with dinner on the table, waiting for Mom or Sis or Wife to walk through the door and bitch about the traffic?"

Pete's drinking not only slowed them down and increased the danger of traveling by bicycle on cluttered roads, but it also made him prone to blubbering. And Campbell did not want any damned blubbering at the moment. The world had already thrown itself the biggest Pity Party of all time, and the clam dip had definitely gone bad.

"Let's check this out and get moving," Campbell said, eyeing the smoky horizon. "We have to find a safe place to crash before dark."

Campbell hoped the rear door of the van was unlocked. He didn't want to open the cab. Pete dropped the purse and said, "Hey, don't you want to—"

—check it out, Bro?

But he was already swinging the door open and Marvin the Martian was definitely very angry indeed, because a blur of bulky movement exploded out of the shadows.

The impact stunned Campbell, and breath exploded from his lungs as he landed flat on the asphalt. The scrabbling creature standing over him smelled like the ozone of an electrical short, spiced with sour perspiration, urine, and a primal aroma that didn't have a name but was known by prey of every species.

He could dimly hear Pete yelling somewhere far away, and the creature's long ropes of hair whipped in his face, blinding him as he tried to roll. A jolt of agony flared in his shoulder, and he kicked upward. The creature seemed to have eight arms, and all of them were searching for a hunk of meat.

Campbell punched upward and hit something soft, and he had the goofy image of his hand vanishing into the creature's face, as if it were Marvin the Martian's black gap of nothingness. Then it rained, and the rain was warm and heavy, and a muffled *krunk* repeated itself as someone were beating a damp drum in a distant jungle.

The creature slumped on top of him, and then its weight moved to the side, and there was Pete leaning over him, a massive pipe wrench clenched in his right fist. The head of the wrench was clotted with hair and gore.

Finally Pete's inane shouting coalesced into language. "Crap, man! Oh, crap."

Campbell touched his shoulder, where the Zaphead had exposed his flesh to the air. It wasn't a deep bite, but electric fire radiated from it like a herpes sore from hell.

"She bit me," he whimpered.

Pete gave the dead Zaphead a kick. "Man up, dude. You were attacked by a chick."

Campbell rose to his hands and knees and looked at the creature that had attacked him. She was petite, about the size of his mother, with the same black hair. For one horrible moment, he thought it *was* his mother—her skull was so caved in that her features were unrecognizable.

By the time he'd risen staggering to his feet, Pete had pulled a clean towel and a roll of duct tape from the back of the van. "You can't get through an apocalypse without duct tape," Pete said, clamping the towel against Campbell's wound.

He gripped the protruding tail of the tape with his teeth and reeled off a foot-long section. Campbell clamped his hand over the towel, holding it in place as Pete applied the patchwork. Blood had trickled down the front of his shirt, but most of the flow had been staunched.

"Think I'll turn?" Campbell asked.

"These ain't zombies," Pete said. "Although it did get a

little close to the throat. I'm giving you the heads-up now. If I see fangs sprouting out of your mouth, I'm punching a stake through your chest."

"Point taken," Campbell said, but the weak pun didn't even elicit a grin. The wound throbbed but Campbell had full movement of his arm. He gave one last look at the woman, who appeared to be in her forties. Her lipstick was smeared, and a flap of Campbell's skin was stuck between her teeth.

Pete gave her one final kick, and her body lay there like a sack of mud. "One down, a million to go."

Campbell didn't like to think about a million Zapheads crawling across the face of the earth, hiding in shadowy crevices and waiting for something to kill. Right now, he didn't want to think of anything, much less whether his mom was somewhere out there jumping survivors.

Pete rummaged in the back of the van and came away with a fat screwdriver. "You risked your life to find out what's in the briefcase, so we may as well have a look."

He jimmied open the briefcase, banging it with the bloody wrench for emphasis. The lid popped open and loose cash fluttered out and settled on the highway. It looked to be tens and twenties, stacks of it.

"Whoopee, we're rich," Pete said, kicking the briefcase so that more bills lifted in the wind.

"You don't need to save for the future." Campbell patted the makeshift bandage. "You'll have a future in medicine after this is all over."

"Who said there was an 'after'?" Pete said.

Campbell had no answer as they collected their bicycles and headed west.

CHAPTER THREE

Rachel didn't want to wait for sundown.

While the vanishing daylight carried a greater risk of exposure, she couldn't bear the thought of one of the Zapheads clutching at her in the dark.

Or a crowd of them creeping up on her while she dozed.

Chain Guy was far up the street. Stumpy had fallen from the bench, and Rachel couldn't tell if he'd been beaten or not. He didn't move, and still, the flies swarmed.

Maybe he died from the infection, or a heart attack, or sudden pneumonia. Something sanely senseless. Please, God, let somebody around here die by natural causes.

After a moment, she added, *Except me.*

The Beard was nowhere in sight, and Rachel decided Chain Guy was chasing him, which would take them both out of the picture. That sounded like wishful thinking, but wishful thinking had not changed anything during the past week, so she knew not to trust it.

The street was clear, at least as far as she could tell by sticking her head out the door. The shadows of light poles and trash cans lay long across the sidewalk, giving her directions. Metal clanged several streets away, like a body falling on the hood of a car or a boot being driven into a Dumpster. She wondered if one of the affected had caught a fresh victim. But there was no scream.

Had the survivors already adjusted past the point of screaming?

Were there any survivors left at all?

She didn't like the thought of being alone, the last human in the universe, and the dead pharmacist's little care package came to mind. But she loathed the pale, grim surrender that had been painted on his dying face. That was the coward's way out, the path of the faithless. If such a time came, she trusted God would first give her permission.

Until then…

Rachel secured the backpack and stepped outside, clinging close to the brick, metal, and glass walls as she eased down the street. She paid absurd attention to each footstep, making sure the rubber soles of her sneakers didn't scuff on the concrete. She didn't know whether the Zapheads were driven to prey by superhuman senses of sight, smell, or hearing, but she figured the apocalypse was as good a time as any to hedge her bets.

She'd lived in Charlotte for two years, taking little time to learn the city. Her world had been largely confined to West Charlotte, where she interned as a school counselor for the Department of Social Services. Rachel knew the beltway and the exits for the larger shopping malls, the libraries, and the uptown area where she'd visited the Mint Museum, but little else. The high, gleaming finance centers were behind her, once busy with moneychangers and loan officers, but were now just seventy and eighty stories of stacked mausoleum crypts. The glass glinted red in the sunset, the towers of Babel gone silent, and small plumes of smoke curling from some of them.

She picked up her pace a little, more confident now that Chain Guy apparently hadn't noticed her. *Charlotte has to end at some point, and then you'll hit the woods.*

The block ended, and she glanced into one of the cars slanted across the intersection in the heart of a traffic jam. A woman's head was tilted back, ponytail dangling over the seat. Behind her was a child's safety seat. Rachel's heart, already galloping, jumped a fence and missed a step.

What if it's alive?

And the little devil on her shoulder whispered: It would be crying. Don't stop.

Maybe it's asleep, or scared, or—

Or dead. Maybe it's dead, and you walk over there and peer in the glass and see its cute little blue face and then you scream, and then Chain Guy comes running with his steel whip, ready to play and play and play until your brains are sausage.

Shut the eff up.

I'm the devil. You can't tell me what to do. And I see you're using profanity, Rachel. That's good. That's very good.

Rachel said a quick prayer and forced herself toward the car, glancing up the street only once. That was the litmus test: If she saw Chain Guy, it was a sign from God that she should run for it. Otherwise, she had a moral duty to save a baby if she could.

As she reached for the handle of the back door, she wasn't sure whether it was morality or loneliness that drove her. With a baby to care for, she had less reason to think about the poison pills.

But she didn't open the door. The safety seat was empty, a rumpled yellow blanket piled around it.

Rachel hoped the baby was off with Grandmother, playing patty cake or whining for her mom's nipple, somewhere secure and far, far from the carnage of downtown Charlotte. She didn't allow room for the Chain Guy's discovery of the infant, or what those steel links might do to tender flesh. No, such things didn't happen under God's heaven.

And even if they did, she didn't need to know about them. She didn't want to know about them.

The sun sank lower, the shadows flattened fatter, and the distant noises clanged more cacophonous, building like tribal drums, only this tribe had been driven mad with one big celestial flash.

She hurried west, figuring the beltway was two miles away, and beyond that, a pine forest broke up the small satellite communities. For some reason, the forest was a more appealing option than the maze of alleys, buildings, and vehicles that could serve up a Zaphead at any second. At least in the woods, the hunt and the flight would feel more natural.

Two corpses lay just ahead, with a sodden aspect that suggested they'd been there since the flash, and she veered closer to the wall, preferring dubious concealment to the easier passage but a higher exposure of the street. A shopping cart blocked her way, and it held four bulging trash bags, a pair of curled and cracked leather shoes on its bottom wire shelf, and a plastic boom box in the child seat. It was a homeless person's portable life, a legacy on crooked wheels.

She raised her hand, not wanting to smell the corpses, but her palm didn't reach her nose.

Instead, a ring of fiery steel clamped around her forearm.

She gasped as she was yanked into a mildewed gap in the storefronts. She'd been so intent on ignoring the corpses that she hadn't even noticed the narrow alley.

And now you'll pay, Rachel. Now you'll play the devil's game, and dance with a creature from out of hell.

And the bitch of it was, she couldn't even scream. Her ribcage clamped around her lungs as tightly as the hand locked on her forearm, and one more tug from *it* cost her the remainder of her balance—then she was in its arms, and flailing, kicking, maybe even spitting, when she heard a grunt of pain.

"Goddamn it, take it *easy*!" it said.

Could Zapheads talk? She hadn't heard one speak yet, but that didn't mean anything. Maybe their language of grunts, groans, and odd chuckling had served them sufficiently well so far.

Rachel pulled back, but the grip remained, and she saw its dark face, one eye gleaming wide in the dim light, and then the contrast of its big white teeth, and she thought maybe she could scream after all, and then—

"You're not one of them," he said. "Or you would have done bit me."

"Of course I'm not," she said. "Any fool can see that."

"Who you calling a fool? I ain't the one walking down the street plain as day."

"You're not...affected?"

"Affected? Is that what you call it when you want to bust open somebody's skull and play piddly-pooh with their brains?"

That uncanny eye was still fixed and unblinking in the ebony face, staring deep into her soul as if exposing every sick secret she'd ever harbored, every bad thing she'd ever done. Then she looked at his other eye, which blinked.

"You think I'm one of them freaks?" he said, and she noticed for the first time that he held a pistol in his right hand, barrel tilted up by his shoulder as if he were ready to level and fire at any moment, in any direction.

"I guess not, or I'd be dead."

"Damn right, you'd be dead. You might be dead anyway."

She glanced longingly at the street and the sunset that washed the pavement like the surface of a river, the cars like so many storm-swept boats, the corpses and trash like flotsam headed for a distant gray sea. "I think we're all dead," she said.

"Don't you got no gun?"

She realized how vulnerable she was, to him and to the rest of the world. "I'm scared of guns."

"Well, I'm scared of *those* things more."

She studied his face, trying to read his expression, but the glass eye kept throwing her off. It gave the impression of coldness, which belied the rest of his expression. The mouth said "mean," the slight pinch of forehead said "worried," and the lifted eyebrows said "easy meat," but his good eye confused the whole picture, because it was dark brown and teeming with so many human things.

He gave a twisted smile. "What? You think I'm going to rape you?"

"No, just—"

"Kill you for whatever's in your backpack?"

She shrugged it off her shoulder a little. "You can have it."

"I don't want your shit."

"What *do* you want? Prove how tough you are? Show your manly power? Why didn't you just let me go on down the street?"

He eased his grip on her forearm, but only a little. It was the below the point of inflicting pain, but still too tight for her to pull away. "I...just wanted to see if you was real."

"I assure you, I am quite real. I may be the only real thing left in Charlotte."

His good eye blinked. "You talk funny."

"What? Now I have to apologize for being a middle-class white woman with an education?"

His good eye grew as cold as his fake one. "Don't pull that shit with me."

"Well, you're trying to play some sort of half-assed stereotype, the bro' from the 'hood jumping the white bitch." The cussing was foreign to her, and she hated herself for it, but she used anger as an excuse.

He released her, and she shook the circulation back into her arm. "Go on," he said, subdued, waving his gun back toward the street. "Git."

"Excuse me?"

"You'd rather be out there with them murdering freaks than hanging with a nigga," he said.

"It's not—"

"It's the eye, ain't it?"

His accusation caused her to inadvertently stare at it. She'd been glancing, she couldn't help it, that shiny glass orb was a magnet. She'd heard of the "evil eye," a belief in many cultures that an ill-intended gaze could bring malady or misfortune. Although she had a hard time attributing such qualities to an inert prosthetic, it seemed to radiate an unsettling power.

A miniature sun casting its own solar flare...

"No, it's not—"

"Just call a spade a spade and get done with it. We don't got time for games."

"I..." She looked back at the street as the insane chuckling echoed down the concrete canyons.

"Bastard Zappers give me the creeps," he said, his finger tightening ever so slightly on the trigger. He didn't seem to be aware of it.

"It's getting dark."

"What you going to do? You got a plan?"

She shrugged. "Go west to the mountains."

"That's not a plan, that's a beer commercial."

"You have anything better?"

He angled his head across the street, to what looked like apartments above a wig shop. "Hole up and lock down for the night, then figure it out. Like I been doing for a week."

"That's not a plan, that's making crap up as you go along."

He grinned for the first time, and it warmed his entire face. Even the glass eye took on a sparkle. "So far, so good."

"Okay," she said. "I have some food, a flashlight, and stuff like that."

"You got it together," he said. "I been faking that part, too."

She held out her hand, the fingers still tingling from the blood returning to her extremities. "Rachel Wheeler," she said, realizing the use of her last name was awkward under the circumstances, as if they were business associates.

He took her hand, gentle this time. "DeVontay. DeVontay Jones."

Then he grew solemn again, edging to the corner and peering out of the alley. He was tall, a few inches over six feet, and a little gangly. In the sunlight, she saw that he wore leather pants and a leather jacket, both of which bulged uncomfortably as if he wore several layers of clothing.

As if he's afraid of being bitten. But I've never seen the Zapheads bite anyone.

"See anything?" she whispered.

"Naw," he said. She couldn't place his accent, but it wasn't Southern. And it wasn't quite inner city. He appeared to be in his mid-twenties, so maybe he'd moved to Charlotte for work.

She didn't seem to have much in common with him.

Except whatever kept us from being killed or affected.

Yeah.

Except for that.

The only thing left that mattered.

He motioned with his free hand. "All clear. Hurry."

And then they were on the street, exposed to the dying sun and the creeping night and whatever chuckled in the far distance.

CHAPTER FOUR

"It's a fire," Pete said.

Campbell didn't believe it. He'd insisted it was electric lights, maybe even automobiles moving beyond the dark trees, the wind causing them to flicker. Then the wind shifted, although there wasn't much of it, and a faint trail of acrid wood smoke drifted past.

"What should we do?"

"Go in."

Pete was drunk. Shortly after the close encounter with the Zaphead in the plumbing van, they'd come across a Budweiser truck. Pete had filled his backpack with 12-ounce cans and even made some makeshift saddlebags with a tool satchel he'd taken from the van. He'd stopped his bike every two miles or so to bust open one of the warm beers and down it. Their pace had slowed considerably as the evening wore on, and Campbell had nearly pedaled headfirst into a jackknifed tractor trailer because he thought he'd seen someone move inside one of the stalled cars.

But Pete wouldn't let him check out the movement, coming back with, "Haven't you learned your lesson *yet*?"

And Campbell had buried his hope that maybe there were others like them, *normal* people, survivors who weren't driven by a homicidal impulse. Now, with a campfire a hundred yards away in the dusk, they were faced with a choice, and Pete's judgment was about three times over the legal limit.

"What if it's a bunch of Zapheads?" Campbell asked.

Pete pulled the tab on a fresh brew, and it *fwooshed* and sprayed into the dusk. "Then we shoot the hell out of them."

"You say that like you'd enjoy it."

"Fuckers trying to wipe us out, man. This is about the survival of the species."

"I think they're the same species we are. They're human."

Pete wiped foam from his mouth with his sleeve. "Humans don't jump on you and rip out a chunk of skin with their teeth. Unless they're Mike Tyson or Jeffrey Dahmer."

The fire was in the forest beside the highway, set down a gentle slope. They'd passed a bridge about three hundred yards back, and a silvery creek slid beneath it, laughing and gurgling as if all was merry with the world. Survivors—human survivors—would likely follow evolutionary instinct and camp by the water.

"Maybe we ought to keep going."

"What if it's like that last camp?" Pete was starting to slur and his sibilants were mushy.

"I didn't trust them."

"You're just mad because you didn't tap ol' Gypsy Rose."

"They were talking prophecies and wacko stuff."

"Well, maybe they were onto something."

Campbell wished they'd snagged some binoculars. Full dark was setting in, and they'd have to make a decision on where to sleep. They usually locked themselves in an empty car for the night, but Campbell always felt trapped and claustrophobic, and Pete's drunken snores pushed away any chance of rest. One night they'd slept out in an open field, taking turns keeping watch. Campbell had jerked awake sometime long before dawn and found Pete had dozed off, leaving them ridiculously vulnerable.

So, maybe the idea of sticking with a group was worth a little risk.

"Okay," Campbell said. "Let's check it out."

Pete leaned his bike against the guardrail and drew his pistol from his jacket pocket. "Lock and load, my man."

Campbell drew his revolver. It didn't have a safety switch, but he'd test-fired it twice on the day he'd found it in the sporting-goods shop. He hadn't shot a gun since he was 12 and his grandfather had taken him squirrel hunting. The double action required a serious pull of the trigger, which meant the gun would be hard to fire accidentally, but also that he'd have to be serious if he wanted to shoot somebody.

Some THING, I mean. These Zapheads aren't "somebodies."

He flashed back to the face of the creature that had attacked him and shuddered at the brief illusion that it had been his mother.

"Got your flashlight?" Campbell said.

"I only got two hands." Meaning that Pete wouldn't put down his beer.

Campbell fished in his wire basket until he found his flashlight, but he didn't switch it on. The purple dusk revealed large, bruised clouds overhead, so the moon would be of little use. He looked up the highway toward the last hilltop they'd crested. Something moved there, a distant stick figure that soon blended with the shadows of stranded vehicles.

Pete chugged his warm beer, then belched. "What you waiting for?"

Campbell swung over the rail and started down the slope toward the campfire. The revolver was heavy in his hand, and he let his arm dangle so the barrel pointed at the ground. He used the flashlight for ballast as he descended. The slope leveled out at a ditch, and briars tore his khakis as he stumbled through the granite riprap.

Above him, Pete stumbled and fell, cursing once before remembering they were supposed to be in stealth mode.

"You okay?" Campbell whispered.

"That better be the good guys or I'm going to be pissed," he whispered back.

Campbell switched on his flashlight, hooded it with his forearm, and illuminated a path for Pete, who kicked, stumbled, and staggered down the hill. Pete's body odor overwhelmed the beery stench.

Sweet. We're all turning into animals.

After crossing the ditch, they entered a thicket of scrub pine, thorns, and ragged rye. The elusive flickers of fire showed here and there through gaps in the trees, and as full dark settled in, the orange light took on the quality of a jewel forged from a mysterious source.

Campbell's hand sweated around the revolver's grip, even though the air had turned cool and moist because of the nearby creek. He didn't know where to point the gun, and he took each step gingerly, in fear of snapping twigs. Pete, however, had no such hesitation. The alcohol delivered a stupid brand of courage, and the semi-automatic topped it off with a bow. Pete soon took the lead, muttering under his breath.

"Maybe they got some meat," he said. "You smell that? Smells like barbecue."

Campbell rubbed the bite wound on his shoulder. *No. I'm not going there. The Zapheads aren't crazed cannibals or zombies. They're just…*

Just WHAT?

And then he did smell it, smoky and acrid and rich, and he had the image of stumbling into a nest of Zapheads, all gathered around the fire and roasting a child on a slim white sapling, fat dripping onto the hot stones and hissing to greasy steam.

"Plenty of canned meat and jerky still around," Campbell said. "Years and years of it."

The wire basket of his bicycle held cans of tuna, sardines, corned beef, and pink salmon. Aside from the one stop at the "gypsy camp," they'd eaten their food cold. But the smoke didn't make him hungry. It was oily and tainted.

A bird *chirruped* high in the trees. The Big Zap had wiped out a lot of animals, but the survivors among them seemed to behave as they always had. It was only humans that seemed to have been affected on a neurological level. So far, anyway. All their homing instincts, territorial boundaries, and migration patterns could have altered in uncertain ways.

A branch snapped behind them, maybe twenty feet away. Pete swung around, bumping Campbell in the arm with his pistol.

At least the dumbass didn't shoot me. But the night is young.

The rustling came closer, *swick swick swick* through the dry brush. Then a pause, as if whomever—or whatever—it was had stopped to listen for its prey.

Campbell strained to hear, holding his breath, but Pete was rasping away, the smoker's rattle rising from deep in his lungs. He wondered if Pete was thinking the same thing he was: *Who shoots first?*

But what if it was a person? A fellow survivor? Maybe there were more, enough to form a group and—

Campbell beat back the faint flutter of hope. In the week since the event, they'd met only four survivors, and one of those had turned and fled when Campbell had called her. The other three were in the makeshift gypsy camp, and Campbell hoped to God that wasn't a sample representation of mankind's future.

Swiiick. One cautious footstep through the weeds.

Pete nudged him. Campbell turned, but Pete was just an onyx bulk against the lesser black of night. Then Pete's mouth was at his ear, spraying saliva as he whispered: "Go left, and I'll go right."

Campbell nodded, trying not to tremble. A Zaphead

wouldn't be subtle. It would charge like a rhino through the veldt, using whatever it had in its hands as a weapon. Such a mad, predictable danger was reassuring in an odd way. *This, however...*

He edged to his left, pushing the barren flashlight before him to test the foliage. The susurration of Pete's passage let him know the gap between them was widening. Campbell was on his own.

Swiiick. Another step forward.

Or had that been Pete's footstep?

Campbell turned again, and he was disoriented. He could no longer see the thin licks of fire in the near distance and the night had blended with the canopy until he was unsure of the location of the highway, the forest, or the creek. He nearly surrendered to the impulse to switch on the flashlight, but he pinched his fingers together until the pain cleared the panic.

It's not a Zaphead. And a survivor has no reason to hurt you.

But the smoke told a different story. The smoke said, "Mmm, tastes like chicken," and "I'll bet you're just dying to join us for dinner" and "We're pleased to serve you."

Screw it. You watched too many horror movies back in the Old Days.

Never mind that the Old Days were July or so.

He looked up at the dim stars and mist-hidden wedge of moon, trying to get his bearings. The constellations themselves seemed alien and strange, as if the massive solar flare had tilted the planet's axis. Maybe the world was all shook up, both literally and figuratively.

Swick swick swick, the steps were fast and close, and he raised the pistol, its sodden weight tugged by gravity until the act was like bringing to bear a field cannon.

And he heard the signature insane chuckling—not in the direction of the steps, but behind him, right behind him—and then the night erupted with a flash and roar. Campbell's ears rang with sudden pain as he dropped his pistol and fell to his knees.

"You okay?" said a gruff voice above him.

"Yuh-yeah." Campbell gripped the flashlight before him as if it was a dagger he could use to impale himself.

"What the hell?" Pete said, some distance away, crashing through the scrub toward them.

"Don't shoot," the gruff voice said. "Your friend's okay."

The man flicked a switch and a bluish Maglite blinded Campbell, although the beam was directed to the side. The light bounced past him and settled on a limp figure pressed face-first into the grass. A dark, wet bloom covered its back and ragged bits of flesh clung to a gaping hole in the back of the shirt. Campbell had the impression of graceful bulk as the man swept past him and stood over the corpse just as Pete burst into the circle of light.

"A Zaphead," the man said.

"Who the hell are you?" Pete said. His Glock was pointed at the man, who gave it an amused glance.

"The king of nowhere," the man said.

"Shit." Pete looked at Campbell, letting his aim waver. "You sure you're okay?"

Campbell nodded, a little embarrassed. He collected his revolver and looked at the man standing over the corpse. The man was bald, a little over six feet, and dressed in a matching gym suit, a khaki hunter's vest over it. Although the suit was dirty, the man appeared well-groomed and fit, despite his age.

"Who is that?" Campbell managed to ask, pointing his revolver at the corpse.

"What," the man said. "*What* is that? These things don't deserve to be called a 'who.'"

Campbell couldn't tell by looking whether the corpse was

once a Zaphead. All he knew was, it had once been human. Yet, Campbell had not heard it approaching, and Zapheads weren't known for stealth and subtlety.

"You sure it's a Zaphead?" Campbell asked the man.

"It's not the first one I've killed."

"It was stalking me," Campbell said. "They're supposed to charge."

"It was creeping up, all right. But not on *you*. It was watching *us*."

"Wait a sec," Pete said. "How come you could see in the dark?"

The man fished around in the hip pocket of his coveralls, eliciting a threatening wave of the Glock from Pete. The man ignored the gesture and pulled out some tinted goggles on a thick strap. "Infrared," the man said. "Nothing but the best in survival gear if you want to survive, right?"

How come WE didn't think of that? Oh, yeah. Because Pete's drunk off his ass and my survivalist training ended in the sixth grade when Mom made me quit the Boy Scouts.

"Is it just you two fellas?" the man asked, tracking his flashlight along the scrub.

"Yeah," Campbell grunted. "How come this one was sneaking? I've never seen any of them sneak."

"They're changing."

"Changing?" Pete said. "Like what, growing a third eye or something?"

"The way they act. Come on, you can ask the professor about it." The man turned and headed into the forest.

"Damn, man." Pete said to Campbell. "Hardcore."

The man stopped ten feet ahead and turned. "You boys ain't dangerous, are you? With them guns?"

"No, sir," Campbell said.

"Didn't think so. I bet you're too scared to shoot if you had to." He continued toward the flickering fire.

Campbell switched on his flashlight and pointed it down at the corpse. He imagined he heard a low chuckling but decided it was the thing's stomach gases. But it didn't look like a thing, or a veggie, or a Zaphead. It looked like somebody's chubby uncle, a bus driver or brake mechanic or off-duty cop. The corpse wore a dark short-sleeved shirt, blue jeans, and scuffed leather shoes without socks.

Campbell wondered where the man had been when the solar flare erupted. Zapheads rarely moved with any sort of real intention besides venting rage on anything that breathed. If they were changing, evolving, and adapting, he hadn't seen such behavior manifested. But hadn't the woman in the plumbing van pounced with a glimmer of intelligence?

"I don't want these things to change," Campbell said. "I was just starting to get used to the idea of a planet full of mindless killers. I don't know if I can handle any more surprises."

"Well, we better catch up with Mister Happy up there."

"And his friends, apparently."

"Wonder if they got any beer?"

Campbell led the way, giving the corpse a wide berth. He wondered how many more Zapheads might be lurking in the bushes, watching the campfire and waiting for an opportunity.

Pete staggered by him, wobbling and cussing, hacking at the saplings with his free hand. "Dude could have let us borrow his goggles."

"I have the feeling he's not the sharing kind. He'd probably say some jock bullshit like 'Only survivalists survive.'"

As they neared the forest, the air became moister and cooler. The creek lay beyond them in the dark, gurgling in oblivious merriment. The clouds had spread out in great purple skeins above, backlit by the psychedelic auroras that came in the wake of the solar storms. Somewhere above them, the moon continued its track across the sky. The world continued to turn, all the great cogs of the universe appeared to fit into their proper slots, and the machineries of time functioned in perfect precision, but the one big piece of it was broken.

Campbell looked back toward the road once, wondering about their bicycles, but the night had swallowed all their travels. Now there was only the bobbing fire, and that pungent, tantalizing smoke, and a future where former humans crouched in a depraved hunger for violence.

"Do you see any of them?" Pete said as they entered the silent corridor of trees.

"Shh." Pete squinted at the crackling fire, playing his flashlight around, wondering where their rescuer was. They stepped into a clearing that contained a couple of tents, a blanket hanging from a wire strung between two trees, and some gray cookware stacked on a sodden stump.

No one was in sight.

Then a deep voice erupted from the surrounding shadows: "Drop your guns and move real slow."

CHAPTER FIVE

They'd decided on a room in a Motel 6 on the outskirts of the city, just below the interstate but away from any commercial developments or residential neighborhoods. A convenience store and a Taco Bell were the only other buildings in the little off-road cluster designed to bleed money from travelers on the way south to Columbia or north to Raleigh. In the murky light of sundown, Rachel couldn't make out any of the vehicles she knew were scattered along the road.

There were fewer cars in front of the convenience store, so they chose that one to explore instead of the Taco Bell. The fast-food restaurant with its darkened glass seemed absurdly like an abandoned temple, a religion whose comforts no longer served the masses. Rachel could smell the spoiled cheese emanating from the place. At least, she hoped it was cheese.

She kept watch out front while DeVontay prowled the convenience store for food and supplies. She clutched the flashlight, afraid to turn it on, figuring that invisibility was the best defense. The world's silence was oppressive and weighty—a new sort of gravity enveloped her in an alien skin. The only sounds were the occasional crashes as DeVontay pillaged the store.

He soon emerged with his backpack bulging, a bag of Doritos ripped open in his hand. He crunched the corn chips as he said, "Got us enough to get through the night."

"See anybody?"

"Just a couple dead folks."

"Were they Zapheads?"

"Why you call 'em that?"

"That's what the media was calling them, before the power went out."

DeVontay headed for the motel and she followed, glancing at the Taco Bell. No more running for the border.

"The solar flares," Rachel said. "Astronomers knew they were coming. They just didn't know what would happen."

"I never was no good at science." DeVontay held the bag of chips out to her.

"You shouldn't be eating that junk food."

"What, it will rot my brain?" He snorted in laughter.

"That stuff's full of preservatives."

"I might need me some preserving, if things get any worse." He pulled his pistol from his belt as they approached the drop-off circle by the motel's main entrance.

A red Fiat was pulled up to the curb, its front doors open. Rachel gave the car a wide berth but DeVontay peered through the window. "Bad ride."

"It's dead, like every other car we tried in the last half hour."

"Why you got to be so negative all the time?"

"Maybe because everybody I know and love is either dead or trying to crack open my skull," she said.

"Well, that's what you get for lovin' people," DeVontay said. "I never had that problem."

He left the Fiat and joined her outside the sliding-glass doors, where she peered into the shadowed lobby. The front desk was unattended. A dark form slumped in one of those stiff, formal chairs that were designed for decoration, not for sitting.

"Somebody's in there," Rachel said. "Should we knock?"

DeVontay tugged his pistol from his belt. "Are they moving?"

"I can't tell."

DeVontay pushed at narrow gap where the two sliding doors stood a few inches from meeting. "No electricity. This bitch won't open."

"Maybe if you yell a little louder, we can get some Zapheads to bust it open for us."

"Ain't nobody here. Not alive, no ways."

Rachel didn't want to think about all the bodies spread throughout the motel. There were at least 30 cars in the parking lot, which meant a big slice of America: business travelers, families on vacation, retired people headed to see the grandkids.

"We could break the glass," Rachel said.

"Like that wouldn't draw attention?"

"I don't know how well those things can hear. We still don't much about them."

"Wait here." DeVontay gave her the bag of Doritos headed back to the Fiat, then he stooped through the driver's-side door. A moment later, the trunk popped open. DeVontay returned with a scissors jack and handle.

"Lucky it had a manual latch, or I woulda had to bust into it," DeVontay said. "Wouldn't be the first time."

"So, we can add 'car thief' to your list of survival skills. Great." She put a Dorito in her mouth and the crunch filled her ears from the inside.

"Says the lady eating a stolen Dorito."

She glanced down at the bag and realized the moral compass, even hers, had shifted with the arrival of the solar flares. Perhaps God's commandments needed a revision.

She might have thought that the catastrophe had been a punishment for the wicked, except that the apocalypse had punished everyone, good or bad, white or black, believer or infidel. But she couldn't worry about the big picture right now. First, she had to survive the night.

DeVontay wedged the jack between the bottoms of the motel doors and cranked the handle until it was tight. At first, the doors held, and then they groaned in protest before yielding. The jack handle quivered under the stress, and Rachel wondered if the glass would shatter after all. Then the doors gave a grudging inch, and then another.

When DeVontay had widened the gap to more than a foot, he stepped aside and retrieved his pistol. "Ladies first."

"You're a real gentleman."

"I told you, I ain't no gentleman. Just a man. Now get in there and just scream if you see any Zapheads."

She stared into his face, which was getting harder to see as night encroached. His glass eye was lost in shadow, but his real one burned with impatience. She pushed her backpack through the opening, and switched on her flashlight, keeping the beam directed on the lobby floor.

Rachel stepped inside, immediately hit by the corrupt air of the three-story mausoleum. She played the flashlight beam over the figure in the chair and wished she hadn't. She had been a maid with a Spanish complexion and dark hair knotted into a bun, perhaps taking a final break without realizing her shift was about to be punched out by the Big Time Clock in the Sky. Beside her was a cart filled with folded towels, linens, and cleaning supplies.

"Grab this," DeVontay said, shoving his own backpack through the opening. She had to wiggle it to get it through, but was uneasy about turning her back on the dark lobby. Once she got it through, DeVontay followed, and she drew comfort from the pistol he now pointed before him into the darkness.

"Smell that?" she said.

He took her flashlight and walked over to the maid's cart,

ignoring the body. He came back with a squirt bottle of hand sanitizer. He squirted some on his fingers and rubbed the goo above his upper lip, into the faint stubble of his mustache. He gave an exaggerated sniff and passed her the bottle.

She understood and aped his actions. The perfumed aroma immediately filled her nostrils and masked the smell of death.

"You're pretty resourceful," she said.

"Saw it on a TV show," he said.

"Wow."

"Don't sound so surprised. We got TV in Philly, too. Before it fried out, I mean."

Outside, a faint dusting of stars stuck to the deep ceiling of the sky, the rippling green bands of aurora borealis painting the darkness.

"Let's get a room," she said.

"I could make a joke here, but it's the end of the world," he said. He crossed the lobby to the front desk, flicking the flashlight down each wing to make sure they were empty. He went behind the desk and into the open office while Rachel shouldered her backpack and waited. A moment later, he came out holding up a key ring.

"Key cards won't work, but one of these gotta be the master key," he said.

"Hurry. I'm getting the creeps out here."

"Let's take the first one we come to," he said. "The nicest rooms are usually closest to the front desk. Might even get a Jacuzzi, for all the good it will do us."

"Pass the apocalypse in pampered luxury," she said. "I can see the television commercial already."

"Except the part where there ain't no TV anymore." He gave her the flashlight and she illuminated the hallway so he could try the first door.

"What if there's somebody in it?" She meant "somebody dead" but she didn't have to say it.

He raised his hand to knock, and then grinned sheepishly at her, squinting against the light. The eyelid covering his glass eye didn't fully close. "We can stand out here all night if you like."

She peered past him down the hall, into the blackness beyond the flashlight's reach. "You hear that?"

He turned toward the end of the hall, where a scuffling noise echoed down the concrete stairwell. "Hear what?"

"That," she whispered.

"Probably just the air conditioning," he said.

"Power's off, remember?"

DeVontay didn't say anything, but his face said, "Oh, yeah," and he selected one of the keys on the ring and tried to jam it in the door lock. It slid in halfway and stuck. He jiggled it three times before he was able to yank it free. The noise was louder now, and clearly sounded like feet shuffling on concrete steps.

"What if it's one of us?" Rachel whispered.

DeVontay pushed a different key into the lock, but it didn't even penetrate. His hands were shaking, causing the keys to jingle.

"Give me the gun, you can go faster," she whispered.

"You know how to shoot?" he whispered back, shoving a fourth key toward the slot.

"No, but I'll feel safer," she whispered.

Before he could answer, the key slid in and he turned it with a loud *click*. He depressed the door handle as Rachel swerved the beam down the hall. A bulky shape filled the opening of the stairwell, moving toward them.

"Hurry, hurry, hurry!" Rachel implored DeVontay, pounding on his back. "He's coming."

DeVontay swung the door open, pointing the gun down the hall as she pushed past him into the room. The air was stale but didn't smell of corpses.

Thank you, God, for small blessings.

"Who are you?" DeVontay yelled down the hall, but he waited only one second before stepping inside and slamming the door closed, quickly throwing the deadbolt in place.

"You know how to shoot?" Rachel mocked, aiming the flashlight at the pistol by his side.

"Smartass. I wasn't the one squealing"—he raised his voice to a thin falsetto—"*Ooooh, help, help.*"

"Shush," she said. "Maybe he won't figure out which room we're in."

They heard him banging on doors, coming closer. Rachel didn't know how smart Zapheads were, but in her observation, they seemed to have varying degrees of cunning. Perhaps the solar flares had short-circuited different people's brains in varying degrees. Most died, some fried, and a few lucky souls were left to sort out the mess.

DeVontay drew back from the door, joining her in the middle of the room. She flicked the light around to make sure the room was empty. It was a suite, with a little kitchenette and a Jacuzzi. DeVontay had gotten lucky after all.

Then the Zaphead was pounding on the door, giving three hard blows with the bottoms of his fists. Rachel instinctively clutched DeVontay and switched off the flashlight, not wanting the beam to attract attention. She could hear DeVontay panting in the dark.

Then the Zaphead was off across the hall to the next door, repeating the pounding as he worked his way down the hall. Soon the banging was muffled, as if he had reached the far wing. Rachel exhaled, not realizing her lungs were burning with held breath and tension.

"Close one," she said, flicking on the flashlight again.

"You got your Jacuzzi after all," he said.

Without thinking, she turned the water tap, but nothing came out. "I haven't had a bath in ages," she said.

"You gonna be smelling worse than these corpses soon."

"Well, just keep squirting that sanitizer up your nose and you'll be fine."

He chuckled, mostly with relief, and wiped sweat from his head. He plopped his backpack onto the bedside table and dug into it. He pulled out a few tins and cellophane bags of food, then a pack of white candles and a Bic. "Save your batteries," he said, lighting a candle and jamming its base into the wrought-iron lamp.

He lit another, and then checked to make sure the curtains were drawn tight. "Guess we're as safe here as anywhere," he said.

"Would you have shot him?" she said. "If you had to?"

He turned, the candlelight soft on his face. He looked young, barely a teen. "Wouldn't be the first."

She couldn't tell if he was just talking tough or trying to reassure her. She didn't press. She wasn't even sure she wanted him to shoot. Even though they were Zapheads, they were still God's creatures.

Do you really believe that, Rachel? Why can't they be Satan's army? Or are you one of those who only believe the convenient parts of the Bible?

She shuddered. "I'm exhausted," she said.

"King-size bed."

"Good." She sprawled on one side, then curled into a ball with the pillow pulled to her stomach. "You can stay way over there."

"I'm eating first," he said. "Sweet dreams."

"Sorry," she murmured.

"Huh?"

"I left your Doritos in the lobby."

CHAPTER SIX

Campbell slobbered over the pork and beans, which were heated in a tin can that had been resting in the embers. The fire was large and crackled with intense energy, and it could have been the primal fire, the first lightning strike that had forever changed the human race. It sent giant fingers of light stippling against the surrounding trees, creating a yellow wall against the black and unknown beyond.

There were four in the group. Donnie, a scrawny guy in a camouflage cap who'd challenged them when they'd entered the camp, had taken his turn at watch while shouldering a mean-looking automatic rifle. A woman named Pam was evidently asleep in one of the tents popped up in the clearing. The group must have settled there for some days, because of the clothesline strung between two trees and a stack of broken limbs piled nearby to feed the fire.

The man who'd stuck the gun in Campbell's back was named Arnoff. He'd collected their guns after Donnie had demanded they drop them. Pete had been pissed at first, but now he was nursing a beer and gazing into the flames as if he were at a frat-house bonfire before the big homecoming football game.

Arnoff sat across the fire from Campbell, tenderly cleaning a disassembled rifle. "You boys made it all the way from Chapel Hill, huh?"

"We had bicycles," Campbell said.

Arnoff nodded. "Yep. Saw you through the binocs."

"That's why we didn't shoot you," said the bald, thin-faced man with huge black spectacles that gave him the appearance of an insect. "We haven't seen Zapheads exhibit such coordinated behavior."

"I woulda shot you anyways," Arnoff said. "Just for target practice. But the professor here said we need to gather as much info as we could."

"He's joking," said the bald man, although Arnoff's eyes held not the slightest hint of mirth.

"How long have you guys been together?" Campbell asked, eager to change the subject. His stomach wasn't doing too well with the beans and he already felt bloated and gassy.

"I teach earth sciences at Wake Forest—I mean, I *did* teach, back when I had students," the professor said, digging into his shirt pocket for a cigarette. Absurdly, he still wore a tie, as if that one senseless symbol of civilization guaranteed that all the pieces would eventually fit back together. "My colleagues in the department were well aware of the approaching solar flares, which tend to come in cycles. Indeed, it was national news, but like most science stories, it was dumbed down for public consumption."

"Yeah, we saw that on Yahoo!," Pete said. "They were talking about the worst solar storm on record, sometime around the Civil War, but they said this one wouldn't be that bad."

Arnoff *clacked* a bullet into the chamber of his rifle. "They never get it straight. Goddamned media. Keep you so screwed you don't know whether to sell your stocks or buy ammunition."

"The 1859 solar flare, the Carrington Event, disrupted telegraph communications and burned some poles," the professor said. "The aurora was spotted all over the country and as far south as Mexico."

"Those freaky green and purple lights in the sky?" Pete asked. "That make you feel like you're on a bad acid trip?"

"Yes, caused by charged particles. Other recent solar flares and sunspot events have caused power outages, but no one could have expected anything like this."

"You mean Zapheads?" Campbell said.

"I mean, 'all of it.' Congress had ordered some research and contingency plans in the wake of massive solar disruptions, but that was mostly in the event of satellite problems and the like. Anyone presenting these types of doomsday scenarios would have been classified as Internet wackos and UFO conspiracy theorists."

"I get the part where it knocked out power and electrical systems, even combustion engines," Arnoff said. "Sorta like short circuiting the whole world at once. But I don't understand what it did to people's brains to turn them into Zapheads. And I sure as hell don't understand why some of us are more or less still normal."

"I doubt we'll ever have those answers now," the professor said. "Assuming the rest of the globe was affected like the United States, there's no way to undertake the necessary research."

Arnoff waved a hand. "Don't get off on no lecture. Knowing won't change the facts, and the facts is there are a bunch of Zapheads out there wanting to kill us."

"You said they've changed," Campbell said. "What did you mean?"

"They seem to be adapting," the professor said. "You might have noticed yourself, if you've had repeated encounters. Just after the flares, the Zapheads"—his face curdled as he uttered the name, as if he found it distasteful and scientifically inaccurate—"engaged in violence at random, attacking any living thing in their immediate vicinity. But we've observed them engaging in communal activity, as if they are organizing."

"That's why I almost shot you," Arnoff said. "Where

there's one, there might be more."

"Great," Pete said. "Nice to see us humans sticking together."

Campbell gave a small shake of his head, trying to signal Pete to shut up. While Arnoff was a loose cannon, at least he was a cannon—Campbell hadn't felt this safe since the apocalypse had started. He set the empty can of beans aside and licked the sauce from his fork.

"How many of us do you think are left?' he asked the professor.

"It's difficult to estimate. I met Mr. Arnoff between Winston-Salem and Greensboro, traveling east on Interstate 40. He was headed for the coast, figuring he'd find a little island and play Robinson Crusoe until things got sorted out. Thirty miles from here, we found Pamela and Donnie four days ago, hiding in a school bus. And now here are you two. It's a small sample size, but I'd guess maybe one person in a million was immune to the electromagnetic disruptions."

"Holy shit," Pete said. "That's sort of like winning the lottery."

"Or maybe losing, in this case," Arnoff said. "I always thought the world was too crowded, but I don't like being outnumbered."

"Which was my next question," Campbell said. "We met a few other survivors, but we've seen a lot more Zapheads."

He told them about their encounter with the Zaphead in the van, and Pete punctuated the story with sound effects to describe how they'd beat the woman to death. He didn't embellish too many of the details, although he came off like the hero of the tale.

"Good for you," Arnoff said. "I never woulda figured you had it in you."

"Maybe we're adapting, too," the professor said, drawing

on his cigarette. "Maybe the need to kill will turn *us* into Zapheads. The lingering magnetic fluctuations could be turning the kettle of our brains up to a boil as we speak."

Campbell didn't like the idea that his internal circuitry might even now be mutating into something treacherous.

"Don't go getting all negative on me," Arnoff said, leaning his rifle on a stump. "Things are bad enough already. Let's keep it on the sunny side."

"Ironic, given the fact that the sun is the cause of our problems," the professor said. He flicked his cigarette butt into the fire.

"So, you guys have been walking?" Pete asked, slurring his words a little.

"I had a horse I found in a stable," Arnoff said. "It threw me when it stepped in a pothole and broke an ankle. About broke my neck, too."

"Let me guess," Pete said. "You had to shoot it, but you didn't get too down about it."

Arnoff glared at him, and Campbell made a surreptitious slashing motion across his throat to signal Pete to cool it. "Some things just need to be put down," Arnoff said.

The professor made a show of looking at his wristwatch, a nerdy wind-up model that had outlasted the planet's digital watches. "Donnie's time is about up."

Arnoff stood and collected his rifle, walking to the nearest tent and lifting the flap, revealing the mesh screen over the door. "Wake up, Pamela, it's your turn."

"So, what's happening in the east?" the professor asked Campbell in a lower voice, to keep the conversation private.

Campbell shrugged. "A lot of dead people. A lot of Zapheads. Stalled cars. Nothing working right."

"Any organization of emergency services?"

"Like, cops and stuff? No, they were as dead as everybody

else. Once in a while, we saw people walking around off in the distance, but we were afraid to check them out. We didn't know whether they were Zapheads or not."

"Perhaps that was a good idea. I estimate the ratio of Zapheads to survivors is on the order of ten to one."

"I just can't believe it's like this all over the goddamned world," Pete said. "It's like the zombie movie from hell."

"It's hopeless," Campbell found himself saying. He had never given thought to the concept of "hope." That was a word for a Hallmark card when a relative was undergoing chemotherapy, not a word that normal people worried about.

"We have food and supplies," the professor said, keeping his voice at the same lecturing level as before. "If our bottled water runs out, we can filter water from this creek and boil it. This is our second day here, and we could easily last a week before making a foraging run into one of the nearby towns."

"I don't see no advantage in staying here," Arnoff grumbled from his position by the tent. "How long before more of those Zapheads locate our camp?"

"That's for the group to decide," the professor answered.

Campbell had a feeling that opinions were divided and, for the first time, felt tension between the professor and Arnoff, whose eyes were like dark, wet beetles. And, Campbell wondered if he and Pete were now considered part of the group.

Safety in numbers, unless those numbers start shooting at each other.

Arnoff strode off into the trees at the dark perimeter of the camp. Campbell wasn't sure whether the man was scouting or taking a leak.

"What about power?" Pete said. "These batteries won't last forever."

"Power might end up being the thing that kills us," the

professor said. "The sun is the biggest thermonuclear reactor in our corner of the universe."

"All this talk about green energy, there have got to be some wind turbines and solar panels and stuff," Campbell said. He'd known a guy named Terrence Flowers, a big energy hippie, who had always drawn up elaborate plans for off-the-grid sustainable systems. They could sure use Terrence now, unless he was a Zaphead.

"Most such devices have electronic components in their converting systems, so they are useless now. I suppose you could replace the damaged parts and they might work, but we can't just order parts online and have FedEx deliver to our door, right? But the problem is even bigger than that. We could soon be looking at four hundred Chernobyls."

"The hell?" Pete said, cracking another beer with an insolent hiss.

"There are more than four hundred nuclear power plants in the world. They use water circulated by electrical pumps to cool their reactor cores and spent fuel rods. Without electricity, it doesn't take long for them to melt down."

"Wait," Pete said. "No damn way. The government wouldn't allow that shit to happen."

"Oh, the nuclear plants have back-up systems." The flames tossed shadows across the professor's impassive face, giving his words an even more sinister weight. "Diesel generators and other electricity-dependent systems. But if the geomagnetic storms wiped those out, too…"

"Like that Japanese plant in the tsunami," Campbell said.

"Yeah." The professor tossed his cigarette butt and it arced like a meteor into the heart of the fire. "The core overheated because the back-up systems failed. The plant was built to withstand a tsunami, and it did. The trouble was, the back-up systems weren't build to withstand it."

"Jesus Christ," Pete said. "You mean we're going to have to start worrying about giant mutant lizards, too? Like Zapheads aren't bad enough?"

"Oh, no worries," the professor said. "We'll be dead long before anything has a chance to mutate due to radiation."

"Scaring the children again, Professor?" came a woman's voice from the opening of the tent. The flap peeled back and a wild mane of red hair spilled forth. The mane lifted and the tangles revealed a weathered but attractive face, a woman of late middle age without the benefit of makeup but with a fierce sparkle in her green eyes.

As Pamela stood up in a rumpled terrycloth robe, a blanket draped around her, Campbell was immediately captivated. She wasn't beautiful, not by modern Photoshop standards, but she projected a vexing allure. She was a little younger than Campbell's mother, slim but with a strong frame. Even Pete took notice of her, rousing from his drunken stupor to grin at her.

"I like to deal with facts, Pamela," the professor said, lips pursing into a pout. "Eventually, we're going to be living with four hundred Chernobyls. No one knows the effects of that kind of radiation exposure from multiple sources. You can't really model that on a computer."

"Sorry, I left my iPad in my other pants," Pamela said, causing Pete to snort into his beer.

Campbell vaguely understood the danger of radiation, but it seemed as distant a threat as secondhand smoke or preservatives in Twinkies. Pamela was flaunting her charisma, which made the professor squirm a little on his fireside stump.

The professor fumbled for a cigarette. "All I'm saying is—"

They were spared a lecture by the booming report of a gun somewhere off in the night. Pete flopped backward in surprise, dropping his beer, and the professor grabbed for the rifle leaning beside him.

"Donnie!" Pamela shouted, heading in the direction of the shot.

"Stay here," the professor ordered, not that Campbell had any intention of wandering off into the dark, especially with Arnoff out there, armed and dangerous.

After the professor and Pamela had both disappeared in the shadows, Pete said, "Man, what if the Zapheads come while everybody's gone?"

"Maybe we ought to split. We can get back to the road and find our bikes and be out of here before they get back."

"And then what? These people might be our best bet. At least they got some weaponry."

Campbell couldn't offer a better alternative. Arnoff made him uneasy, but at least the group had established some basic order. And Campbell found that he missed order. He liked clocks and homework and responsibility and a schedule. Maybe such things were useless in the new world, but he could find substitutes by belonging to a group with a common purpose.

And no common purpose was as compelling as survival.

"Okay," Campbell said. "Let's give it a couple of days."

Pete opened another beer, and this time, Campbell joined him. Minutes later, Arnoff, the professor, and Pamela came back. Donnie had apparently been freaked out by a stray dog and shot it. Pamela found blankets for Pete and Campbell, who sacked out beside the fire. Campbell was just drowsing off when he saw Arnoff enter Pamela's tent.

He hoped Donnie wasn't the jealous type. He didn't want to wake up to the sound of more gunfire.

CHAPTER SEVEN

When Rachel awoke, she thought she was in her grandmother's house on Puget Sound. As a young child, she'd slept in a guest room facing the sea. In winter and spring, the Pacific sky was often gauzed with gray that penetrated every opening. No amount of electric light could push back the dismal gray.

Rachel fought through the pillows to reach for the bedside lamp, but the table was in the wrong place. The only break in the darkness was a fat line of gray that appeared to be shrinking. She couldn't shrug off the gravity fast enough to crawl toward it, and she was sure that the gap would close before she could climb through. Then she'd be trapped inside the darkness, and Grandma would never hear her screams.

A hand gripped her elbow and she fought against it.

"Easy there, Blondie," said the man whose voice sounded like sand in honey.

And she saw one wet eye catching the light, a miniature mirror of that vanishing grayness. It all came back—the solar flares, the ensuing chaos, the sudden deaths of billions of people, and a world in which Grandma would never again pile stuffed animals around her for comfort.

"Is it tomorrow?" she asked.

"It's now, is all I know," DeVontay said. "You talk in your sleep, did you know that?"

Her mother had said something about it once, but when one slept alone, it was hardly the kind of thing to worry about. "What was I saying?"

"Mostly gibberish, but you were saying a name. 'Chelsea.' Friend of yours? A sister?"

She sat up, aware that she'd slept in her clothes. DeVontay eased back over to the far side of the bed, his eye now swallowed by the black. A moment later she heard the *snick* of his lighter and one of the candles burst to life. It had a faint lilac smell.

When she knelt by the bed to say her morning prayers, he didn't comment.

"Has our little friend come back?" she asked, sitting up and smoothing some of the wrinkles from her clothes before realizing how absurd that was.

"Brother's been making the rounds. Door to door, all night long."

She tried to read his face in the candlelight, to see if he'd stayed awake all night watching over her like a creepy Robert Pattinson in a *Twilight* movie. She forced herself not to whine, although after nearly two weeks in After, she feared numbness more than distress. "What do you think he wants?"

DeVontay, carrying his pistol, crossed the room to the thick line of gray, which had now brightened to a shade of mustard between the curtains. He peeked outside. "Who knows? Mighta been a guest who was checked in when the Big Zap hit and never checked out."

"Or maybe his wife's behind one of these doors? Lying in bed and rotting?" The notion reminded her they were surrounded by dead people, not just in the Motel 6 but all around the Charlotte metro area and probably the world. The faint but putrid odor of decomposition assailed her and she crawled across the bed to the little bottle of hand sanitizer on the table beside DeVontay's midnight snacks. The bottle was half empty, surrounded by Slim Jim wrappers, crumpled cellophane, an empty bottle of Sprite, and a pack of Goody's headache powder.

That's what happens when you leave the grocery shopping to a man.

"Don't see nothing outside." DeVontay parted the curtains to let more light into the room.

"So?"

"We can't stay here."

"It's safe."

"And what's your plan? Just stay here until room service decides to bring us breakfast?"

"Where were you going before?" She had to pee but was too embarrassed to say anything.

"Out of the city, away from them things."

"I meant before that. You know...*before.*"

"Wasn't going nowhere. I was already there. Had me a good job with a roofing company. When you got a job, no reason to go nowhere else."

His silhouette filled the window, his shoulders broad but thin, graceful like an athlete's. His hair was cropped close, with narrow stripes of sideburns on each cheek. That fixed, hooded eye gave him a menacing aspect. Rachel wondered if she would ever have voluntarily take a seat next to him on a bus. "I guess we have a new job," she said.

"What's this 'we' stuff? We need to talk about that."

The words shocked her. She had survived alone, for days and days, running, hiding, learning the rules of After, but she could feel herself wearing down, her options narrowing. "We're alive. We're human. And we can't let them win."

He looked out the window and spoke with his back to her. "What if I decide you're slowing me down? And what else you got to offer besides an extra set of eyes? You don't even got a gun."

"I can find one," she said, hating the desperation in her voice.

He went to the kitchenette and opened the mini-fridge.

"Damn. Looks like it's junk food again."

She really had to pee now, and she felt herself squirming. The bathroom door was closed, and she hadn't remembered them checking it. What if one of the Zapheads was inside? Or a dead body?

"Okay, then," Rachel said. "Go on. Pack up your shit and get out."

He faced her, his good eye widening with surprise. "What you doing cussing? I thought you were one of them goody-goody girls."

"'Shit' is not taking the Lord's name in vain. You're thinking of 'goddamn,' and I'm not calling you a goddamn asshole, even if you are one."

His lips pursed into a frown of contemplation and the silence was thick between them. Somewhere on the floor above, they heard the resident Zaphead banging on a door. DeVontay grinned, showing broad teeth. "All right, so you got a little fire after all. Maybe we can make this thing work as a team until we find something better."

She hadn't even imagined a "better." It was nearly impossible to imagine "good."

"So, since that's settled, what now?" she asked.

"Maybe I ought to go up on the roof and take a look around."

"What if that guy gets you?"

DeVontay waved the gun. "I got an answer."

Rachel didn't want to be left alone. But she wasn't about to let DeVontay know that. "Let's just pack up and get out of here. We can go up on the highway and get a better look. I don't want to risk getting caught in the stairwell. Plus, we don't know how many more of those things are around. The others might not be as noisy as our little friend."

He nodded, apparently taking their partnership seriously.

"Yeah, if it's all clear on the road, I'd just as soon head north."

"Okay, you pack up and I...uh, have some personal business." She didn't want to ask him to check the bathroom. She was embarrassed enough as it was.

Funny, it's the end of the world and I still have something to be shy about.

Rachel felt his one eye tracking her across the room. He chuckled. "What, you going to put on some make-up?"

She frowned at him, gave the doorknob a vigorous twist, and peeked inside. It was dark, but at least no one jumped her.

"Want a light?" DeVontay said.

"No, I'll just leave the door cracked a little."

"I already used it, so don't mind the smell. I saved the flush for you."

"Thanks for sharing." Inside, as her eyes adjusted, she poked with her foot to find the porcelain bowl. As she peeled her jeans down, she listened to the brooding hotel. The banging was several floors above, fixed in one place now, and she was relieved the Zaphead had stopped making the rounds. Maybe the guy had found his room.

Then she heard something below that sound, thin, reedy, and barely piercing the unnatural silence. At first she thought DeVontay was whistling, but it was coming from her left—the room to the other side of their suite.

"Do you hear that?" she whispered, startled by the echo in the tile-covered bathroom.

"You say something?"

"It's music."

"Can't be no music. The pulse blew out all electronics. Didn't you hear the news?"

She didn't point out the contradiction. Instead, she listened more carefully as she wiped. The notes plinked with a metallic coldness, yet they varied in tone and rhythm. After she fastened her jeans, she felt along the sink counter until she found one of the plastic sanitary cups. She shucked the cellophane sheath and placed the mouth of the cup against the wall, then placed her ear against the cup's bottom.

She didn't turn when the door swung open behind her and DeVontay called. "What you doing?"

"Shhh." When Rachel was nine, before the divorce, her father had given her a little music box with Walt Disney's Barbie-fied version of Cinderella on top. By twisting the little brass key, she could make Cinderella spin around and around, never losing a slipper. The music box had issued the same sort of brassy tonality she now heard.

"Somebody's over there," she said.

"Ain't nobody over there. They would have heard us and said something."

"Maybe they're scared."

"And maybe it's a Zaphead."

Rachel thought about banging on the wall and yelling, but if the person *was* scared, that wouldn't help. "We need to open that door and check."

"The hell we do," DeVontay said, his good eye narrowing in annoyance. "We already got a plan, and it don't include saving the world."

"All right, then," she said, pushing past him, not bothering to flush the toilet. "Give me the gun and you can wait here like a sissy."

"A sissy? Nobody calls nobody a 'sissy' anymore."

"Well, sorry I'm not up on my hood lingo, dude. Or homey. Or whatever gangsta thing you want to be called. But I'm not going anywhere until I see who's in that room."

Rachel was surprised by her own anger, but she understood it. She'd felt so helpless watching everyone die from the pulse, or turn into Zapheads, or commit suicide, and finally, she had a chance to be useful.

DeVontay exhaled a long sigh. "Okay, damnit. We get packed, check the room, and then we're outta here."

She met his gaze and they stared at each other for a full ten seconds, neither willing to flinch. "Deal."

As he packed, he cussed under his breath. Rachel collected her backpack, checking the vial of Nembutal the druggist had given her. No, she wouldn't surrender, not while someone else might need help.

DeVontay drew his gun before flipping back the security bolt and opening the door. Rachel pressed close behind. Once in the hall, they could clearly hear the Zaphead banging away above them.

The room next door was 202, and judging from the spacing of the doorways, it appeared to be a suite as well. They paused before the laminated door, listening, but the music had stopped. Rachel nudged DeVontay, and he slipped the master key in the lock.

The tumblers clattered in their own loud music, and the banging upstairs stopped.

"Shit," DeVontay hissed.

Rachel pushed him into the room. The curtains were parted, throwing a wash of gray light across the carpet. Blankets were wadded over a hump on one of the beds, and the air was rank with decay. A boy of about ten knelt on the floor, a doll clutched to his chest. The doll was undressed, and the boy was twisting a knob back and forth that protruded from the doll's back.

He looked up at them with wide brown eyes, his face stricken with guilt. "It broke."

Rachel knelt and put her hands on his shoulders, trying not to weep. DeVontay peeled back the blanket to verify what their noses had already told them.

"Is that your mother?" Rachel asked gently, afraid the boy might see her tears and have his own breakdown.

"She didn't wake up," the boy said.

"We better get out of here," DeVontay said. "I don't think the guy upstairs is going to wait for the elevator."

"Come on," Rachel said, taking the boy's hand and pulling him toward the hall.

The boy gave one last look back at the figure on the bed, at a past that no longer made sense to any of them, and allowed her to lead him into After.

CHAPTER EIGHT

Marina was crying.

Not out loud, which would have disturbed him. They were safe, he was pretty sure of that, as safe as anyone could be these days. But still Marina's sniffling and small grunts unsettled him. He couldn't show it, though, not with Rosa about to shatter.

Jorge Jiminez let his face harden into a mask, the same expression he wore when the boss man, Mr. Wilcox, ordered him to shovel llama manure into the flower garden. Jorge liked the llamas, even though one would occasionally spit in his face. He liked them a lot better than he liked Mr. Wilcox.

He even liked the poop better than he liked Mr. Wilcox.

But now the *gringo* was dead, and so were the sixteen llamas. Jorge had been outside when the flash occurred, his wide-brimmed hat pulled down low over his eyes. The llamas collapsed almost instantly, and so did Barkley, the loud border collie that constantly pestered the animals. The chickens barely paused in their scratching and pecking, though, so Jorge thought it must have been some strange sort of gun, although he couldn't figure out how a gun could kill so many animals at once without making a sound.

But then his mind jumped immediately to Rosa and Marina, and he dropped his shovel and bolted for the tiny mobile home at the back of the property, which was tucked behind a thicket of Douglas firs so that it couldn't be seen from Mr. Wilcox's house. His wife and child hadn't noticed the flash of light. Rosa was stitching a patch on the knee of a pair of jeans and Marina was sprawled on the floor, coloring in her big book of princesses.

That had been over a week ago.

They'd moved into Mr. Wilcox's house two days ago, and although Jorge instinctively sensed it was safer, he wasn't even sure what the danger was. After all, everyone else seemed to be dead.

"Maybe we go to town to see," Rosa said. She sat at the fine oak table, uncomfortable, a glass of water perched in her hand as if she were afraid of leaving spots on the finish.

"I told you, the truck doesn't start," he said, as if explaining to a child. "Neither does the car, and neither does the motorcycle. Everything's *dead*."

He didn't mean to say that last word with such anger. He didn't mean to say it at all. Such a word was bad luck in times like these.

"What if we walk?"

"We could do it in a day. Marina can't walk that far, so we'd have to take turns carrying her."

"I can, too, walk that far," Marina said, her voice cracked and strained. "I'm not a baby."

Her English was very good, better than Rosa's and almost as good as his. Jorge had taken classes at the community college because he knew he'd never see Baja, California, again. Even though the silver mines of La Paz had paid a fair wage of 200 pesos a day, the United States offered the kind of wealth a man needed to raise a family. Like many of his migrant countrymen, he'd planned to work for a year or two and return, but there was always a bill to be paid first, or paperwork, or some legal obstacle.

Luckily, Mr. Wilcox offered employment year round. In the spring, there was gardening, and in the summer, the crew mowed grass at various gated subdivisions built by the boss man, and in fall, they cut hay and prepared for the Christmas tree harvest. In winter, Mr. Wilcox dispensed a list of repairs around the property, which Jorge had once heard him brag consisted of "nine hunnert acres of East Tennessee's mountain heaven." All year round was the task of shoveling of manure: chicken manure, llama manure, pig manure, horse manure, and, once when the septic tank was clogged, people manure.

This week, there had been no shoveling. If one didn't count the graves.

"No, you're not a baby," he said to Marina.

"Maybe we walk to the neighbors' house," Rosa said, glancing out the window.

The closest neighbor was half an hour's walk, even with a nine-year-old. Jorge wasn't afraid of the distance. He was afraid of what they might find when they arrived.

Perhaps they would discover more people like Mr. Wilcox, whose face had been blank and eyes staring wide, as if the flash had blinded him forever. Or more like the Detoro family in the trailer next to theirs, with Alejandro and Sergio dead on the floor and mother, Nima, dead on the couch. Jorge had found Fernando Detoro in the barn, collapsed over the open hood of the tractor's engine, his hands black with grease. Jorge thought perhaps Rosa and Marina survived because they had been inside, and so, that was part of their luck, but being inside had not saved the Detoro family.

"I don't think we should risk leaving," he said. "We have all we need right here."

"But we don't know—"

"*Sí.* We don't know. So we stay."

Before Marina, they had talked only in Spanish when they were together, but Jorge wanted an American daughter. She would have had enough trouble because of her skin, although her straight black hair and onyx eyes surely made the paler girls jealous. Not that there were many paler girls around to worry about, now.

Jorge crossed the living room and drew back the thick velvet drapes. For a bachelor, Mr. Wilcox had put a lot of trouble into his home decorating. The front lawn was now getting ragged, and Jorge had to shake off the itch to mow it.

Nothing moved outside, except for a few crows perched on the white fence. Crows would enjoy this new situation. Plenty of meat to scavenge.

Jorge sat on the couch and stared at the big flat-screen TV. Its size was absurd, like many of the furnishings in Mr. Wilcox's house. Now the blank screen was a mockery of all the things that had once played across it.

"I should try the tractor again," he said. "If anything runs, it will be the tractor."

Rosa didn't challenge the flawed logic. Although they had been raised in a patriarchal culture, Jorge encouraged her to express her opinion. He valued her wisdom. Except now, she was frightened, and fear always hindered wisdom.

"We will be alone," Rosa said. Marina looked up from her drawing.

Jorge glanced toward the kitchen pantry where he'd leaned a loaded shotgun against the racks of wine, spices, and canned goods. "Not alone."

"Hurry back, Daddy," Marina said.

"I will, *tomatilla*," he said, using her toddler nickname of "Little Tomato." "You be good for your momma, okay?"

Marina smiled, nodded, and went back to her drawing. Jorge wondered if she would ever go back to school, or ever again have the normal American life he had wished for her.

He drew back the deadbolt and paused by the front door. He wasn't sure whether he should be afraid. He didn't know enough to be afraid.

Jorge didn't want to retrieve one of the guns from the closet, because that would scare Marina. He fastened his work belt around his waist as if he prepared to weed the landscaping. The machete hung from his belt as it always did.

"Lock up behind me," he said to Rosa before slipping outside.

The day was bright, the sunlight made even fiercer by the amount of time he'd spent inside. He stood on the porch, looking out between the high white columns. Birds chattered in the trees, but their chirps and whistles were spread across the surrounding woods, eerily sparse for late August.

So, not all the birds have died.

The trees were still, and the pastures vacant. The corn swayed slightly in the garden, the tassels just beginning to turn golden. Whatever had killed people and animals didn't seem to have affected the vegetation.

Jorge stepped off the porch and walked past Mr. Wilcox's silver SUV. The vehicle probably cost two years' worth of Jorge's salary, but now it was worthless. Jorge had found the keys in Mr. Wilcox's pants when he'd searched the man's body, but the SUV was just as dead as his boss. Jorge had even swapped out batteries with the tractor, but the engine hadn't turned over.

Jorge wasn't as skilled a mechanic as Fernando Detoro, but he was convinced that whatever had killed Fernando had silenced the engines as well.

He surveyed the road as he continued his trek to the barn. Mr. Wilcox often had visitors from town, fat men wearing ties who never set foot in the fields. Rosa said they were bankers and lawyers who used Mr. Wilcox's money to make more money with no work. Jorge wanted Marina to have that chance one day. He'd been saving cash buried in a jar under the trailer. It was Marina's college fund.

If she ever went to school again.

He entered the two-story barn. Jorge had lied to Rosa. The

tractor had no hope of starting. The engine was in pieces, the radiator removed, spark plug wires and hoses arrayed on a greasy drop cloth.

"Willard?" he called.

On the day of the deaths, Willard White had been mixing chemicals to spray on the shrubs. Willard was the only one whose body hadn't turned up, and Jorge wanted to be sure his family was alone on the farm. He also didn't want Marina stumbling across a decomposing corpse.

Perhaps Willard is as afraid as I am. Perhaps he is hiding.

Willard was a local man, a *gringo*, even if he was unkempt and smelly. He also talked constantly, which is why Jorge couldn't imagine him hiding for days. Willard ranted about "my old bitch of a wife, Bernice," "the guddam government," "guddam sun in my eyes," "my bitchin' back acting up again," "that cheap bastard Wilcox," "guddam milk thistles taking over the pasture," and a long litany of life's constant miseries.

Jorge checked the barn stalls, where a row of horses whinnied uneasily. Mr. Wilcox liked to show off his horses, even though he never rode them. Horses were a luxury, taking valuable pasture and providing no food in return, unlike the cows and chickens. But Jorge liked the horses, because they treated him as an equal, unlike the men.

He patted each on the nose and promised them grain. Unlike the llamas, they had survived the sun sickness.

Jorge entered the cluttered tack room, where Willard liked to take breaks and drink brown liquor called Old Grand-Dad's. Metal trash cans full of sweetened grain stood in one corner. Harness dangled from one wall, and a row of saddles were perched across three sawhorses. One of Jorge's duties was to ride the horses once a week to keep them all trained and in shape, but the leather gear was far from broken in.

The shovel Jorge had used to bury the people was hanging on the wall, along with axes, crosscut saws, sledgehammers, chains, animal harnesses, pulleys, fan belts, loops of twine, and all the other tools needed to operate the farm. Jorge couldn't be sure, but the bags of chemicals and the backpack sprayers appeared untouched.

Thud-dunk.

Something had fallen overhead, up in the hayloft.

The suddenness of the sound kept Jorge from calling out. If it was Willard, the man would have heard him and responded. The barn was large but open, and sound carried well under the corrugated tin roof.

Jorge kept perfectly still, his heart leaping in his chest.

Nothing to fear. Everyone is dead.

Another heavy sound came from above, as if someone was dropping sacks of feed.

Jorge eased out of the tool room, careful not to let the door creak. He headed for the loft stairs and climbed, gripping the machete. Dust motes spun in the open windows like tiny insects. His ascent startled a chicken, which squawked and exploded from under the steps in a blur of feathers. It must have been nesting under there. Jorge wouldn't trust those eggs, not with everything dying.

A rough, wooden-planked door waited at the top of the stairs. When he reached it, Jorge didn't lift the rusty hasp that was held in place by a bent ten-penny nail. Instead, he leaned forward and peered through a crack in the planks.

Willard White paced in the middle of the loft, weaving and wobbling like he did after a quart of Old Grand-Dad's.

But Willard wasn't muttering or singing the way he would if he were drunk. No, he wasn't talking at all, which was the first sign that something wasn't right, because Willard never shut up.

As Jorge spied through the crack, Willard staggered between the stacks of hay bales, plastic water barrels, and sacks of cracked corn like he was looking for his bottle. He stumbled into a loose pile of hay and fell onto his face with a soft *thump* that shook the floorboards. That was the cause of the sound. Willard must have fallen twice before.

Despite his uneasiness, a wave of relief washed over Jorge.

Maybe this is a different kind of drunk. At least he's alive. We aren't alone.

Jorge lifted the hasp and swung open the door.

"Mister White?" Jorge called.

Willard didn't move.

Maybe he's sick. Maybe he was afraid to be alone so he spent his time with Old Grand-Dad.

Jorge stepped into the loft, one palm riding the butt of the machete's grip. He wasn't sure someone could stay drunk for three days, even Willard.

"Something bad happened, Mr. White," Jorge said, louder than he normally would have. He wanted the man to wake up, even though that would mean Willard would be in charge, because Mr. Wilcox made sure his Mexicans knew their place. And if he brought Willard White into the house, Willard would become the new Mr. Wilcox.

The sunlight was soft on the hay, creating a golden bed around Willard. Wire mesh covered the windows, which allowed the breeze to drift through and push the chaff around. The hush of the farm was unnatural, and even the frantic chicken had fallen quiet.

"Mr. Wilcox and the others…they are dead," Jorge said, now ten feet from Willard. The man didn't seem to be breathing, and Jorge was afraid again. If people could still die from whatever had happened, that meant Marina and Rosa were at risk.

He suddenly wanted very much to be back in the house.

But he had to know.

He knelt by the man, sniffing. There was no sweet stench of liquor about Willard, although the man's dirty clothes and body odor were plenty strong.

Jorge touched his shoulder. He whispered, "Mr. White?"

The man turned suddenly, grabbing Jorge's wrist with knotty, calloused fingers. With a yelp, Jorge tried to fall back, but Willard clung with a fierce intensity. The wide eyes glittered, the pupils almost completely filling his sockets, and the remaining whites were streaked with scarlet.

Willard's mouth moved, and Jorge saw a large cavity in one of the yellow molars. "Yuh...yuh..."

"Yes?" Jorge said, still trying to pry his arm free.

Willard wheezed and brought his other hand from the depths of the hay. It held a ball-peen hammer. That must have been what had been hitting the floorboards.

"You're afraid, too," Jorge said.

Now Willard was smiling, although the twisted mouth was open far too wide. "Yuh...yuh..."

"Let me help you up," Jorge said.

Willard swung the ball-peen hammer while tugging Jorge toward him. Jorge swerved just in time. The hammer bounced off his upper arm, sending a dull, icy knot through his body.

"Mr. White?" Jorge twisted away, but Willard kept his grip on Jorge's wrist, cutting off the circulation.

Willard still grinned, but there was no humor in his brightly sparkling eyes. The man hadn't blinked at all and specks of straw were stuck to his eyeballs. Willard raised the hammer again, unable to muster a good swing because he was still lying down.

The hammer came close to Jorge's skull, close enough that he felt its wind, and he unsheathed the machete with his free hand. Willard was drawing the hammer back for another blow when Jorge struck.

Willard's forearm wasn't as limber as the saplings Jorge weeded from the Christmas tree fields. The machete's blade cleaved the flesh and struck bone with a wet, splintering sound. Blood spattered from the wound and onto Jorge's face, but Willard didn't release his grip.

Worst of all, Willard was still grinning, as if the chop was a joke between co-workers killing time. "Yuh...yuh..." the man said, with no passion or pain in his voice.

It was when Willard drew the hammer back for another blow that Jorge chopped again, scared and fierce. This time, the shattered bone yielded. Willard's stump spouted thick jets of blood in rhythm with his heartbeat, and the grizzled farmhand sat and watched it with detached curiosity.

Jorge fell backward now that Willard's weight wasn't serving as an anchor. His arm was heavy. He wondered if he had been injured by the hammer, but when he looked down, he saw Willard's shredded hand still circling his wrist.

Horrified, Jorge tried to shake off the amputated limb. It wouldn't budge. Jorge tucked the bloody machete in his armpit and started peeling back the fingers. One of them twitched and wriggled as if it had a mind of its own.

Finally, he shucked it free and it bounced off the hard wooden planks.

As Jorge ran to the door, he gave one last glance at Willard White. The man stood and began staggering again, as if Jorge had never been there. Blood dribbled from his ragged wound, but his face showed no shock. He dropped the hammer and it made its trademark *thunk*.

"Mr. White?" Jorge said, desperate to see the slightest human emotion in that unshaven face.

Willard turned toward the door. "Yuh...yuh...."

The spidery hand still twitched. Jorge stepped forward and drove his boot into it, sending it spinning across the floor to Willard, who picked it up and looked at it, then stuck it at the end of his arm like a child trying to fix a broken doll.

Jorge slammed the door and dropped the hasp into place, breathing hard. He found some baling wire and twisted a loop to secure the hasp. Willard White could easily remove the chicken wire from the windows if he wanted, but Jorge hadn't seen any glint of remaining intelligence in the man's face.

Jorge hurried down the stairs, wondering if he should remove his shirt so Marina wouldn't see the blood stains. He couldn't come up with a convincing lie, and he still was unsure of the truth.

All he knew was that he didn't want to leave his wife and daughter alone if men such as Willard White existed.

If he's even still a man…

In the house were guns and ammunition, and even if Jorge didn't know what was happening, he could defend his family. He gripped the machete, too frantic to holster it.

After the shadowed dimness of the barn, the sunlight was blinding. He shaded his eyes and headed for the house.

He stopped after a single step.

Two men stood between him and the front porch, their faces as slack as Willard's, their eyes devoid of emotion but glittering with mad energy.

CHAPTER NINE

"Hola," Jorge said.

The man on the left was dressed like one of Mr. Wilcox's banker friends, although his suit was rumpled, the sleeves ragged and his necktie twisted to one side. He was short, fat, and balding, with thick hands and pasty, wormlike fingers. He was a man who'd never performed manual labor.

The other man was close to the porch steps. Despite the heat, he was dressed in brown coveralls and there were dark blotches along the front.

Blood?

The man in coveralls was tall and lean, his face pocked and stubbled. He looked familiar, with his slicked-back hair, green baseball cap, and thick eyebrows, but Jorge was pretty sure the man wasn't one of the farmhands. Perhaps he worked on one of the construction crews.

Neither man responded to his greeting. Jorge lifted the machete, which had been dangling along his right thigh. Jorge wasn't sure whether they were sick like Willard White. They didn't look dangerous, but their quietness disturbed him.

He pointed the machete at the banker and waved the blade down the driveway, indicating that the man should go.

There is no car. How long has he been here?

Maybe the man had walked from town, but that would have taken a day. Jorge couldn't imagine the plump man walking the length of the gravel drive, much less the ten miles to town. Not in those fancy leather shoes.

"You," Jorge said to the man in coveralls. "Move away."

The man turned his back and started up the steps. The banker finally blinked, the first motion to cross his face since

Jorge had emerged from the barn.

Jorge pictured little Marina inside the house, and Rosa frightened of the noises outside and unable to hide it. "Stop," he said, afraid to shout.

The man in coveralls ignored him, crossing the porch to the front door, his heavy boots drumming the wooden boards. Unlike Willard, the man in coveralls moved with purpose, although his gait was jerky and unbalanced.

He's trying to get in.

Ignoring the banker, who at one time would have commanded almost as much polite respect as Mr. Wilcox, Jorge ran for the porch. If he moved fast enough, the man in coveralls wouldn't reach the door.

But as Jorge raised the machete and prepared to launch himself up the steps, he sensed motion to the left. The banker closed in with a speed that belied his girth. He slammed into Jorge, wrapping him in a hug and knocking them both to the ground. The machete flew from Jorge's fingers.

Jorge rolled, scrabbling for purchase on the lawn. The banker gripped him around one thigh, and Jorge kicked backward, pounding into the man's shoulder. The man's face was pink with effort. He appeared to be grinning.

"You *blanco culito*," Jorge muttered, not wanting to raise his voice.

The "white little asshole" clung to Jorge, his expensive jacket ripping. Jorge kicked and spider-crawled backwards. The crazy attacker still clung to him.

The man in coveralls reached the door and rattled the knob.

While the banker was definitely afflicted with whatever had contaminated Willard, the man in coveralls acted with intent and intelligence. Jorge considered him as the more dangerous of the two, but first he'd have to deal with the banker.

Jorge used a trick he'd learned while wrestling the boars. Mr. Wilcox made them castrate the young male pigs that weren't needed for breeding. Jorge resented the blood and violence of the act, but now he was grateful for the experience.

Treat the banker like a pig.

The banker didn't have the strength of a young boar. Jorge straddled the banker's upper chest with his legs, squeezing him in a scissors grip. The banker bellowed and pushed forward, scraping Jorge's back but moving them both closer to the machete.

The man in coveralls slammed his fist against the front door.

If you make Marina cry, I will castrate you.

And that was when Jorge recognized him. He was the farrier who visited once a month and trimmed the horses' hooves and replaced their metal shoes. While the banker had been inside the house, probably sipping lemonade or brown liquor in the den, the farrier had no right seeking entry. Workers never went inside the Wilcox house.

The machete lay five feet out of reach, and the banker wasn't letting Jorge gain any traction. Jorge squeezed the man harder between his knees. His thighs trembled with fear, rage, and exertion.

The farrier pounded on the door with both fists, the noise like a horse galloping across a wooden bridge.

Jorge thought he heard a scream inside the house.

That would be Rosa. Marina is the calm one. Marina would never break her promise to be good.

He was almost as angry at Rosa as he was the two men. Marina would be an American, not so weak with her emotions.

But the scream fueled him. He grabbed the banker's head

and slammed his face into the ground. A soft *merp* of surprise flew from the man's mouth on impact. He hardly seemed to notice the pain.

The banker's head lifted. Those dry eyes looked right through Jorge and into the Badlands beyond everything.

The man's pink skull enraged him. The banker became the symbol of all the times he'd had to stand with his hat in his hands, all the nodding and sweating in the immigration offices, all the frowns and smirks in the feed store when Jorge picked up farm supplies. The banker was bacon in a world where Jorge could only afford salted fatback.

Jorge punched at the man, banging against one rubbery ear. He drew back for a second blow, but the banker crawled forward when Jorge's legs unclenched.

Now the banker was on top of him like a lover, a stench of musky sweat mingled with faint fancy cologne. Jorge swung again but the blow was stunted. It bounced off the man's shoulder.

"Get off," Jorge grunted at the man.

The banker wriggled higher onto Jorge's chest, his bulk making it difficult for Jorge to toss him aside. Then his breath was on Jorge's face and it stank like a barn stall.

He's smiling. Like this is American football.

Jorge angled his neck until he could see the farrier at the door. The man had stopped pounding and was fishing in one of the thigh pockets of the coveralls. He emerged with a set of metal pinchers, a tool used to trim hooves. Jorge shoved the banker as the farrier clamped the tool on the door lock and began twisting with a *skree* of metal.

The banker lunged forward again, his glistening forehead now right at Jorge's chin, and Jorge had to fight an urge to bite into pink flesh.

Instead, he used the momentum to slide them both

forward another foot until his fingers found the machete handle.

He waggled the blade through the air, unable to get a clean arc. The side of the steel blade slapped against the banker's back with a *thwack*. The banker, apparently not able to understand that the blade could harm him, ignored it and continued to grind himself against Jorge as if to smother him.

Jorge got a better swing the second time and the blade cleaved through the fancy jacket and struck meat. Blood spouted from the wound.

The banker's face curdled in confusion. Jorge hewed another opening across the man's back.

Now the banker relaxed his grip enough for Jorge to kick free and roll to his knees, just in time to see the door open in front of the farrier.

He's broken in—

Jorge's heart fluttered in fear. He used the adrenalin to hurtle toward the porch, blood dripping from the machete blade. He was off balance, the bright sun blinding him, and the creaking of the door hinges seemed as loud as an animal's scream.

He wasn't going to make it in time. The farrier entered the house, the wicked tool dangling at his side.

He waited for Rosa's scream. He leaped up the steps and raised the machete.

But before Jorge could enter, a loud *ka-doom* poured through the doorway. Jorge entered to the acrid smell of gun smoke in the air.

The farrier lay facedown on the floor, a patch of crimson blossoming across the back of his coveralls. Rosa stood by the kitchen counter, the shotgun in her slender arms.

A blue thread of smoke curled from the barrel as if she'd just burned the toast instead of killing a man.

Not a man. A thing. A pig.

"Marina?" Jorge asked her.

"In the closet."

Where the guns were. Jorge pictured Rosa shoving Marina in there and grabbing the gun. Maybe he didn't know his wife at all.

"Who is he?" Rosa asked.

"The horseman."

"He's dead?"

Jorge nudged the corpse with his boot. It lay like a sack of rotted potatoes. "*Sí.*"

"Who are these people?"

"Something has changed." Jorge laid the bloody machete on the granite countertop, crossed the kitchen, and opened the pantry door. Marina sat hunched on a cardboard case of wine, her hands over her ears, hair trailing over her face.

He knelt and brushed her hair away until she peeked at him.

"Is the bad man gone?" she asked. Her voice wasn't trembling or whiny, just cautious, like she'd done something bad but wasn't sure what.

"Yes, *tomatilla*, he's gone."

"It's not like on TV, is it? Where the bad man comes back after you think he's gone?"

Jorge hugged her, glancing back into the kitchen. From there, he could see the farrier's feet. "No, this isn't TV."

But he'd forgotten about the banker. Jorge had delivered several vicious blows with the blade but probably not enough to kill. "Stay here, okay? *Un momento.*"

He was slipping, using Spanish. Marina would never become American if he didn't control himself. She nodded and even gave him a tired smile. He reached behind her and took the hunting rifle with the big scope. He didn't know what caliber it was, but the shell he'd put in the chamber was nearly as thick as his pinky.

Yes, smile in the face of danger and you will fit in here. Because America is a dangerous land.

He closed the pantry door and Rosa was waiting, still cradling the shotgun. Her eyes were wide and wet with fear, but her jaw was firm.

"Is the other one dead?" she said, quietly so that Marina couldn't hear, although it seemed as if the boom of the gun still echoed off the kitchen tiles.

"I need to check."

"I saw through the window. And when he came up on the porch—"

"You did well. Stay while I check on the other one, the banker."

"Will we be in trouble? For killing these white men?"

Jorge didn't tell her about Willard. "I don't know who would cause trouble. Mr. Wilcox is dead. Who would call the police?"

"The phone doesn't work."

Jorge took a position near the big window, parting the white curtain with the tip of the rifle barrel. The banker was on all fours, crawling away from the porch. His jacket was shredded and his tie dragged in the dirt. Jorge wondered if he should shoot the man. Was the man in pain, or was he beyond feeling? The anger that Jorge had felt when his family was threatened washed away and left him tired and confused.

"What do we do now?" Rosa said behind him.

"We could stay," he said, not liking his indecision. He's always been the patriarch. And now his wife was a protector, a killer, while he let a man crawl away who had attacked him and threatened his family.

"What if there are others? Mr. Wilcox had many friends."

"He had no friends. He had people who wanted his money."

And now we have everything he once owned.

Jorge glanced at the giant TV mounted to the wall in the living room, the shadows of the tree branches from outside swaying across the black surface. The high glass cabinet held carved wooden ducks, fish, and turtles, as well as ivory elephants that Mr. Wilcox had boasted were illegal to own. Above the marble fireplace was a painting of black people cutting wheat with hand scythes.

Upstairs, in the dresser beside Mr. Wilcox's puffy and waxy corpse, Jorge had found eight thousand dollars in a cigar box. He had been afraid to take the money, sure that rich people had a way to track cash.

Everything Mr. Wilcox owned is now worthless, except these guns and the food in the pantry.

Jorge glanced at the farrier's cooling corpse and the pool of blood that was already coagulating around it.

And horses.

"Get Marina ready," Jorge said.

"Ready?"

"Load some backpacks with food we can eat on the road."

"So, we're not staying here?"

"More people may come. I don't want to wait."

Jorge felt a surge of strength as he took control of the situation. He was still *masculino*. But he kept the rifle, even though he sheathed the machete. Locking the front door behind him, he checked the banker's progress. The banker was halfway down the drive, flies already circling him in black clouds.

Soon the vultures will have him.

Jorge studied the sky, wondering whether his family would change, would become like *them*.

But such worries would make him weak, and Marina and Rosa needed him to be strong. Plus he had the rifle. He thought again about Mr. Wilcox's money and all the useless comforts of his boss's life. He wasn't an overly religious man, despite his Catholic upbringing. But perhaps the meek truly did inherit the Earth.

It was as good an explanation as any why the three of them had been unaffected by the sun sickness.

He went to the barn to saddle the horses.

CHAPTER TEN

"What road are we on?" DeVontay said, peering at the crumpled map.

They sat in the shade of a large oak, careful not to touch the poison sumac that was already turning fierce red with the end of the summer. The boy had quickly grown tired and had asked for his mother once. But they kept moving, determined to get away from the population centers where Zaphead encounters were more likely.

"That's I-77," Rachel said, pointing to the four-lane highway below them. They'd walked parallel to the road, staying in the vegetation even though the traveling was more difficult. Rachel didn't trust the vehicles, especially since so many of them had tinted windows. On the crest of the slope, they were able to see movement in any direction.

DeVontay squinted through the treetop at the rising sun. "Which way we headed?"

"The sun rises in the east," Rachel said. "I learned that in Girl Scouts."

DeVontay scowled, the expression almost comical because of his glass eye. "Wish I'd left you back at the hotel."

The boy stiffened and shuddered beside Rachel, and she shot DeVontay an angry glance and shook her head.

We're his parents now. We have to pretend everything's going to be all right, just like real parents do.

I failed Chelsea, but I won't fail this boy.

The boy's blonde hair and freckles suggested a fair complexion that would sunburn easily. At their morning stop at a convenience store, she'd found him some sunscreen and made him put on a Carolina Panthers ball cap. She'd also collected some of the healthiest offerings she could find, including some apple juice she hoped hadn't spoiled. DeVontay had collected the map, a pack of butane lighters, and half a box of Reese's Peanut Butter Cups.

Rachel fished a bottle of water from her backpack and held it out to the boy, who still clutched the naked doll to his chest. "Here, honey. I'll bet you're thirsty."

The boy shook his head. He'd barely spoken a dozen words all day. Rachel wondered if he was in shock. She hadn't studied much basic health, but she knew shock tended to kill people before they had a chance to die from more horrible things.

She put the water bottle by his sneakers and offered him a granola bar. He shook his head.

"You gotta speak the language," DeVontay said. He opened one of his Reese's and held a cup of chocolate and peanut butter out to the boy. The boy's mouth visibly watered and he licked his lips.

"It's okay." Rachel gave an encouraging smile, hoping the boy didn't crash from a sugar high while they were putting in some miles.

The boy let the doll fall into his lap. He took the candy, which was soft from the heat. As he bit into it, DeVontay said, "Melts in your mouth, not in your hands."

"That's M&M's," Rachel said.

"Whatever. Same principle."

"No, it's not. M&M's has a hard shell so instead of smeary chocolate, it leaves artificial food coloring on your fingers."

"Do you got to argue about everything?"

"No, only when you're wrong. Oh, wait a minute. You're wrong about everything."

The boy's blue eyes tracked back and forth, from one of them to the other. He had returned to the world a little, back from whatever private hell inside his head.

"Here," she said, reaching out for the other peanut butter cup. She held it in her palm until the chocolate ran. Then she popped the candy into her mouth. It was so sweet that it made her teeth hurt.

She showed her palm to both of them. "See? A gooey mess."

"That looks like poopie," DeVontay said.

Rachel made a show of studying her palm as if making a scientific observation. "Hmm. You're right, it does."

She licked her palm, making sure to smear chocolate all over her lips. "Mmm. *Tastes* like poopie, too!"

DeVontay laughed, and the boy giggled. "Yuck!" the boy said, in a small, delighted voice.

"Hey, watch this," DeVontay said. He dug his fingers into the skin beneath his left eye, then touched the glass orb and rolled it a little so that it appeared the eye was gazing far to the left.

Whoa, don't freak the kid out. We're trying to get him back to normal, not make him think you're a Zaphead.

But the boy gazed with intense interest. DeVontay smiled, then lifted up the skin just beneath his eyebrow and rolled the glass eye into his fingers. He held it up like a marble. "Here's looking at you, kid."

"Can I hold it?" the boy said.

"Sure. But only if you let me hold the doll for a minute."

The boy nodded and made the trade. It was the first time Rachel had seen him without the doll since they'd rescued him. She decided to bring him all the way out. "What's your name?"

"Stephen."

"That's a nice name."

The boy shrugged, focused on the glass eye. He turned it

so it caught the light. "How did you lose your eye?" he asked DeVontay, his lips pressed into a solemn line.

"Messing around. You know how kids are."

"Mommy says if you play with sticks, you'll poke your eye out."

"She's pretty smart," DeVontay said.

Rachel noted he used present tense. *He's got a good instinct. Maybe he has more social experience than he lets on.*

DeVontay stroked the doll's kinky hair. "What's her name?"

"Miss Molly."

"That's a pretty name," Rachel said.

"Does it hurt?" the boy asked, passing the glass eye back to DeVontay.

"Not anymore. It's just something you get used to. But it took a while."

Rachel noticed his street grammar had softened, and his former aggressiveness was buried. "Just like this—this *After*—is something we'll all have to get used to," she said to Stephen.

The boy touched the bill of his cap. "Like not having football this year."

"Probably not," DeVontay said. "But the Panthers wouldn't be no good anyway. The Eagles would have whooped them bad."

As DeVontay plopped his glass eye back in place, Rachel scanned the road below. *All those people rotting in the August heat.*

"Mommy said only the wicked people changed," Stephen said.

"Lots of people have died, Stephen," Rachel said. "None of us are perfect, but most of us are good."

"Then why did my mommy die? Does that mean she is wicked?"

DeVontay gave Rachel a look like: "I'm not touching this one." He gave Stephen his doll back and the boy immediately clutched it to his chest, apparently lapsing back into his near-catatonic state. Rachel knew this might be their only chance to pull the boy out again.

"Your mommy wasn't wicked," Rachel said. "God just needed an extra angel in heaven, to make things ready for when the rest of us arrive."

Crap. Maybe this wasn't such a good direction. But they didn't cover this in Counseling 101.

"Then how come some people died and some just walk around being mean? Aren't they wicked?"

"We don't know that, honey. That's why we need to stay away from everyone until we can figure out what is happening."

"So, it's just the three of us forever?"

"We'll find others like us."

"Other good people?"

Rachel wasn't sure why she'd survived. She'd always felt special, but not in an arrogant way. Even from an early age, she'd always felt God made her for a reason, and made only one person like her in the whole world, and she was supposed to be Rachel all her life. She'd felt it even before her mother took her to Catholic services or her dad gave his grumbling rants that took her years to understand as atheism.

She wasn't even sure if she'd ever accepted his atheism, because she couldn't comprehend a world without purpose and order. After Chelsea's death, Dad had shut off any pretense of faith, insisting that no merciful God would allow such a tragedy. She wondered what Dad would make of this apocalypse.

"Yes," Rachel said, realizing the silence had stretched too long, filled by the twitter of birds and the soft flapping of leaves overhead. "Other good people."

"Do you know where they are?"

DeVontay, studying the map again to avoid joining the discussion, pointed to the northwest and said, "Yeah, little man. They're that way."

"Is that way Mi'sippi?" Stephen asked. "My daddy's in Mi'sippi."

Rachel found herself nodding. Little white lies didn't make her wicked, did it? "Yes, Mississippi's that way."

"I hope Daddy's good. I don't want him to be one of the mean people."

Stephen's eyes welled, and Rachel scooted over to hug him. He sagged into her arms and she patted his back. "With a boy like you, I'm sure he's good. We'll find him for you."

She imagined an older, pudgier version of Stephen, a bloated corpse lying in bed or on a sidewalk or roasting in a car. Then she saw him staggering along the street, looking for something to attack. She pushed the vision away.

Please, God, give me strength. Show me Your purpose and help me be part of Your order. Even if I don't understand it.

DeVontay folded the map backwards, so that it was lumpy and the corners uneven. He pushed it into his backpack, along with the leftover food. He pulled the pistol out, making sure Stephen wasn't watching, and said, "Hey, we better get started if we got to walk all the way to Mi'sippi, right?"

Rachel brushed Stephen's hair back from his freckled face and kissed his forehead. "You're a good boy. And I don't believe wicked people can hurt good people, do you?"

He shook his head no, bumping her cheek with the bill of his cap. She smiled and helped him to his feet. DeVontay had eased back into the shade until he was behind the tree. He tilted his head toward the highway.

Rachel saw four of them, coming up the pavement

between the jumbled lines of cars. Their clothes didn't look ragged, and they didn't jerk and shake, but she knew they were Zapheads. Something about them was off. Maybe it was the way they peered in each vehicle as they passed, as if searching for any movement they could make still forever.

They were about three hundred yards away, and it was unlikely they would notice anyone on the slope above them. From Rachel's observations, Zapheads had a suppressed sense of perception, as if they could only process information in their immediate vicinity. Maybe their focus on destruction was so all-consuming that they had no larger awareness of the world.

Perhaps that is the definition of "wicked": pure selfish destruction.

"I need you to be very quiet, Stephen," she said calmly, in her regular voice. "Can you do that for me?"

He opened his mouth and caught himself, then nodded. He looked at DeVontay and saw the gun.

"We're going to Mississippi now," she said.

"I'll be good," Stephen whispered.

"This way," DeVontay said, waving them into the scrub vegetation that dotted the top of the slope. Rachel nudged Stephen toward DeVontay and collected their backpacks. On the highway below, one of the Zapheads pounded an iron bar against a car hood. The brutal *thwack* was an intrusion on the pastoral serenity of a few moments earlier, and Rachel was reminded that After was not paradise.

It was a land where the wicked walked.

When three of the four Zapheads disappeared from view behind a tractor-trailer rig, Rachel hurried into the bushes to join DeVontay and Stephen. Glass shattered below them, followed by a strange inhuman cry that might have been glee.

They hurried without speaking, DeVontay beating back

the branches and briars with the arm that held the gun, Stephen hunched low so that the bill of his cap hid his face, and Rachel repeatedly glancing behind her. They were still moving roughly parallel to the interstate, although they'd put more distance and vegetation between them and it. The morning coolness had given way to an intense heat that had burned away the dew, and the air held all the promise of an oven.

After ten minutes, they could no longer hear the crazed vandalism, and DeVontay slowed a little, tucked his gun in his belt, and picked up Stephen. He must have noticed the dark circles of exhaustion under the boy's eyes.

"I know you're big enough to walk, but I want you to rest so you can tell me bedtime stories," DeVontay said.

"Are you going to shoot the wicked people?" Stephen said, letting the doll nestle between them. It must have been uncomfortable for DeVontay, but he said nothing.

"No wicked people are going to get you while we're around, okay, little man?"

"Okay."

Rachel peeled away Stephen's backpack to help lighten DeVontay's load. The act caused the doll to fall to the ground, and Stephen gave a bleat of alarm. She hurriedly collected it before he could scream and alert the Zapheads. They continued through the vegetation, which had thinned considerably and occasionally allowed them a view of the cluttered highway.

After a few minutes, Stephen was asleep and DeVontay slowed to reduce the bouncing of his gait.

"Did you see what I saw?" Rachel asked.

"'fraid so. But tell me anyway, so it's not my imagination."

"The Zapheads were moving in a group. They weren't doing that before."

"Maybe it was random. They just happened to bump into each other and said, 'Yo, muthas, let's break some shit together, whaddya say?'"

"Either way, I don't like it."

"I don't like any of this. Things were bad enough without no wicked-ass gangbanger shit."

He'd reverted back to his street persona. She didn't blame him. Maybe it was a useful survival mechanism, and they might need all such mechanisms they could find.

"You were good back there," she said. "With Stephen."

"So, I'm one of the good people for a change," he said. "Don't be getting used to it."

CHAPTER ELEVEN

Campbell was dreaming of Gina Bellinari, the first girl he'd ever kissed. In the dream, they were behind the bleachers at the Idlewild High School football stadium, and it must have been a school day, because he could hear kids running and laughing on the practice fields. Gina was saying people would notice they were missing, and she couldn't afford to get sent to the office again, and Campbell knew her reputation and figured just a kiss was being cheap. But when he went in again, his lips puckered out like he was about to suck down a sour gummy worm, she kicked him hard on the shin.

"Fuh," he said, knowing he looked uncool, and uncool didn't cut it when Gina had her choice of any straight boy in the school, except the artists and the geeky band students who'd probably be virgins all the way through college.

"We're moving out," Gina said, but her voice was gruff, cracked, and masculine, and she didn't look all that happy about being kissed.

Campbell opened his eyes to find Arnoff standing over him, dressed in camouflage overalls. The encounter with Gina had given way to an ROTC nightmare and all the chisel-jawed goons in high school who'd waved their flags in his face and had strutted around spouting word like "duty" and "honor." But this wasn't some high-school faker, this was a grown man, although his cheeks were shaven as brightly pink as a teenager's.

Then Campbell remembered the camp, and the solar storms, and the world with six billion dead people. And his back was killing him from sleeping on the ground. "Hell," he groaned.

"Yep, same as yesterday," Arnoff said, walking away to the fire, where the professor was tending a blackened coffee pot.

Campbell peeled back the thick blanket and the stench of his rumpled clothes crawled over him. He hadn't changed since they'd left Chapel Hill, and he'd only bathed once, half-heartedly swabbing his armpits with creek water. If the Zapheads didn't get him, flesh-eating fungus eventually would.

He glanced over at Pamela's tent. Donnie was helping Pamela break it down. Donnie was slender and had bad teeth, like an ex-con who'd been deprived of decent hygiene. His black, greasy hair was combed straight back over his head, and he wore a sleeveless denim jacket and his arms were covered with crude tattoos. In high school, Campbell would have called him a redneck, but never to his face.

"Make sure you shake the leaves out," Pamela said to Donnie. At least Pamela had taken the time to brush her red curls, and Campbell couldn't be sure, but she apparently was wearing mascara and foundation. In the firelight, he'd taken her for thirty-ish, but the harsh morning sun added a good decade to her face.

"A little bit of dirt never hurt nobody," Donnie said.

"I didn't say it would hurt, I just said I didn't want them."

"It's my tent, too."

"Don't push your luck."

"I push what I want, where I want."

"Enough of that, lovebirds," Arnoff barked. "I'm making a scouting run and I want everybody ready to roll when I get back."

Roll? On what, bicycles? Some armored column you got here, Rambo.

Campbell crawled out of the blanket and looked around

the camp. It was shoddier in daylight than it had appeared last night, with filthy clothes flapping from a sagging piece of twine that was stretched between two trees. Ten feet behind the professor was a mound of cans, plastic bags, and coffee grounds. Pete lay bundled up on the edge of the clearing, apparently having rolled away from the fire during the night.

Campbell stood and stretched the stiffness from his spine. Pamela glanced his way with a smirk and said, "Is this the best Generation Y has to offer?"

Donnie scowled, not passing up a chance to bicker. "Dead weight. I don't know what the hell Arnoff thinks he's doing."

"Pissing you off, Donnie. And just maybe saving your life."

Campbell nodded at the professor, who focused all his attention on making the perfect cup of coffee under the most trying circumstances, as if the apocalypse was just a crude chemistry lab. The bespectacled man was perched as if he'd spent the entire night gazing into the flames. Campbell would never be caught dead in such company under normal circumstances. But normal was a distant memory.

Two weeks? It's not even been two weeks?

While Donnie and Pamela wrestled their tent into a nylon bag, Campbell woke up Pete, whose bedroll was surrounded by half a dozen crushed beer cans. Pete blinked his bleary eyes and said, "Ugh. I must have turned into a Zaphead, because it feels like somebody cracked my skull open like an egg and took a big electric dump in it."

"You don't have time to enjoy your hangover. Sgt. Rock has ordered us to move out."

"We don't have to stick with these clowns. We were doing pretty well on our own."

"Really? Your idea of a Plan A is to go from beer truck to beer truck until we're in Milwaukee."

Pete sat up and wiped the crust from his eyes, then grabbed his wool cap and pulled it down to his eyebrows. "Give me a break. At least I'm not thinking I'll crash my parents' house and sleep in the basement until I can get back on my feet."

"Dude, it's a thing called 'hope.' When the shit hits the fan, you hold on to it."

Pete looked around, spied his sodden cardboard case of beer, and fished out a warm can. It spewed as he popped it. "This is the only thing I'm holding on to."

"Hey," Pamela called to them. "You party boys coming with us?"

"Safety in numbers," Campbell said to Pete.

"Not numbers like these. Look at the professor. You want your life in his hands?"

The professor poured dark, thick fluid from the coffee pot into a tin cup and blew on it. "At least he wouldn't eat your liver if you were snowed in together," Campbell said. "And Sgt. Rock seems to know his way around a gun. Unlike you."

"Yeah, then how come he didn't give us our guns back? I don't think this is such a good time to be a control freak. Because there's shit out there beyond everybody's control."

Donnie sauntered over to them, a backpack, a rifle, and the bagged tent slung over his shoulder. "So, which one of you is the momma's boy?"

"Excuse me?" Pete said.

"Come on, guys like you? You kidding me? You're doing everything but holding hands. I need a momma's boy to carry this tent for me."

"Screw you," Pete said, still sitting with his blanket wadded around him.

With the ferocity of a wolverine, Donnie slung the tent bag down his arm and hurled it at Pete. The bag knocked the beer from his hand and forced the wind from his lungs with an *oomph*.

Pete rose from the ground and wobbled a moment, still woozy from his hangover, but rage twisted his face. Campbell had to hold him back, but Donnie was unimpressed.

"Look at the lover boys hugging," Donnie said, grinning with black teeth. "Ain't that sweet?"

"Knock it off, Donnie," Pamela said. "Arnoff won't like you messing with the guests after what happened last time."

Last time? Campbell didn't like the sound of that.

"Look, Donnie," Campbell said, taking a chance and calling the guy by his name, not knowing how he would take it. "We're basically what's left of the human race. If we go fighting each other, we're no better than the Zapheads."

"Shit on them," Donnie said. "I got enough ammo to take care of all of them."

"We don't know how many are out there," the professor said, sipping his coffee like he was kicking around theories at the local barista. It was the first time he had interacted with anyone that morning. Maybe he needed caffeine before he could face the horrors of modern life.

"That's why Arnoff wants us to stick together," Pamela said.

"Arnoff this and Arnoff that," Donnie said. "We were getting along just fine until you made him king of the world."

The smoky air was ripped by an explosion of gunfire.

Arnoff emerged from the brush. "Good thing I wasn't a Zaphead, or you'd all be meat."

"Come on, Arnoff, you'll scare the children," Pamela said.

"They ought to be scared. How come you guys aren't packed?"

Pete and Donnie glared at each other for a moment, and then Donnie gathered the tent from the ground. The professor tossed his coffee into the fire and said, "How was the reconnaissance mission?"

"It's clear to the west, so we'll be heading that way."

"Yesterday, you wanted to go east toward the coast," Donnie said.

"Changed my mind. People change their minds from time to time."

"And sometimes the sun does it for them," the professor said.

"What about our bikes?" Campbell asked. He assumed Pete was sticking with the crowd. Campbell certainly was, at least for now.

"We move as a unit," Arnoff said. "But it wouldn't hurt to have fresh legs to do some advance scouting."

Donnie smirked. "Hear that, pretty boys? Fresh legs."

"Don't be an asshole, Donnie," Pamela said, shouldering her own backpack. Campbell wondered if she had a firearm tucked in one of the bulging pockets of her thin cotton jacket. Even the professor had a rifle leaning against a tree near his pile of gear.

"Do we get our guns now?" Campbell asked Arnoff.

"Get packed up. Then we'll see."

Campbell helped Pete roll up his blanket. When Pete reached for a fresh beer, Campbell kicked away the cardboard box. "You're going to get us killed."

"If these creeps don't kill us first. Don't you think they're a little unhinged?"

"We're all a little unhinged. We just got hit with the apocalypse. What do you expect?"

"Yeah, but you'd think they'd be banding together. Instead, they're ripping each other to pieces."

"Stress. We're in a war zone now."

"We'll play it your way for a day or two. But if this is the best they have to offer, I'm taking my bike and flying solo." Pete shouldered his backpack and headed out of the clearing.

"What do you think you're doing?" Arnoff shouted.

"Getting my bike."

Arnoff pointed his rifle ninety degrees to Pete's left. "You might want to head in the proper direction."

Pete gave an insolent wave and slipped into the woods, Campbell following. When they came to the place where Arnoff had shot the Zaphead, the corpse was gone. Only a crushed section of grass and a rusty brown stain remained.

"What do you think happened to it?" Pete asked.

"Maybe somebody buried it."

"You serious? You think Arnoff would pass up an opportunity to put us on gravedigger detail? And why would he bother, anyway? They knew they were breaking camp and leaving. So what's one more corpse?"

"Or maybe he wasn't dead, just wounded."

Pete peered into the surrounding trees. "I don't like it."

"Come on. Let's get our bikes before the others catch up."

As they emerged from the trees and climbed the rocky slope to the guardrail above, Pete said, "At least the professor seems to have his shit together. Maybe we can learn something from him."

"All he's got is theories," Campbell said.

"Beats what we got." Pete began clambering up the rocks but only made it about ten feet before he stopped.

"What's the matter?"

"You smell that?"

"I don't smell anything but your body odor."

"Seriously. Smoke."

"The campfire."

"No. This is like plastic and garbage and stuff instead of wood."

"Maybe the professor made them clean up their trash. 'Leave no trace' and all that."

Pete kept climbing, and by the time they reached the guardrail, Campbell was out of breath. He could only imagine how Pete felt, with last night's beer leaking from his pores. The morning was already muggy.

"Look," Pete said, pointing to the east.

Several massive pillars of smoke boiled in the far distance, shimmering in the heat. "The hell is that?" Campbell said.

"That would be Greensboro," Arnoff said.

They both turned in surprise to see Arnoff perched in the bed of a pickup truck, scanning the horizon with binoculars. They hadn't even heard him come up behind them.

Damn. What if he'd been a Zaphead?

"What's going on?" Pete asked him.

"The reason I decided we're heading west. Looks like the cities have gone to the Zapheads."

"What do you mean?" Campbell asked, his stomach tightening with renewed dread. "I thought they were pretty much brainless killing machines."

"Like I told you, they're changing." Arnoff lowered his binoculars and slipped on a dark pair of aviator glasses. "And until we know more about why they're changing, or what they're changing into, we're keeping clear."

The others had reached the bottom of the slope and Donnie was helping Pamela keep her footing. The professor ascended with the stubborn grace of a goat, showing himself to be in decent shape. Arnoff watched Donnie like an eagle might watch a mouse.

"All right, soldier," Arnoff said to Pete. "You want to be point?"

"Not sure what that means."

"Take those two wheels of yours and head up the highway

about a mile, to the top of that next rise. We'll be heading your way. If you see any Zapheads, ride back and give us a warning."

"I have a better idea. Why don't you give me my gun back, and if I see anything, I'll fire a shot in the air."

Not bad. Campbell was impressed with his friend's shrewdness.

Arnoff gave a curt nod. "Good plan."

He fished in one of the pockets of his camouflage cargo pants and pulled out Pete's pistol. Pete rolled his bike beside the truck bed and accepted it. Campbell couldn't help thinking Arnoff was getting off on authority, a position that only the end of the world could have granted him.

We've all discovered our worst.

No, not "worst."

Because that assumed things would get better.

As Arnoff's crew assembled on the asphalt, Pete mounted his ten-speed and pedaled between the stalled vehicles, his silhouette growing smaller and smaller. Then he swerved around a cattycornered dump truck and was gone.

CHAPTER TWELVE

Jorge had given Marina a few riding lessons, but it was Rosa's first time on a horse. He spent most of the first hour just keeping her calm, not wanting to spook either the horses or Marina. Rosa's horse, Tennessee Stud, was an older, thick-bodied stallion, not much for speed but with plenty of durability. All she had to do was hold onto the reins and Stud would do the rest.

But even that seemed almost more than she could manage, sliding from side to side atop the saddle.

"Just settle into his motion," Jorge said. "Don't fight him."

"I'm not fighting him," Rosa said.

"Look how white your fingers are."

"Maybe I'm turning into a *gringa*."

"No, you're just gripping too hard."

Jorge's horse was a spirited mare named Sadie, but she was tame and responsive. Sadie's biggest problem was that she wanted to release her pent-up energy and explode into a gallop. Jorge felt her power beneath him, like a wagonload of dynamite waiting for a match.

Marina was riding a pinto pony that Mr. Wilcox kept around for his grandchildren to ride. Jorge would saddle the pinto about once every three months, and a few of the kids would make a circuit around the wooden corral by the barn before heading off for cake, ice cream, and video games. Marina took to the equestrian arts better than her mother, rocking back and forth in sync with the pony's gait.

Jorge had led them along the logging trails that wound around the Wilcox farm. Jorge had made up his mind to go east, mostly because the crews had shipped their Christmas trees downstate, to the wealthy people of Raleigh, Charlotte, and the Outer Banks, lands where people didn't grow trees. Jorge wanted to avoid the highways because he didn't trust the gringos not to steal their horses.

Plus, he wasn't sure what had happened to Willard or the others. He didn't know if everyone else had become starry-eyed and murderous. He couldn't risk his family on uncertainties.

"What do you think is happening in Mexico?" Rosa asked.

Jorge didn't want to talk about it in front of Marina. Before he could answer, though, Marina said, "Do you have to shoot crazy people?"

"Shooting people is wrong," Jorge said.

The rifle he'd taken from Mr. Wilcox's house was stuck in a bedroll slung across the back of his saddle, the stock protruding. His machete was hanging from his belt in its leather sheath. He was ready if necessary. But with Willard and the banker, he'd only been able to fight back after being attacked.

Rosa had saved Marina. All Jorge had done was drop a sheet over the dead farrier in the kitchen.

"When can we go back and get my crayons?" Marina asked.

"Soon," Jorge said. "We just have to make sure everything's okay."

Rosa gave him a worried look and struggled to keep her balance atop Tennessee Stud. "Where does this trail go?"

"It connects to the parkway."

The Blue Ridge Parkway was part of the national forest, Mr. Wilcox had explained to Jorge. America had set aside some of its most beautiful land for the people, although Mr. Wilcox said the government took too much from the people. The parkway was just across the border in North Carolina.

"Mostly used by them Yankee tourists," Mr. Wilcox had said. "But they make the rest of us pay for it."

They started down the back side of Jefferson Peak, a thickly forested slope pocked with granite. They were about ten miles from the Wilcox house, and Jorge's backside was already getting sore. He could only imagine the pain Rosa must be in, due to her rigid perch, but Marina seemed almost drowsing.

"Marina?" he said, worried.

Please, Father in Heaven, don't let her be sick.

She jerked erect in the saddle, pulling back on the reins. The pinto pony stopped, as did the other two horses.

"*Sí, padre?*" she said.

He didn't like her use of Spanish, but he let it pass. "Are you okay?"

"A little tired."

Rosa put a hand over her mouth, but her eyes showed fear. Jorge didn't know if the Detoros had fallen sick before dying, or if the sun sickness came to Willard and the others before they became murderous.

"Let's rest a moment." Jorge slid out of the saddle and tied his mare to a tree, then helped Marina off her mount. Rosa hesitated, uncomfortable with putting her weight on one of the stirrups.

Jorge let Rosa lean over onto his shoulders so he could guide her to the ground. She whispered, "She is pale."

Jorge didn't think so, but it was difficult to tell with the sun dappling the understory of the forest. He'd always prided himself that she was not as dark as either of her parents. None of the doctors at the clinic had ever expressed any concern for Marina, but her check-ups rarely lasted more than five minutes.

The water in the Wilcox house had been fed by a pump

that had gone out with the electricity. The only standing water had been in the toilets, aside from a quart that had been left sitting in a saucepan on the stove. Rosa had collected it in a canning jar, and Jorge had packed several soft drinks and a bottle of grape juice he'd found in the pantry.

A trickle of water seeped between two cracked slabs of gray granite, and Jorge decided to trust it. The water in the valleys would be tainted, but up this high, few people had built houses or roads, and the chemicals used on the Christmas trees would not reach across the miles they had covered.

Rosa checked Marina's temperature by pressing her wrist to the girl's forehead. She said nothing, but her lips pursed. Jorge brought water in a canteen he'd found in Mr. Wilcox's camping gear and gave it to Marina.

"Don't the horses need water, Daddy?" she asked.

"They will drink when we reach a creek," Jorge said. "Water runs all over this mountain."

"I like riding," she said to Rosa. "Can I keep the pony if Mr. Wilcox doesn't come back?"

"We'll see," Jorge said. Marina knew about the dead people but she was maintaining the fantasy that Jorge had spun, about Mr. Wilcox taking the Detoros to an agriculture exhibit.

"We don't keep things that don't belong to us," Rosa said. "That brings bad luck."

"Wait here," Jorge said. "I want to have a look."

The trails split just ahead, with one continuing up to the peak and the other starting a slow descent into the valley. The trees were thin on a small jut of rocky soil, and Jorge pushed through the wild blueberry shrubs and laurel. The sky opened up to him and he stood on a mossy ledge, nearly dizzy after the oppressive density of the forest.

The ribbon of highway stretched below, curving around the base of the next mountain and only visible in segments. He counted three vehicles stopped on the road, and an RV was pulled onto the grassy shoulder. No one moved.

Jorge drew comfort from how little the road was traveled, since it was closed to commercial traffic. Mr. Wilcox had often grumbled that the tourists could use the parkway all they wanted but the Christmas tree trucks had to go 20 miles out of the way to hit the interstate. There was still risk of running into more of the starry-eyed people, but they would have an easier passage by following the parkway.

Does it matter how easy the journey is if you don't know where you're going?

Jorge judged that it would take half an hour to climb down to the road, which would allow them time to prepare for possible encounters. Jorge had reluctantly left the shotgun behind, mostly because Rosa would have had to carry it and it would have been visible to Marina. He wondered if stress was eating away at his daughter's little tummy.

He liked that possibility better than sun sickness.

Jorge emerged from the shrubs, thinking about how he would get Marina down the mountain if she was sick, how far they might travel before sundown, and where they would spend the night.

Perhaps we could stay in the RV if there are no—

He nearly bumped into the man standing on the edge of the trail. Jorge hadn't seen him because the man wore a solid green jumpsuit, with a hood drawn tight around his face. A pair of goggles gave him the appearance of an insect, and his bushy, salt-and-pepper beard billowed beneath a cloth mask. The man stood motionless, unarmed, his hands sheathed in gloves.

Jorge looked past the man, making sure Marina and Rosa

were out of sight around the bend. He felt foolish for not taking the rifle with him. He hadn't wanted to alarm Marina. But he had the machete, and he cupped his palm around the butt.

The man appeared unarmed, but his stillness was even more disturbing than a violent assault would have been. Jorge recalled the agitated behavior of Willard, the banker, and the farrier, and he had accepted violence as a symptom of the sun sickness. If this man had the sickness—and Jorge couldn't tell from the concealed eyes—then perhaps the sickness had taken on different symptoms.

This made him think of Marina. The sickness might be changing her and the helplessness to fight that change made him angry.

"Hello," Jorge said, parting his legs a little and unconsciously going into a slight crouch, tensing for action.

Ten feet away with those cold round eyes, the man didn't respond. The cloth mask was the only movement, drawing in and out slightly with the man's breathing. A moist oval in the fabric revealed the set of his mouth.

Jorge waited another few seconds, aware of the birds in the trees, the laurel leaves rattling, and the distant rush of whitewater as a creek tumbled down the broken Blue Ridge slag.

He drew the machete.

The man still didn't move.

If he was sun-sick, he would have attacked by now.

Willard and the banker hadn't exhibited any understanding of the machete, and therefore, had no fear of it. Even after it had cut them, they still didn't try to dodge its sharp edge. Perhaps they didn't feel pain or were unaware of the danger. Or maybe they simply had no fear of death.

"I'm going that way," Jorge said, pointing the blade down

the trail behind the man.

The man uttered something, but the words were muffled by the cloth mask.

Jorge took a step forward, letting the machete dangle loosely in his hand. "We know this isn't our land," he said. "We're leaving."

The man spoke again, louder and more clearly. "Got a card?"

"Excuse me?"

"Green card. You legal?"

Jorge didn't think the man had sun sickness, but that didn't mean he wasn't dangerous. "I am in the United States on an agricultural visa, yes."

"Where do you work?"

"I work for Mr. Wilcox in Titusville."

"The tree farmer? Is he still alive?"

Jorge wasn't sure how much to tell. Perhaps the man didn't know about all the deaths. Maybe he would accuse Jorge of something, and Jorge wanted to avoid confrontations. That's why they'd taken the trail in the first place.

He thought about turning and fleeing down the trail, away from Rosa and Marina, in the hope that the man would follow him. But he didn't know what weapons the man might have concealed in that jumpsuit. He decided to tell the truth.

"Mr. Wilcox is dead. So are five of his workers, and two of his friends who were visiting."

The man didn't alter his position, the mask moving in and out as he considered the remark. "You sick?"

Jorge shook his head. "I don't feel any different."

"You hold that machete like you know how to swing it."

"I cut weeds on the tree farm."

"I'll bet you did."

Jorge squinted, trying to make out the man's eyes through

the goggles. "I mean no harm."

"Wouldn't expect you to say any different," the man said. His accent was like that of most mountain people, the vowels drawn out and sometimes difficult to understand. People here didn't talk like the *gringos* on television.

Jorge stepped onto the trail and gave the man a wide berth. One of the horses snorted and the man in the jumpsuit turned.

"How many others are back there?" the man said.

"None. I left my horse."

Two horses whinnied, exposing his lie. Jorge kept walking, letting the machete dangle at his hip, until the man called to his back: "I'd stop if I were you, unless you want this bullet to do the stopping."

If the man had the sun sickness, he probably wouldn't use a gun or speak in clear sentences. That meant he was like Jorge and his family—but it also meant he was scared and confused and therefore dangerous. Jorge couldn't risk running.

He faced the man, daunted by those black lenses. The gloved hand held a slim, silver pistol. Even if Jorge charged, he'd be lucky to raise the blade before the man shot him.

"We mean no harm," Jorge said.

"We? Changing your story on me?"

"Please, *señor*. My daughter is not well."

"Your daughter?"

"Yes. My wife is with her. We stopped to rest on our way across the mountain. We're headed to the parkway."

"Is your wife sick, too?"

"No, you don't understand. My daughter doesn't have the sun sickness—"

"Sun sickness? Is that what you call it? You haven't heard of the Zapheads?"

"Zap? No, I know nothing of that. We only know it was

the sun that killed people."

Jorge was surprised to find himself near tears. *Be strong. Rosa and Marina need you.*

The man's pistol dipped just a little, now directed at Jorge's knees. "Your girl? How old is she?"

"Nine."

"Damn." The man slipped the pistol into one of his pockets. "All right, let's go get her."

CHAPTER THIRTEEN

They'd covered perhaps three miles since leaving the roadside, and Stephen was still slumped over DeVontay's shoulder, sound asleep. They'd been reluctant to stray out of sight of the interstate but also didn't like being in the open. They'd descended from the hill into a suburban neighborhood, with silent cars in the driveway and menace in the shaded windows.

The bedroom community outside Charlotte looked beyond sleepy. It looked dead.

"You getting tired?" Rachel asked DeVontay.

"Not too bad," he answered, although she imagined his muscles were screaming.

"Why don't we rest a minute?"

"I want to put a little more distance between us and them Zapheads back there."

"I think they're oblivious," Rachel said. "I doubt they'd be much interested in us."

"Oh, they're interested in bashing our brains out. You've seen 'em."

The gunshot boomed up from one of the houses ahead, shattering glass and reverberating across the valley. Stephen stirred in DeVontay's arms, moaned a little, and pulled his doll close against one cheek as DeVontay knelt into a crouch.

Rachel hurried to a grimy white picket fence and scanned the street ahead. At first, she saw no movement. Then she saw a man in the yard of a brick ranch house. The man was slightly slumped, moving toward the house's broken picture window with the prototypical confused steps.

Zaphead. But Zapheads don't use guns.

"What is it?" DeVontay hissed in a whisper behind her.

"Trouble."

"I figured that. The gunshot was a pretty decent clue."

"Somebody might be trapped in that brick house," she said, lifting her head so that she could see without exposing herself. "I see a Zaphead."

"What's a Zaphead?" Stephen asked in a drowsy voice.

"Never mind, little man," DeVontay said.

"Is it like that guy in the hotel who kept beating on the doors?"

"Something like that."

The Zaphead staggered toward the broken window, a tool in his hand. It looked like a rake with a broken handle. The Zaphead dragged it behind him like a shell-shocked gardener. He looked to be in his forties, overweight, wearing a plaid shirt and jeans. Two weeks ago, he probably had been standing over a barbecue grill, bitching about the Yankees' starting rotation.

"He's not one of the good guys," Stephen said.

"No," Rachel said, relieved that the boy was emerging from his earlier catatonia. "Probably not."

"Wait here," DeVontay said. "I'll check it out."

Rachel grabbed his forearm as he rose to slink around the back of the house. "You're going to leave us here unarmed and defenseless?"

DeVontay looked at her and shook his head. "You and the Little Man here will be all right. You took care of yourself just fine before I came along, right?"

Yeah, but then all I had to worry about was myself.

"Okay, but don't be gone long," she said.

DeVontay looked like he wanted to offer her the gun but didn't want to say that word in front of Stephen. Rachel waved him on his way, watching the Zaphead gardener climb into the shattered picture window. DeVontay slipped along a hedge of azaleas and was gone from view when Rachel saw the other Zapheads.

Two Zapheads emerged from the open garage, moving in tandem. One of them was an elderly woman in a floral housecoat, wispy white hair drifting in the breeze. A pink fuzzy slipper covered her right foot, and her left foot was bare, covered with thick blue veins. She shuffled like an Alzheimer's escapee from a nursing home.

The other Zaphead was a young man with a feminine haircut and thin arms, wearing a striped sailing shirt. He resembled the pop star, Justin Bieber, but with a less-masculine jaw. Rachel nicknamed them Miss Daisy and the Bieb. It somehow made them less threatening.

"Are they going to get DeVontay?" Stephen asked, hugging his doll under his chin.

"No, DeVontay's smart."

"Are they going to get *us*?"

"No, they're not getting us, either."

"If they did, would they eat our guts like on TV?"

"No, these things don't eat people."

Although I'm not sure I can vouch for the Bieb. He's slobbering a little.

"Will DeVontay get shot?" Stephen asked.

"He'll stay out of sight until he figures out what's going on. But there's probably a good guy trapped in the house, and only good guys shoot guns."

"I thought guns were bad."

"Guns are dangerous, but sometimes you need them. And Zapheads don't shoot…I mean…"

"What's a Zaphead?"

Rachel peeked over the picket fence again. Miss Daisy was wobbly, taking two steps to the left for every step forward.

The Bieb had passed her and made for the shattered window, stepping over the corpse. Rachel debated the possibility of throwing Stephen into shock against the necessity of education.

He needs to know the rules of After. Guns are now good. And Zapheads are bad.

She wiggled one of the pickets until it was loose, and then peeled it back to create a gap. "Take a look."

Stephen put his face to the gap, and then held up the doll so it could take a gander, too. "See that, Miss Molly? That's what bad people look like."

Glass shattered, and someone shouted from inside the house. It was a man's voice, yelling, "Get back."

Then Rachel heard DeVontay shout, "Hey, man, I'm here to help—"

The gunshot boomed through the house, rattling the windows. Rachel's heart clenched in her chest like a fist around barbed wire.

DeVontay?

She was ashamed that her first thought was a selfish one, that she'd be stuck alone, to care for Stephen. She pushed aside the thought and debated whether to rush into the house. The Bieb was climbing through the picture window, his legs kicking as he tried to drag his body inside the house.

Rachel looked around. There was a little utility shed behind the neighboring house, the door sagging open. "Come on," she said, grabbing Stephen's hand and pulling him through the forsythia hedge toward the shed.

"I'm scared," Stephen said, and Rachel realized he was talking to the doll, not her.

They crossed the secluded lawn, with Rachel hoping no Zapheads were attracted by the commotion in the house. After making sure it was unoccupied, Rachel slung her backpack in the shed. The shed was cluttered with garden and carpentry tools, a ladder, a wheelbarrow, and milk crates full of wires, electrical outlets, and metal hardware. A stack of shelves held an array of paint cans, bags of potting soil and pesticides, and plastic sacks of herbicide. Through the light of a grimy window, Rachel saw something that might be useful.

She grabbed the can of Raid ant spray and put it in Stephen's hand. "If anybody comes in, squirt that in their eyes. Okay?"

"You going to leave me?"

"Just for a sec. But I'll lock the door behind me."

"You'll come back?" Stephen looked wildly around, perhaps comparing the shed to the hotel room where he'd been stuck with his mother's corpse.

Rachel knelt before him, grabbed his shoulders, and looked him full in the face. "Do you believe in God, Stephen?"

He nodded. "Me and Mommy went to church."

"God will watch out for you. Just pray and you won't be alone."

"But God made the Zapheads, didn't He?"

"God makes everything."

"Why? Why not just make good people?"

"I'll be right back. I promise."

Rachel scanned the wall. The sledge hammer was far too heavy, and the hoe's long handle rendered it unwieldy. A broken pair of pruning shears leaned against the bench, one blade curving like a rusty eagle's beak.

Could I hack somebody's skull if I had to?

They weren't people, not anymore. But could she be sure of that? Did Zapheads have souls? Even if they didn't, did she have the right to kill them?

She closed the door, smiling back at Stephen's worried, puppy-dog face. She hated leaving him alone, but until she knew what had happened to DeVontay, she couldn't choose a course of action that might expose them both to danger.

By the time she reached the fence again, the Bieb had disappeared, probably inside the house by now. Miss Daisy was doing her peculiar Texas two-step, banging her scrawny shoulder into the screen door as if she had some memory of entrances but didn't quite have a destination in mind.

Rachel checked the street for other Zapheads, recalling the group behavior of the ones back on the interstate. But apparently none had responded to the noise, or perhaps no more were in the vicinity. She decided to go behind the house and follow DeVontay's route.

Clenching her fists so tightly that her fingers ached, she crept along the fence until she reached the back yard. A swing set and sandbox were surrounded by bright plastic toys, and two garbage cans were overturned near the fence. Rachel wondered if the children were dead inside the house, maybe facedown at the table, or maybe all tucked into their beds with prayers and bedtime stories.

She found an unlatched gate, probably the same one DeVontay had used, and she slipped into the back yard. A set of four wooden steps led to a screened-in porch, and she couldn't see through the mesh. She listened for a moment but all she heard was a dull thumping that might be Miss Daisy.

Rachel hesitated, picturing Stephen in the gloomy shed, but that was wiped away by the fleeting image of him lying on the floor with blood leaking from his body.

Angry at herself, and refusing to acknowledge her fear, she sprinted across the yard and up the steps. She flung open the porch door and burst into the house, felling a little silly at being weaponless. Ahead was the kitchen, its door open. She stepped inside the house and had just a moment to register the mess—dinner that had once been underway, sliced onions on a cutting board, and spaghetti clinging to the stove—when the man grabbed her.

CHAPTER FOURTEEN

They'd gone about two miles along the highway, with Arnoff playing drill sergeant and urging the group forward, when they came across Pete's bike.

It was lying on the pavement, with no sign of Pete's backpack. The bike was right at home among the surrounding vehicles, as forlorn and forgotten as any of them. Campbell leaned his own bike, which he'd been pushing since this morning, against a blue Nissan sedan. He glanced into the driver's-side window and saw a gray-haired man with his head flopped back and mouth open. In death, his dentures had slipped and were perched along his swollen lower lip.

"Doesn't seem to be any sign of violence," Arnoff said.

"You shouldn't have sent him ahead," Pamela said. She fanned herself with a bandana, her makeup running with her sweat.

"We needed a scout."

"We needed to stick together."

"Hush it, Pamela," Donnie said. He stuck a plug of chewing tobacco into his mouth and mashed it together twice with his teeth, and then pushed the lump into his jaw with his tongue.

"He might have abandoned his bicycle and continued on foot," the professor said.

"No, Pete's way too lazy for that," Campbell said. "If something was wrong with the bike, he would have sat on the bed of that pickup and waited."

"I don't see no blood," Donnie said. "So, he probably wasn't attacked by a Zapper."

Arnoff picked up the bicycle and bounced it. "Tires still

have air and it seems to be in working condition."

Donnie walked twenty feet up the highway, his rifle slung over his shoulder. "Nothing up the road."

Campbell cupped his hands around his mouth and yelled, "Pete!"

"Shut up, *now*," Arnoff barked. "Do you want to draw every Zaphead for miles around?"

"He's my friend."

"And it looks like he ran off and left you. Maybe he figured he liked his odds better on his own."

"In that case, you made a strategic blunder," the professor said, "because if you sent him ahead as a sacrificial lamb, you lost an asset without getting anything in return."

"What do you mean, a 'sacrificial lamb'?" Campbell said.

"Canary in a coal mine," the professor said. "A loss leader. Bait."

"He was point man," Arnoff said. "He knew the risks."

"You're crazy," Campbell said. "This isn't a war movie or a chess match. This is one of the survivors. He's one of *us*."

"Don't lose your cool, soldier," Arnoff said. "Your friend might be sitting up there in the trees, snoozing in the shade. Like the professor said, it doesn't look like the Zapheads attacked him. Besides, he could have locked himself in one of these cars if he thought he was in danger."

Campbell pounded his fist into the side of the Nissan. The body inside shifted slightly and the dentures fell into the corpse's lap.

"Don't hurt yourself, honey," Pamela said, rolling her eyes toward Arnoff. "You might need that fist later."

Donnie opened the rear door of a nearby van and the stench rolled over them like a solid wave. A fleet of flies boiled out, their green wings iridescent in the sun. Campbell buried his face into the crook of his elbow, using the sleeve of his shirt as an air filter. It didn't help much.

Campbell didn't get close enough to count, but it looked like half a dozen people of his own age piled in the back of the van. They might have been taking a road trip. One girl's face was turned toward him, and though her flesh was mottled and corrupted, he could tell she had once been attractive. Her fine blond hair had not yet lost its sheen.

What a goddamned waste.

Donnie reached into the mass of slumped bodies and pulled out a purple bong. "Looks like these hippies was having a pot party," he said, standing strong in the face of the stench. "Guess they didn't know their brains was getting fried for free."

"Don't mess around in there," Arnoff said. "You might get some diseases."

"Not likely," the professor said. "If the bodies harbored infectious diseases, they usually die with the host. Some pathogens like HIV can survive for up to two weeks, but it still requires a direct transfer of bodily fluids. Cholera outbreaks after natural disasters are usually due to contaminated water. The biggest risk we face is gastroenteritis."

"You mean, the shits?" Donnie said, wiping the bong on his pants leg and looking into the bowl to see if held any marijuana.

"Still, I wouldn't put that to your mouth," the professor added.

"Donnie will put anything in his mouth," Pamela said.

"Yeah, and I've put a lot of *your* things—"

"Shut up." Arnoff raced forward and knocked the bong out of Donnie's hands. "Unless it's immediately necessary for our survival, it's off limits. We're carrying around enough dead weight as it is."

Campbell didn't like the way Donnie and Arnoff were looking at him. "I don't know why you recruited me and Pete, anyway. We were doing just fine on our own. And if we had stuck together, maybe he'd still be alive."

As soon as the words left his mouth, Campbell realized that was what he had been thinking: Pete was dead. But he didn't quite believe it. Despite all the death around him, Pete seemed like a constant around which the madness of the world revolved. Cities could burn, mountains could melt into slag heaps, all the trees could wither, but Pete would be sitting there grinning stupidly and sipping a warm beer.

Campbell tugged his bike away from the Nissan and mounted it as it rolled forward. He nearly slammed into the open van door, and Donnie jumped back to keep from getting struck by the handlebars. Campbell recovered his balance and pumped the pedals.

"Where do you think you're going?" Arnoff shouted behind him, but Campbell was intent on maneuvering through the stalled vehicles—a dump truck here, an SUV with its airbags deployed there, a motorcycle spilled on its side with the leather-clad driver rotting in the heat. He half expected to hear a gunshot—*Arnoff isn't that crazy, is he?*—and then realized he'd probably be dead before the percussion reached his ears.

He pumped his legs hard to gain momentum for the next rise. He heard Arnoff's little band arguing in the distance, punctuated with Pamela's brittle feminine laughter.

So, when society breaks down, we all turn into sociopaths. Guess we should have seen that one coming.

Campbell topped the rise, breathing hard, and a cramp rippled through his right thigh. His backpack seemed to have doubled in weight, although it only held about ten pounds of bottled water, a blanket, and a few cans of food. He didn't know how far he would go, but he was grateful for even a few minutes away from the group. He would soon turn around and pedal back, and he muttered at the irony of having turned into Arnoff's new point man.

Below him, the interstate ran in twin ribbons of speckled gray, sporting the usual clutter of stalled vehicles. A tractor-trailer was upended on its side, the cab mating with a mangled mini-van. Campbell marveled at the chaos and calamity he'd missed during the solar flares that had forever changed the world. To him, that moment had been marked by annoyance that the television screen had gone blank. Meanwhile, the rest of the world had had its plug yanked in the most horrible and permanent way.

To the left, about two hundred yards off the asphalt, a giant scar in the trees marked the path of a downed jet airliner. Bits of frayed metal littered the raw dirt, and one full wing jutted at an angle into the sky like a massive sun dial. The nose and much of the fuselage had plowed through a row of houses, leaving sagging roofs and splintered siding in the wake. Swatches of color were scattered here and there in the wreckage.

Luggage. And people.

Campbell coasted down the hill, riding the hand brakes and weaving between the cars, trucks, and vans. In this section, the vehicles were in an orderly line, with few rear-end collisions, as if traffic had been moving slowly when the big electromagnetic eraser had wiped out their engines. The stench of rotted bodies hung in the air, the putrefaction hastened by the greenhouse effect of the windows. Campbell did his best to avoid looking inside the vehicles, but curiosity suckered him in again and again.

Part of it was his faint hope that maybe he'd see a survivor, injured and unable to escape. The other part was his coming to grips with the scale of the apocalypse.

If the professor's right, and this is a worldwide deal, then I'm one of the last men on Earth.

And what the hell did I do to deserve it? Why am I upright and breathing while that poor lady with the blue hair at the wheel of the BMW is maggot food?

He swerved around a spare tire lying in the road and slowed the bike even more. Tools, clothing, and oil jugs were scattered on the road, and the trunks of several cars hung open. The back doors of a bread truck gaped wide, with plastic racks of molded bread spilled from the opening. A clutch of blackbirds flew away from the spoils. The flapping of their wings was the only sound in what should have been a rush-hour melee.

A man's corpse flopped out of the driver's side of a Toyota sedan. The passenger door was also open, and a woman sprawled dead on the pavement several feet from it.

Someone has moved those dead people.

Campbell stopped the bike and dismounted, looking at the nearby cars. The doors were open on about a dozen of them, the corpses inside apparently disturbed from their original positions. Most often, victims had died on the spot, collapsing wherever they happened to be. Many of the vehicles had endured collisions, although the loss of engine power had minimized much of the damage. A driver might flop over the steering wheel or loll back in the seat, but these people had been carelessly shoved out of the way of...*what?*

A survivor—maybe a group of survivors—might have prowled through the vehicles for food and supplies. That made sense. Campbell had done the same thing, except he'd not touched any corpses. Whoever had conducted this search had been disrespectful, almost to the point of obscenity. His unease was confirmed when he saw that a young woman's blouse had been torn open, her pale breasts left exposed to the sun.

Zapheads?

No, the Zapheads he'd encountered wouldn't have bothered with desecration, because they sought to inflict destruction on the living. To a Zaphead, the dead were no different than a tree or a car. They were inconveniences and obstacles, nothing more. Only a human—a human unaffected by the cataclysmic solar flares—could have indulged in such behavior as this.

A chill crept up Campbell's neck, even though the morning sun was now high and hot in the August sky. He was mounting his bike, eager to return to Arnoff's tribe, when he spied a blue backpack on the asphalt beside an empty child-restraint seat. Pete had a backpack just like that one.

Campbell ran to the backpack and peeled back the zipper on the pouch. He dug into the pocket and brought out a melted Snickers bar. The backpack smelled of beer and chocolate and stale sweat. It was Pete's, all right.

Why would he toss his backpack here?

But maybe Pete hadn't tossed his backpack to the pavement. Maybe it had been tossed for him.

CHAPTER FIFTEEN

Rachel wasn't sure whether she'd blacked out or had been knocked unconscious.

The first vestiges of grayness brought no pain, only confusion. She remembered entering the house to look for DeVontay—

Stephen. How long have I been here? Wherever I am.

She rubbed her eyes and then realized it wasn't her vision that was blurred. The room's windows had been covered with sheets, blocking out most of the light. She was sitting on a hard wooden chair. Dim shapes stood around her at various intervals.

"Are you one of us?" a man said.

Rachel turned in his direction, unsure if the man was addressing her. He stood near the window, so she could barely make out his silhouette. He was tall and broadshouldered, appearing to glance out the window and back again.

"Who is 'us'?" Rachel said. She tried to stand and realized she was bound to the chair. That made no sense, because she didn't feel any ropes. She wriggled her hands. They were so numb she could barely tell where they ended.

I must have been sitting here for a while. Real charmers, these guys.

"If you are one of us, you know what we are," the man said.

She nicknamed him The Captain, even though she was pretty sure he wasn't a Zaphead. She peered at the shapes of men. Four that she could see, maybe more standing behind her. At least two of them appeared to have rifles.

None of them looked like DeVontay.

"We heard a shot," she said. "We thought someone might need help."

"We?"

"Me and DeVontay."

"The dark one," the man said.

Dark one? Well, I guess it could be worse. Could be calling him the N-word.

She raised her voice. "Are you here, DeVontay?"

A muffled moan came from somewhere inside the house. The Captain moved from his post by the window and crossed the room. The additional light gave definition to the edges and shapes. Rachel could make out a desktop computer, the dull rectangle of the window reflected in miniature on its blank screen. Loose papers were piled around it, and unkempt shelves were stuffed with books, board games, and ceramic cats. An exercise bike stood in the corner, a windbreaker dangling from one handlebar.

Rachel turned her head, working blood flow back into her fingers. She couldn't see them, but she sensed several more people standing behind her. The air in the room was stale, body odor mingling with dust. Someone smelled of tobacco, and the cloying corruption of rot lay under it all, the new base aroma of the planet.

A hand gripped her shoulder, not hard enough to hurt, but not gentle, either. "You know what this is, correct?" The Captain said.

She shook her head. "We were only trying to help. We saw the Zapheads coming for the house—"

"Zapheads?"

"Yeah. The crazy people. The ones who changed after the solar storms."

"We've all changed."

She couldn't argue with that, and she had a feeling The Captain wasn't in a mood for arguments anyway. "Yeah, but they're the ones trying to bash our brains in."

"You may have noticed that we—that is, if you are one of us—are no different. Morally, you could make a case that ours is a greater sin, because we're aware of our violent actions."

Whoa. This guy's been out in the sun a little too long.

"You're aware you're giving a morality lecture to a woman you've tied to a chair, right?"

"Shall I gag her?" one of the shadowy figures to her left said. "Like we did with the other?"

So DeVontay's alive.

"No," The Captain said. "We need to find out if she is willing."

Willing? These guys can't be rapists, or they would have done their business while I was unconscious. And it's not like I can resist all that much right now.

"Like I said, we heard a shot and saw some Zapheads headed for the house," she said, doing her best to sound calm even though she wanted to scream. "We figured somebody was in trouble and came to help."

"And these…Zapheads, as you call them…what do you think makes them attack?"

"I don't know. Different theories, you know. The sun boiled their brains. The radiation mutated them. The electromagnetic pulse scrambled their wiring."

"Have you considered that maybe they are enlightened?"

"No. I haven't considered that at all. Been kinda busy staying alive."

"Do you believe in an all-powerful God?"

"What is this, the Spanish Inquisition? What next, the rack?" She struggled against her bonds. Feeling crept back into her limbs, in tingling pinpricks of fire. She rocked back and forth, testing the sturdiness of the chair. It was a cheap dining-room model, the legs loose and the slats digging into the backs of her thighs.

"We have to know if you are one of us."

She whipped her head around, taking in the perimeter of the room, at least as much as she could see. Three of The Captain's chums had changed position, one taking up a post by the window. Rachel couldn't tell if it was a man or a woman until the person spoke.

"Movement on the street," the woman said. Her tone wasn't quite military, but it was all business.

These guys have either spent some serious time together, or had something going on before the sun went nuts. Before After.

"Is it one of the enlightened?" The Captain asked.

"Appears to be." The woman tracked the barrel of a gun across the veiled window.

"Stay quiet, everyone," The Captain said. "We don't want to hurt it."

"Let me get this straight," Rachel said. "You jump me and tie me up but you let those things wander loose?"

"Live and let live," The Captain said. "They're children of the sun."

"The Sixties are over," Rachel said. "In case you haven't noticed, we're all that's left. And we should be helping each other. We're on Team Human. Right?"

"We are here to serve," The Captain said.

The woman at the window raised a hand. "There's somebody else outside."

"Enlightened?" The Captain said.

"Hard to tell. Looks like a boy, maybe ten."

Rachel's heart froze in her chest. *Stephen!*

"Time for the test," The Captain said. "We shall see if she is worthy."

The doorknob gave a brassy squeak behind her and the shadowy forms moved toward it. The female sentinel reached up, one skinny arm silhouetted against the daylight beyond the sheet. Then the makeshift curtain came down with a rip and sunlight poured into the room. Rachel squinted against the sudden yellow brightness, and by the time she'd recovered her sight, the room was empty. Footsteps echoed down the hall and The Captain said, "She's all yours."

Rachel scooted in little hops until she was turned and facing the door. Her first impression was correct. The room was a home office or den, bookshelves lined with paperbacks, loose sheaves of papers stuffed among them with the haphazard care of someone who loved information more than artifacts. A globe on a swivel and a heavy oak lamp stood on a small bureau near the door, with statuettes and photographs behind the glass of the cabinets. The floor was tiled with pressboard, but the hallway beyond the door was carpeted. She twisted against the ropes, chafing her wrists as she cast about the room looking for a sharp edge that could sever the ropes.

Maybe there's a letter opener or scissors in the desk.

Rachel tried not to think about Stephen wandering around the yard, lost and looking for her, or the circling Zapheads that might kill him. She couldn't bear another death. Billions had died and she had been helpless, God had abandoned her in her time of greatest need, like He had Jesus when the flesh of his palms shredded beneath the steel spikes and his lungs sagged in suffocation.

Or when the cool water had pulled her little sister, Chelsea, into its deep blue heart.

I don't like this theme. God is never there when you need Him most.

She gripped the edges of the seat and lifted as she pressed

down with her toes. The chair slid forward a good three inches, and she repeated the movement twice, three times, gaining more distance with each bounce. She was so intent on her goal, the metal desk with the computer atop it, that she didn't notice the person in the doorway until a lamp crashed to the floor.

Rachel twisted her neck around. Budget Bieber came toward her, eyes brightly vacant beneath the brown bangs but somehow fixed on her, just the same. He carried himself in an insouciant slouch, stooping to the floor to retrieve the lamp. He appeared to test its weight with one short swing of the wooden base, as if first learning of its potential as weapon. Satisfied, he yanked at the flimsy lampshade until it tore free.

Rachel pitched forward, away from him, forgetting her feet were tied. When she felt herself falling, she twisted so that the chair toppled to the right. Her elbow banged against the floor, but the flimsy chair broke apart. She tried to roll, but the back of the chair clung to her, dangling from the ropes that bound her wrists.

Budget Bieber hovered over her, the lamp raised. His mouth parted wide as if about to embark on the first note of a churlish pop song, but only a strange deep chuckle emerged. He brought the lamp down toward her head, the bare gray bulb leading the way.

Rachel barely had time to scoot to the left before the bulb smashed into the floor, sending shards of glass into her face. The Bieber Zaphead raised the lamp again, the jagged broken bulb now resembling a row of teeth. This time, Budget Bieber rammed it toward her, as if to pin her against the floor.

She took advantage of his lunge to sweep one leg against his shin. Off balance, he clattered to the floor, again issuing his peculiar low chuckle as the lamp bounced out of his hands. Rachel's elbow throbbed as she struggled to her knees, shaking violently to rid herself of the remnants of the chair. One ankle slipped free and she was able to stand.

Still splayed on the floor, the Bieber Zaphead made a grab for her leg. She danced out of reach and then jumped forward again, driving the heel of her sneaker onto his wrist. He moaned in the monotone of unheralded pop stardom, although it didn't seem a reaction of pain. His inner rage was driving him now, the way it apparently compelled all Zapheads to crush, pummel, and slash any living creature that wasn't like them.

Rachel backed against the desk and yanked open the top drawer. Keeping one eye on the Bieber Zaphead crawling toward her, she rifled among the papers, business cards, and zip drives, looking for something sharp and shiny. She heard a whimper of frustration and realized it had crawled from her own throat, making her angry at herself. Only the faithless gave in to despair.

On the desk was a clay jar stuffed with pencils, pens, and postage stamps. A thick plastic handle protruded from the collection, and she snatched it, sensing the Zaphead's approach. The object was a flat-head screwdriver, its tip gleaming silver.

She raised the screwdriver like a knife, ready to plunge it into the Zaphead's vacuous face. But before she could skewer the bangs-covered forehead, she looked into those eyes and saw a glimpse of the human he had once been.

Somebody's son, somebody's brother. Maybe somebody's favorite singer.

His eyes were brown, glittering with a manic golden flecks. She hesitated, holding the screwdriver a foot above his face.

Then he went for her and she fell back onto the desk, knocking the computer to the floor.

Should have killed him while I had the chance. But maybe I've killed enough.

She kicked the broken bits of chair and loose rope from her feet and fled toward the door, Budget Bieber in pursuit. Before she could escape, The Captain stepped from the hall, blocking the doorway, and clapped his palms together. "Halt," he shouted.

Rachel thought he was speaking to her, but no way in hell was she going to stop running until Budget Bieber was shrinking in the rearview mirror of her life. When The Captain repeated his command, she realized he was addressing the Zaphead, and by then she was at the door.

She shoved past The Captain and reached the relative safety of the hall, turning to see how close the Zaphead was to catching her. The Captain stepped into the room, raising one arm and pointing a revolver. "Stop now!"

The Zaphead paused only long enough to take his eyes from Rachel and fix them on The Captain. Rachel backed down the hall, even though the Zaphead had already forgotten her. A new target was closer. The Zaphead hunched for an assault, just out of arm's reach of The Captain.

"Do not cross this line," The Captain said to the Zaphead.

He thinks he can communicate with it. He's even crazier than I thought.

Budget Bieber looked at the gun as if harboring some dim memory of its capacity for harm, then snarled and jumped with outstretched arms. The gunshot roared and echoed down the hall, cordite filling the air. The Zaphead's skull exploded like a bloated melon, spraying the study with flecks of red and gray.

"I told you to halt," The Captain said, his voice just as steady as before.

Rachel looked from the Zaphead to The Captain,

assimilating this new discovery of After. "Did you expect that thing to listen to you?"

"They must learn that violence is not the answer," The Captain said, plucking the screwdriver from her hand. "A lesson you apparently need to learn as well."

"But you and your goons jumped me and tied me to a chair. Doesn't that count as violence?"

"You are worthy," he responded. "He didn't kill you."

The Bieber Zaphead trembled in the center of the room, as if destruction was the source of his passion and grace. Without the raging intent to kill, he was just a teen. Harmless and lost, abandoned in a world that had changed for all of them. *All* of them.

"Great, so I'm worthy," she said. "What about Stephen?"

"Who is that? Your dark-skinned friend?"

"No. The little boy who was out in the street."

"Oh, him. I'm afraid...I'm afraid he *isn't* worthy."

CHAPTER SIXTEEN

We would have ridden the horses right past it and never noticed.

Jorge cradled Marina against his chest and pushed through the thick rhododendron branches. The trail was little more than an animal path winding through the dense vegetation, but the man in the green jumpsuit navigated it as sure-footedly as a goat. The man paused once in a while to look back and make sure they were following, although he hadn't removed his cloth mask.

Rosa held back the branches as best she could so they wouldn't scratch Marina. Jorge had cuts on his cheeks and the backs of his hands, but he'd been able to shield his daughter from the worst punishment.

She is so light. Like a dream.

Jorge didn't like that idea because it made her seem even more fragile and vulnerable, so he shifted his thoughts to the man in the jumpsuit. Why was he helping them? If he was truly afraid of catching a sickness, he would have watched them pass by on the logging road and gone about his business.

The man had even let Jorge keep his rifle, although he insisted they leave the horses tethered on the road. Jorge wasn't sure why, but he suspected the man was afraid they harbored some kind of disease.

"How is she?" Rosa asked, wrinkles appearing around her frown. He'd never seen wrinkles on her before, and he wondered if perhaps the sun had changed them all.

Some changed more than others. Yes, Willard would gladly trade a few more wrinkles in exchange for his hand, and Mr. Wilcox would have given up his "hunnert acres" for another day above ground.

"She is well," Jorge said. Lying came more easily when one was trying to comfort others. But Jorge wasn't far enough along in his new morality to believe his own lies. Marina was pale and sweaty, even though her skin was cool to the touch when he pressed his cheek against it.

The trail opened up onto a twin set of ruts that marked another logging road. Or it could have been the same road they had just left. Jorge had been so obsessed with protecting Marina that he hadn't paid attention to their route, although he suspected they'd been trudging through the dense vegetation for at least twenty minutes.

"Watch your step," said the man in the green jumpsuit, pointing to the ground near Rosa's feet. A thin metal wire stretched six inches off the ground. Jorge thought of the American movies he'd seen where the tripwire sprung a trap of sharpened spikes that punctured anyone in its path or detonated a crude explosive device.

The man must have read Jorge's face, because he said, "Don't worry none. It's just a signal wire, not a booby trap. I don't kill unless I got no choice."

Jorge thought of the bodies back at the farm. Most people never knew the line they would cross before they could kill, but it was thin and almost invisible. Most horrifying of all, it could be triggered completely by accident.

The sun was no accident. It was simply there, doing sun things, with no consideration of the men beneath it.

Rosa stepped carefully over the wire and watched with dread as Jorge also crossed it. The man in the jumpsuit dug his gloved hands into a thick tangle of red vines—"Poison oak," he said—and retrieved a hidden strand of rope that descended from somewhere in the trees above. He threw his weight against it and with the squeal of a pulley overhead, the vegetation blocking the logging road parted. The metal gate had been so cleverly concealed that, if Jorge turned his head for a few seconds, he wouldn't have been able to locate it if the gate were closed again.

The man ushered them through the gate, gave a slow scan of the road and surrounding forest, and entered behind them before closing it. They were in a compound that blended with the trees and boulders and was constructed with such genius that Jorge doubted it could be detected by a low-flying airplane. If airplanes still flew, that was. He hadn't seen one since the solar storms.

Rosa gripped his arm, and then felt Marina's forehead. "Her fever is worse."

"Get her in the house," said the man in the green jumpsuit, motioning to a massive maple tree with low-hanging branches. A structure was built into it, sided with sheaves of bark so that it blended with the tree. Narrow slits of windows glinted here and there. A couple of smaller sheds, roofed with rusted tin, stood in a cleared area that featured a garden and a pen where goats and chickens scratched at the ground.

The man led the way to the cabin. He opened the thick wooden door, stood on the log that served as a front step, and motioned to Jorge. "Can you carry her? Hand her here if you can't."

Jorge didn't want those gloved hands touching his daughter. "I can do it."

"Suit yourself," he said, entering the tree house.

Rosa whispered, "Can we trust him?"

"He could have killed us on the trail, or just let us pass," Jorge said. "Besides, he let me keep the gun."

"Why would this strange gringo help us? "

"Not all gringos are like Mr. Wilcox. Some of them are human beings."

"I don't like this."

"What choice do we have? We have to let Marina rest and recover. And if she has the sun sickness…"

Neither of them wanted to contemplate the thought. Before Rosa could respond, the man stuck his head out the door. He'd removed his mask, but his mouth was still disguised by his bushy beard and mustache. "You folks coming or not?"

Jorge gave Rosa his backpack and the rifle, balanced Marina on his left shoulder, and ascended the rungs. The interior of the tree house was surprisingly spacious and bright, with the windows placed for maximum sunlight. The man removed his gloves and placed them on a shelf which also contained an assortment of hand tools, two pistols, a pair of binoculars, and an oil lantern.

"Put her down over there," the man said, motioning to a bundle of blankets on the floor. Jorge thought for a moment the man was going to extend his hand, and Jorge wondered if he would shake it. But the man turned his attention to an old radio on a hand-hewn table, fidgeting with the dials.

Rosa smoothed the blankets, giving them a suspicious sniff, and Jorge laid Marina among them. Her eyelids fluttered and parted, and Jorge tried his best to smile at her, but his face felt as if it were carved from wood. "*Hola, tomatilla*, how are you feeling?"

"Where are we?" the girl said, her voice so small that Jorge had to lean forward to make out the words.

"Somewhere safe," Rosa said, immediately taking the caregiver's role.

"Will you have to shoot anybody else?"

"No, there are no sick men here. They were all back at Mr. Wilcox's farm."

"But I'm sick, too. Will I be like them?"

Rosa looked at Jorge, who bent forward and kissed her

forehead. "No, you just have a small fever. We will rest and then be on our way."

"Our way where?"

"Hush, *pequeña tomatilla*, you don't have to think about that."

"Where's my pony?"

"Eating sweet grass. He's resting, too, while he waits for you to get better."

"There's water in that pantry," the man in the jumpsuit said, and Jorge walked over to a wool blanket suspended on a wire. He pushed the blanket to the side, revealing a small closet sporting shelves packed with food, some in cans, some in glass jars, with bulging burlap sacks on the top shelves. The pantry was cool and moist, with a sink at the far end, clear water streaming into it from a pipe.

Jorge found a clean glass jar by the sink and filled it with the frigid water. Looking out a window above the sink, he saw the metal pipe angled up into the rocks on the slope above the tree house, allowing gravity to carry the water from a spring.

This man has been planning for something like the sun storm.

After taking the water back to Rosa, he joined the man at the table. The man barely looked at him, intent on calibrating the radio, which was a jumble of glass tubes, wires, and plastic knobs connected to a series of car batteries.

"I want to thank you," Jorge said.

"I should have let you go on about your business," the man said. "I hate meddlers."

"My daughter—"

"Better keep an eye on her. These solar shenanigans might not be over yet. These things tend to come in spurts."

Jorge hadn't even considered that the worst wasn't yet over, that even now they might be exposed to whatever strange radiation had killed most of the people around them and turned others into mindless killers. What would he do if Marina showed a violent streak, if she became like Willard or a lame horse and needed to be put down?

There is no such thing as a mercy killing. Only killing.

Rosa gave Marina some of the water and Jorge was comforted to see his daughter sipping it. The sweat on her forehead had dried, and her complexion had returned somewhat to its usual almond color.

"Were there many of the solar storms?" Jorge said. He had little understanding of science, having attended vocational school to learn welding, a craft that hadn't led to a job back home.

"Hard to tell without any astronomy gear," the old man said. "O' course, all that went out with the first big pulse, when the magnetic fields got all scrambled. But if what they were saying is true, then we might have been hit with storms for a solid week, wave after wave of radiation. Might still be going on now, for all we know. It's not like you can really see them."

Jorge thought of all the time he'd spent in the fields over the past few weeks and wondered about the invisible rays and currents that might have washed over him. Worse, in his ignorance, he'd exposed this family to danger. He glanced at his daughter huddled in a coarse blanket.

"You were prepared for this disaster?" Jorge asked.

The man waved a hand, still fiddling with the radio. "This, or something else. It was bound to happen sooner or later. Personally, my money was on nuclear war, considering all the idiots in Washington."

Jorge had heard of survivalists, who were often painted as well-armed crackpots who barricaded themselves in bunkers and dared federal agents to come and get them. But this man didn't seem angry or confrontational. No, he almost seemed *happy* that the world had taken a turn for the worse.

"My name is Jorge, and that's my wife, Rosa, and daughter, Marina." Jorge opened his palm in case the man wanted to shake hands, but the man kept his attention on the radio.

"You can call me Franklin."

"This is national park land," Jorge said cautiously. "I thought no one could live on it."

"Means the people own it, right?" Franklin said. "I paid taxes. At least for a while, 'til I wised up and saw every single dime I mailed to the I.R.S. was going into killing us all one way or another. The government was bound to either starve us to death or drop bombs on our heads."

A low whine issued from the radio's speakers, and the man fidgeted with the thick copper wires attached to the slender antenna. He plugged in a handset microphone and keyed it with click. "Do you read?" the man asked.

Jorge thought this was odd. If someone was listening on another radio, that person likely wasn't reading. The man turned the knob, yielding a scruffy burst of static, much like Mr. Wilcox's TV. He spoke into the microphone several more times before giving up.

"Too much atmospheric interference," Franklin said.

"Do you think others are out there?"

The man scrunched his bushy eyebrows. "Others like us, you mean?"

Jorge nodded and glanced at Rosa. This man apparently didn't care that they were Hispanic, only that they weren't crazed killers. "Like us."

"Oh, hard to figure," the man said. "But you can bet bear against cornmeal that the U.S. government got itself a dozen little hidey holes around D.C."

"The capital," Jorge said, to assure the man that he knew

his U.S. civics lessons.

"I wouldn't be surprised if the bastards had months of advance warning and took the time to make sure they were safe and living in luxury. Probably got a new bureaucracy running already, figuring out how to tax the hell out of the survivors."

"Did you hear that on your radio?"

Franklin didn't answer, concentrating instead on turning the knobs and listening intently to the whining pitch emanating from the speakers. Rosa came over and took Jorge's hand, squeezing it as they watched their sleeping daughter.

"Her fever is passing," Rosa said.

"Good," Jorge said. "We must leave soon."

"Might not want to be in too big of a hurry," the man said. "The way I've seen them Zapheads acting, you wouldn't have much of a chance if you ran into a pack of them."

"We don't want to trouble you," Jorge said.

"I got plenty of food and water, and my solar panels, and the wind turbine. This is about as close to modern living as you're going to get, at least this side of D.C. Plus, I could use a little help around here, to get ready."

"Ready?" Rosa said. "Ready for what?"

"Let's hope we don't have to find out. But I've learned to plan for the worse, and then the worser, and then the worst of all. We're just now barely on the 'worse.' The survivors out there will soon be going at each other's throats once they realize the resources are dwindling. And if anybody figures out I got electricity up here, and a radio, and supplies, they're all going to want in."

"Why does your equipment still work?" Jorge asked as the man's nubby, wrinkled fingers worked the dials.

"Stored it all in a Faraday cage out back," Franklin said, hooking a thumb to indicate somewhere outside the cabin.

"Shielded metal, it protects against electromagnetic currents."

"Do others have this equipment?"

"Some," the man said. "The smart ones. But as you probably figured out already, there ain't a whole lot of smart ones on this planet."

The radio's whine turned into a crackle, and then a male voice cut in. It was clipped, British or Australian, and the words faded in and out: "*...anyone there?...now is the time for...approximately one in three hundred survived...we are in need of...situation grave...*"

The radio signal sharpened into a keening wail, and the man's urgent voice emerged again from the static. "*Situation grave...repeat, situation grave...*"

Then it faded, like the ghost of the airwaves, emitting one last message before becoming swallowed by the endless high hiss.

"*Situation grave...*"

CHAPTER SEVENTEEN

Two of The Captain's goons shoved Rachel into a dark room and slammed the door.

They weren't gentle about it, either, and she burned her elbow on the carpeting. She guessed she was in a bedroom, although there was no gray square that would suggest a window. She crawled forward cautiously, feeling in front of her with an outstretched hand.

She met something spongy and drew back, horrified that it might be a corpse.

"Took you long enough," DeVontay said.

She sat up on her knees, peering in the direction of his voice but unable to see him. "Hey, you're the one playing hero. Are you okay?"

"Yeah. They roughed me up a little, but I think they're just playing. Got some kind of skinhead thing going on, from what I can tell."

"Their leader, The Captain—"

"Captain? What the hell? You think this is a Batman movie or something?"

"I had to nickname him," she said. "Psychologically, that makes him less of a threat. A kind of gallows humor."

"Yeah, well, gallows humor is all well and good until the noose tightens. Speaking of which, why don't you untie me?"

She scooted forward until she found the thick wooden bedpost and fumbled around the thick lump of knots against his skin. "These are like the ones they used on me. Might take me a minute to get them loose."

"I ain't going anywhere. Did they...*hurt* you?" he said in a low voice as she tugged.

Rachel guessed from the pause that he meant, "Did they rape you?" but she brushed past it. "The Captain threw a Zaphead at me as some sort of screwed-up test. The guy's a little brain-fried himself, I think."

"When I heard that gun go off—"

One of her fingernails split to the quick as it snagged on a knot. "You're not getting rid of me that easily. Not until we get you and Stephen to Mi'sippi."

"Where's he at?"

"I left him in a hiding place, but The Captain's goons found him and turned him loose out there with the Zapheads. I guess these guys think everybody has to pass some sort of survival game to prove they are worthy."

"Shit. Is the boy okay?"

"Put it this way. I haven't heard him screaming yet."

Rachel didn't want to think the worst. Faith required hope, and hope required action. Starting with these godforsaken knots. "I wish I could see," she said. "Maybe I could find a tool."

"The lighter," DeVontay said. "In my pocket."

"They didn't search you?"

"Nah. They don't give a damn about me. I'm a one-eyed black jack."

That made no sense, but she didn't question him. She felt along his hip until she found his belt, and then slipped her hand along the fabric of his pants. She found the hem of the pocket and hesitated.

"Go on, girl," he said. "Nothing in there will bite you."

"It's just…"

"I ain't telling nobody if you ain't."

That made her smile despite the gravity of the situation. She shoved her hand inside the opening, pushing past what felt like a rumpled wad of bills, some flexible, rubbery things she suspected were Slim Jims, and a keychain. Then her fingers stroked the cool, smooth curve of the Bic lighter and she fought it free, hooking the keychain as she went.

With a flick of her thumb, the area immediately around her was illuminated with a dim orange glow. The flame was reflected in each of DeVontay's eyes, brighter in the glass one. His lip bore a small, wet cut, and one cheek was swollen. She gently touched his wound and he flinched away.

"I ain't telling nobody if you ain't," she said, imitating his Philly-street accent.

"I'm okay. Just get me loose and let's get the hell out of here."

She waved the Bic around, revealing that the room was bare, with an unmade bed, a dusty dresser with the drawers open, and an open closet with a single suit jacket hanging in it. Clothes littered the floor, as if the room had been ransacked. Her impression of a windowless room was confirmed.

"Doesn't look like much in the way of hardware," Rachel said. She jangled the keys. "Guess I'll have to use these."

She held the light aloft with one hand as she dug into the knot with the longest key. The knot's author must have been a Boy Scout, because his handiwork refused to come loose. She began sawing the serrated edge of the key across the strands, sending a snow of frayed nylon to the floor.

"What are you doing with keys, anyway?" she asked him. Her fingers chafed to blood and her wrist ached from working the key, but she kept on.

"Got doors to open."

She extinguished the lighter to let it cool. Its imprint was burned into Rachel's retinas, fat sparks dancing in the sudden darkness.

"Got any ideas on getting out of here?" she asked. The first strand of rope gave way and she unraveled the rest of the knot as he anxiously flexed his forearms.

"Gun's in my backpack, wherever that is," DeVontay said. "After they jumped me, I went down for a while. I didn't get a good layout of the house."

"That's a privacy lock on the door. They can't lock it from the outside."

"We could sneak out, yeah. But what if they're still playing survival games? Could be a dozen Zapheads out in the hall."

"We'd hear them banging into the walls."

"Maybe. And maybe that guy—the whatchamadude, The Captain—is waiting there with his gun."

"Well, it's the only way out that I can see." The severed rope untangled beneath her fingers and DeVontay wriggled his wrists to free himself. He shook his hands to restore the circulation as he glanced around the room. He grinned as his eyes settled on the closet.

"You're just not looking in the right place."

He stood, rubbing his palms together, and she followed him with the Bic. He shoved aside the lonely jacket and looked up at the ceiling. "Give me some light."

Rachel shoved the lighter toward him, thinking he'd lost his mind. Stephen was out there somewhere, at the mercy of those soulless killers, and all DeVontay wanted to do was play hide-and-seek?

"Ha," he said. "That little square is an access to the attic. I had a job blowing ceiling insulation one summer. Hottest damn work I ever did."

"Great. So, once we get up there, and then what? Wait for the world to end?"

"Funny, ha ha. I gotta boost you up. No way can you lift me."

"You kidding? You're only, what—two-twenty?"

"Two-oh-five. I ain't et that many Slim Jims."

He stooped and cupped his hands. Rachel hesitated, released the fuel lever on the lighter, and put her sneakered foot into his hands. Something thumped against the door.

"Damn," DeVontay said. "Hurry."

He propelled her upward and she put one hand against the wall to steady herself, patting for the ceiling with the other. She found the access and pushed, feeling it slide away with a *skiff* of abrasion. Rachel reached into the warmer air of the opening and found the ceiling joists, then dangled for just a moment, testing her weight.

"Higher," she whispered, and DeVontay tightened his arms and lifted her. She put one foot on the closet rod as she scrambled into the attic. The dust nearly made her sneeze, and the attic insulation caused her skin to itch almost immediately. She rolled around, careful to keep her weight on the sturdier ceiling joists, and flicked the lighter again.

"How am I going to pull you up here?" she said.

DeVontay looked up and shook his head. "You ain't."

"I can't leave you."

"You got to. Ain't you ever seen a horror movie? The goody-goody white chick always survives."

"Don't be an asshole."

"And don't waste time here when Stephen's in trouble."

She looked at him for a moment, pondering ways to help him up. But he was too heavy, the closet rod too weak. "The dresser," she said. "Move it over here and stand on it."

"Okay, but—"

Something thumped against the door again, louder this time. DeVontay waved her toward escape. She killed the flame and saw the slatted ventilation windows on each gabled end of the house. The closest one was only twenty feet away. She crawled forward, bumping her head once and getting fiberglass insulation in the creases of her elbows and gaps of her fingers. When she reached the slats, she peered through them to the neighboring property.

A Zaphead wobbled up the street, far enough away that he wasn't a threat. He didn't exhibit the excitement and agitation of a Zaphead intent on violence, which might mean Stephen had safely hidden somewhere.

Or it could mean he's already dead.

The idea angered Rachel, and she flipped onto her butt and raised her legs, pointing the bottoms of her feet at the thin wooden slats. She kicked outward and several of the slats shattered. She kicked again and created a wider opening. Shoving splinters aside, she perched in the opening and surveyed the surrounding landscape.

No movement. Even the Zaphead up the street had taken a turn somewhere and was lost in one of the neighborhood houses. From beneath her came the sound of a struggle, and DeVontay shouted something.

His next word was clear through the access hatch: "Go!"

Rachel climbed out enough to minimize the drop to the ground, which was about twelve feet. Not too bad by itself, but it wasn't a good time for a twisted ankle.

"Just my luck," she said. "Roses."

The rose bushes extended in a border around the side of the house, meaning Rachel would have to jump outward several feet instead of merely dropping to the ground. She shoved the lighter in her pocket.

Here goes nothing.

Rachel resisted the urge to yell "Geronimo" as she flew through the air. She had the presence of mind to roll as she landed, taking the brunt of the force on her left leg before tumbling across the grass. Gathering her balance, bruised but otherwise uninjured, she glanced around to see if anyone had spotted her. She wasn't sure whether to be more afraid of the

Zapheads or The Captain and his minions.

She sprinted as best she could with her aching legs, quickly reaching the concealment of the neighbor's azalea thicket.

Okay, you're free. You can give up on DeVontay and Stephen and make a run for it. Your chances are better alone. They're just deadweight anyway, right?

She glanced heavenward, starting to ask for guidance, but realized prayers were never answered with a simple yes or no.

God had granted her longer life for a reason. And that reason wasn't just to keep on surviving.

She had a mission.

CHAPTER EIGHTEEN

Campbell was still searching the trees on the side of the road when Arnoff's tribe caught up with him.

Campbell emerged from the woods to see Arnoff poking Pete's backpack with the tip of his rifle. Pamela, Donnie, and the professor hung back a little, warily checking the vehicles on the highway. "Looks like your buddy chickened out," Arnoff said.

"Somebody got him," Campbell said.

"Hell, yeah," Donnie said. "Zapheads."

"It wasn't Zapheads. There's no blood."

Arnoff knelt and plucked one of the warm beers from Pete's backpack. "Well, he didn't abandon ship, or he'd have never left this."

"So, what do you think happened?" Pamela asked, fishing a cigarette from a pocket of her floral-print blouse. She was sweating from the heat, and the wind carried a faint whiff of the distant burning cities. Campbell thought about what the professor had said, about the four hundred nuclear reactors that would eventually melt down, but he was pretty sure he wasn't going to live long enough to worry about radiation poisoning.

"Post-traumatic stress disorder, psychological strain," the professor said. "He might have just snapped and wandered off somewhere."

"Turned into a Zaphead, you mean?" Arnoff said.

"We've not seen any evidence of latent effects. The experts predicted the solar event was a one-time phenomenon."

"Hell, some horny old bat might have roped him into the back of one of these vans for a go," Donnie said, grinning at

Pamela. "You know how women are."

"Hush your mouth or I'll hush it for you." She glared back, taking a deep puff of her cigarette, but she seemed bored by her own threat.

Campbell's guts knotted in frustration, but he forced himself to remain calm. He didn't know these people. They were acquaintances of circumstance, and bleak circumstance at that.

The end of the world makes strange bedfellows.

Arnoff walked ahead to a BP tanker truck. The silver petroleum tanker reflected the sunlight, causing Campbell to squint. Arnoff shouldered his rifle and climbed a metal ladder on the tanker's rear. Standing atop the giant cylinder, he scanned with his binoculars in all directions.

"Zapheads are going to see him," Donnie said, checking the chamber of his automatic pistol. "This is a time to lay low, not play gold-medal dumbass at the Special Olympics."

"Hush your mouth," Pamela said, sitting on the hood of a green Mercedes. A man was slumped over the wheel, body swollen with rot around the confines of his suit jacket and tie. Campbell was grateful the car's windows were sealed shut. The man likely had the air-conditioning going, probably some Eagles twanging on the stereo, on his way to rake in money off of other people's work. And then life made other plans for him.

Big, big plans.

"See anything?" the professor called to Arnoff.

Arnoff lowered the binoculars and shook his head. "No Zapheads, no survivors, no Pete."

"Too bad we can't get a vehicle going. There's enough gas to get us across the country and back a hundred times."

"You're the egghead," Donnie said, banging on the roof of a Ford Escort. "Why don't you hotwire one of these?"

"As I explained, modern vehicles have electronic ignitions, computerized operating systems, alternating-current batteries and—"

"Blah, blah, blah," Donnie said. "Everything got zapped. I know all that. But the zap's over, right? Why can't we rebuild one?"

"Possible," the professor said. "But we'd need newly produced parts, which means manufactured parts, because all the existing circuitry is fried. And it takes high-technology equipment and electricity to make the parts you need. Catch-22."

"Sort of like needing a fish for bait so you can catch a fish, right?" Donnie said.

"Sort of like that, yes," the professor said.

Campbell hadn't thought that far ahead. Sometimes at night, before falling asleep, he'd had little fantasies of the world rebuilding itself, everyone pitching in like it was a community-pride clean-up event. But he always assumed "somebody," either the government or people from some unaffected part of the globe, would eventually ride to the rescue and restore all the essential services. But what if they were on their own? What if they had to save themselves?

What if human civilization had come down to isolated clusters like Arnoff's tribe?

Then we're screwed.

"Zaphead at ten o'clock," Arnoff said, dropping the binoculars so they dangled from a cord around his neck. He raised his rifle and sighted down the barrel.

Donnie jumped from the Mercedes hood and ran toward the tanker. "Save some for me. I ain't killed a Zaphead in three days and I'm getting a little twitchy."

"I'm not shooting it," Arnoff said. "I'm observing it."

Campbell eased over to where the professor and Pamela

were standing. The tang of tobacco smoke overwhelmed the stench of bodies and distant fires.

"What do you make of all this?" Campbell asked the professor. He almost asked for the man's name, but the group seemed to function better with anonymity. Names didn't seem to matter now.

"Our tenuous situation as survivors, or the geological effects of the solar storm?"

Pamela pursed her lips. "I love it when you use them big words."

"A little of both," Campbell said. "I mean, it's hard to separate them now, isn't it?"

Donnie hoisted himself up on the tanker's ladder and climbed toward Arnoff, who was still peering through the rifle scope.

"We can't be certain of the long-term effects on the environment," the professor said. "But short term, in human terms, we've lost our infrastructure. We've lost all the systems that connected us with food, safety, shelter, and companionship. And, as I said, manmade problems like the nuclear radiation and other pollutants add to the mix."

"Doesn't sound real good," Pamela said. "Then again, I never expected there to be a 'long term.'"

"But surely we can adapt," Campbell said, although the argument sounded hollow even to his own ears. "We're smart and tough and adaptable—"

"That's how smart we are," Pamela interrupted, pointing to the top of the tanker. Donnie had opened a little metal access hatch and was urinating into the opening.

The professor shook his head in grim amusement. "I think the Zapheads are in far better position to adapt. From what I can tell, they have none of the moral baggage and ten times the survival instinct."

"Do you have any theories on why they turned violent?" Campbell asked, warily scanning the sides of the highway. Arnoff and Donnie were so transfixed with one distant Zaphead, they wouldn't have seen any others approaching from the woods. And if Pete staggered out into the open, Campbell wanted to be the first to spot him so he could prevent Pete from getting shot by the trigger-happy Donnie.

"Electroconvulsive therapy is used to treat depression," the professor said. "Everybody thinks of the Jack Nicholson movie, 'One Flew Over the Cuckoo's Nest,' where troublemakers get their brains fried, but it has proven clinical benefits. However, the treatment also can cause severe personality change, memory loss, and cognitive impairment. So evidence suggests that exposure to cataclysmic electromagnetic fields could cause varying results, depending on the individual."

"So, I guess this proves I'm lucky, huh?" Pamela said.

The professor dug into his backpack and pulled out a plastic water bottle. "In some ways, we're better off," he said, twisting the cap and taking a swig. "Fewer of us to consume the finite resources at our disposal."

"What do you mean, 'finite'?" Campbell asked. "I know we can't build automobiles, but we can return to an agrarian society."

"With what knowledge?" the professor said. "How do we save seeds and know which plants to eat? How do we know the proper planting time? How do we build gristmills powered by water wheels to grind wheat into flour? We can't just get on the Internet and Google it."

"Dang, you're a real bummer, doc," Pamela said.

"I see no need to indulge elaborate fantasies. A realistic assessment of our situation gives us the best chance of survival."

Campbell was reluctantly forced to agree. "I'd say the first job—after finding Pete, of course—is to locate others like us and form a bigger group."

"That might not be so wise," the professor said. "Look at the pecking-order problems we have just with a group this small. Put a dozen well-armed, desperate Alpha males in the same place at the same time, and I think they'd make Zapheads look like refined pacifists."

"I don't know exactly what you said," Pamela said. "But if you're saying it's not too smart to put a bunch of Arnoffs and Donnies together, I'd say you're onto something."

The two men stood atop the tankers like statues. Arnoff was ramrod-straight, shoulders back, still holding his rifle barrel steady on his target. Donnie was hunched, but he'd also raised his weapon, pointing it in the same direction as Arnoff.

"If they shoot, every Zaphead within a mile's radius will come see what's going on," the professor said. "They seem to react to stimuli like sudden loud noises and movement."

"They can't be that dumb," Campbell said.

"You don't know Donnie," Pamela said. "He might do it just for the fun of it."

A muffled *ka-pow* sounded to the west. Arnoff instantly shifted his rifle in that direction.

"A gunshot," Campbell said. "Other survivors."

Campbell started up the road toward the tanker, but the professor grabbed his arm. "Remember what I said. Bigger isn't necessarily better. If there was any lesson learned in the Technological Age, it was that."

Campbell shook free and walked away, imagining what the other group was like. Had Pete joined them? Did they have adequate food supplies or transportation better than bicycles or horses? Did they have any young women among them so the race could procreate?

Thinking of sex at a time like this. Sheesh.

Another distant gunshot sounded, and Arnoff scrambled the length of the tanker and descended the ladder. The professor and Pamela gathered their bags and went to meet him, but Campbell climbed astride his bicycle, determined to solve the mystery.

"Where do you think you're going?" Arnoff said.

"I'm your scout, remember? Just doing my job."

"You might want to stick with the winners. Sounds like things are getting hairy out there."

"Hairier than a gorilla's cooter," Donnie said from atop the tanker.

"Just how would you know about that?" Pamela said.

"'cause I been sleeping with you, ain't I?"

Campbell was tired of the prattle. "My friend's out there somewhere, and I'm going to find him."

"Your first responsibility is to the tribe," Arnoff said.

Campbell glared at the professor. "What do you have to say about that?"

The professor shook his head. "Survival of the fittest."

Another gunshot sounded, causing Donnie to whoop and jump from the tanker to the cab of the truck for better surveillance. If Donnie was the pinnacle of human fitness, then Campbell wasn't sure whether he wanted to stick around. Evolution had just taken a stinking piss and washed away every grain of hope.

"I guess some of us have a different idea of what it means to be human." Campbell pedaled in the direction of the gunshots.

CHAPTER NINETEEN

Rachel worked the shadows and shrubs, keeping low as she searched for Stephen. She was reluctant to leave the house where DeVontay was held captive, but she didn't see how a frontal assault would do much good, since she was without a weapon and vastly outnumbered. Instead, she decided to check on the shed where she'd left Stephen. She found the door open and Stephen's can of Raid lying on the floor.

The Captain's goons had left her backpack, and she slung it over her shoulder. The garden tools taunted her as if to say, "*So, violence isn't the answer, huh? Then what's the question?*"

Faith into action.

Even if there's hell to pay.

Rachel picked up the pruning shear. The bolt connecting the two handles had broken, so she gave the single handle a test swing. She liked the balance of it, as well as the short metal hook at the end. It wasn't too heavy to carry, and she liked its prospects better than those of the double-headed ax and the flimsier hand scythe.

A gunshot sounded somewhere down the street, a couple of hundred yards away. Maybe the goons were hunting Zapheads for sport, although they might be shooting stray dogs, car windows, or even other survivors. Rachel had a feeling that The Captain had imposed a quasi-military protocol in an attempt to control his creepy little platoon.

Slinking back to the street where she had a better line of sight, Rachel crouched behind a Volvo and considered her options. If Stephen was on the loose, he probably hadn't traveled far.

Assuming he's still alive.

Rachel was about to take her chances and sprint across the street when she heard shouting and cursing. She peered over the Volvo's hood and saw two people in camouflage coveralls dragging a young, dark-haired man who struggled in their grip.

"Goddamnit, I'm one of the good guys," the man said. He was in his early twenties, hair slick with sweat, wearing a grimy T-shirt.

The goon on the left, a gaunt-faced woman whose mouth was twisted into a bitchy snarl, put a spidery hand on the hilt of a knife at her belt and said, "Shut up, or I'll gut you like a fish."

The man sagged so that the goon on the right had to grab his arm with both hands and hold him upright. The pair was half-dragging him toward the ranch house where The Captain apparently had set up headquarters and where DeVontay was still confined. Through the Japanese maples on the front lawn, Rachel could see the shattered window and the legs of Miss Daisy's corpse dangling from the glass-strewn windowsill.

"You got any beer?" the captive man said. The gaunt woman jabbed him in the ribs with her knuckles, eliciting a hiss of pain.

The man jerked his elbows out, causing the goon on his right to lose his grip. The man seized the opening and started to break free, but the woman slid her leg forward with practiced grace, tripping him and sending him skidding across the asphalt.

She chuckled as she bent to pull the man from the road. "We're trained in the art of pain."

The other soldier drove the bottom of his boot against the fallen man's thigh, causing Rachel to flinch. They were beating him like two television wrestlers who'd caught their quarry in a corner with the referee's back turned. Rachel gripped the handle of the pruning shear, knotted with anger but helpless. After all, the soldiers had semi-automatic weapons slung across their backs.

The two goons were so intent on inflicting punishment that they didn't notice movement along the side of the street. A withered vegetable garden stood at the corner of a lot, fenced with two rows of sagging white clothesline strung between wooden posts. The tasseled corn rattled and swayed, and a hunched figure emerged from between the rows. At first Rachel thought it was another soldier, given the swiftness of the movement, but the figure wore a soiled windbreaker and jogging pants, not camouflage gear.

Zaphead.

But she barely had time to consider whether to shout a warning when another Zaphead came out of the garden, a middle-aged woman in a business suit, pantyhose pocked with holes and trendy haircut now in tangles. Rachel unconsciously dubbed her "Bridget Jones," except this particular career gal was carrying a sharp, heavy stick instead of a diary. The corn rattled behind her, with yet another Zaphead following, a squat, Asian-looking man with no shirt.

What struck Rachel most forcefully was the way they seemed to move in concert, stealthy and intent. In the city, the Zapheads were brainless and shambling, almost like the zombies depicted in film and books but without the taste for flesh. But these were like cunning predators, lurking in the shadows and then sneaking up to deliver their brand of destruction.

The man on the ground saw the Zapheads and pushed himself along the pavement on his back, trying to get his feet beneath him. The soldiers didn't allow him to escape, though. The woman jumped knee-first on his chest while the other soldier urged her on. "Captain will love this one," he said.

Rachel circled around the Volvo to get closer. The closest Zaphead rushed across the narrow grass border to the street. Three weeks ago, it might have been an insurance salesman out for a morning jog, but now it was a killing machine instead of a workout warrior.

"Get off me, you assholes," the struggling young man on the asphalt said. "Here come some Zappers."

The sadistic woman soldier chuckled again, and Rachel wondered if somehow she had been affected, too—that maybe the Zapheads were evolving and the surviving humans were degrading until they all would meet in a wordless, violent misunderstanding.

The jogger Zaphead closed the distance in the blink of an eye, leaping onto the male soldier's back and driving a grunt from his lungs. They fell forward, the four of them tangled in a pile as the other two Zapheads moved in.

The female soldier rolled away and tried to free her weapon from her shoulder, but Bridget Jones was on her like a shark after a baby seal. Bridget Jones swung her garden stake and caught the soldier under the chin, the bone-shattering *thwack* audible to Rachel.

The shirtless Zaphead joined the first in assaulting the male soldier, while the captive scrambled free of the pile. Rachel could see the fear and determination in his eyes.

He's a survivor.

Rachel stepped from behind the Volvo and raised her makeshift weapon. The guy must have thought she was a Zaphead, too, because he scrambled to his feet and started down the street before Rachel yelled, "This way!"

The guy ran toward her and Rachel passed him, heading for the Zapheads. Even though the soldiers were part of the group that had tried to kill her, Rachel couldn't let them get mauled.

When it comes down to it, we're still on the same side. Barely.

The female soldier had recovered enough to pull her knife from its hilt. The blade glistened in the sun for only a moment, and then she drove it into Bridget Jones's abdomen. The Zaphead mouthed a wet *uurk* but continued to attack, even as a blossom of red spread across her formal white blouse.

Rachel struck the asphalt with the curved metal tip of her pruning shear. "Come and get it," she yelled.

The two Zapheads clawing at the male soldier turned to Rachel, snarling, their eyes burning cold with some hidden hate.

Then they did something odd.

They looked at one another as if in telepathic communication, and the shirtless Zaphead tightened his grip on the soldier's throat as the soldier flailed helplessly to reach his rifle. The other, the jogger Zaphead, shoved away from them and ran toward Rachel.

She barely had time to register the sudden change in tactics when the Zaphead was upon her. She swung the shear handle from its position near her hip, tentative and afraid to draw blood. The wooden part of the handle bounced off the Zaphead's arm as if striking rubber, then the Zaphead grabbed her.

His breath stank like molded cheese as he closed rough hands around her throat. Up close, his eyes burned with a liquid malevolence, the roiling lava of a hidden volcano. She kicked at his shin, but he didn't react to pain.

Rachel had never had any self-defense training. Aside from playing tackle football with the neighborhood boys in Seattle, she'd learned most of her moves from movies. But she discovered that it wasn't as easy when your would-be killer wasn't following the script.

Her throat was tight and sore, the pressure of his fingers

constricting the blood to her head. Her vision swam as the Zaphead lifted her from the pavement, pulling her against him. Her arms were heavy and her grip loosened on the shear.

She heard a man yell "Back down, bitch," and then the Zaphead shuddered from a blow to the head. The deathly clutch eased enough for Rachel to suck in a lungful of air and regain her balance.

The man who'd escaped the soldiers swung a fist at the Zaphead, but the Zaphead flinched away, apparently learning to dodge. But while its attention was diverted, Rachel whispered a prayer of apology and swung the handle of the pruning shear.

The metal tip gouged deep into the base of the Zaphead's skull, opening a gap in the flesh and revealing a red weal of raw muscle and gristle. Blood spurted from the wound.

So they bleed just like we do.

"Hit him again," the man said, dancing just beyond the outstretched arms of the Zaphead.

Rachel thought of the bruises she'd be wearing as a necklace for the next week, then swung the wooden handle overhead in a two-handed grip and brought the blunt end flush upon the top of the Zaphead's skull, like the Biblical Samson standing knee-deep in Philistines swinging the bloodied jawbone of an ass.

The sickening crack pierced the sounds of grunts and screams as the other two Zapheads pummeled the soldiers. The concussed Zaphead staggered for a moment, then wheeled and looked at Rachel. The fire in its eyes gave way to a look of hurt confusion, and Rachel wondered whether she'd knocked some wiring loose in his brain—as if maybe she'd pounded some humanity back into him.

"Better hit him again," the man said. "Don't play around with these monsters."

"Thou shalt not kill," Rachel said.

The man looked at her and shook his head. Behind him, the female soldier drove her knife into the Bridget Jones Zaphead a second time, opening another bright gash in her torso. A bit of pink intestine bulged out of the cotton blouse, but the Zaphead didn't seem to notice. She drove her small fist into the woman soldier's face, shattering her nose and sending a tooth flying.

"Let's get out of here," the man said, grabbing Rachel's hand and pulling her toward the yard of a nearby house. The gesture reminded her too much of DeVontay, and she pulled free.

"I have to stay," she said. "I have friends here."

The man's face curdled in resentment, then he grabbed her weapon and shoved her back. "Thou shall not kill, maybe, but I, for sure, goddamned *shall*."

The man swung the blade against the Zaphead's temple, and this time, the guy went down like a jogger after a marathon. A shot rang out, and the shirtless Zaphead's shoulder erupted in a glut of blood and gore, but still, it kept attacking.

"I don't see any friends around here," the man said to Rachel. "Come on."

"This way," Rachel said, pointing to the house where DeVontay was still being held.

"Fine," he said. The rancid odor of old beer hung about him and his bloodshot eyes suggested either a lack of sleep or an abundance of alcohol.

Rachel broke into a run, the man right behind her, hanging onto the grisly, blood-coated pruning shear. When they reached the landscaped shrubbery, Rachel burst through and headed for the side yard, where a high wooden fence offered concealment. They ducked behind it just as another gunshot erupted, then another one.

"New around here?" the man said, wiping sweat from his greasy brow.

"Only since After," she said.

"After?"

She shrugged, lifted her hands to indicate the world. "This end-of-the-world thing. Thanks for saving me back there. I'm Rachel."

"Name's Pete," he said, between gasps of exhilaration. "Just a suggestion, but I'd ditch the Ten Commandments. At least five of them no longer apply."

"That's how I was raised. It's not something you can turn on and off like a light switch."

"Guess so. I wouldn't know anything about that. One Sunday morning in the Catholic church gave me enough horrors of hell to last a lifetime."

"How did they find you?"

"I was bicycling on the highway, stopped to check out a car, and then those unsung heroes jumped me and said The Captain wanted to see me."

"The Captain? Yeah, I've met him." So, The Captain had a rank. She dug into her backpack and found the small bottle of Nembutal the pharmacist had given her. Her fingers slid away until they hit a water bottle, and she pulled it out and passed it to Pete.

He twisted the cap and tossed it into the weeds, then took a grateful gulp. "What's up with these guys?"

"I can't say for sure," she said. "But I think they were stuck in the bunker a little too long and started getting funny ideas. The Captain thinks he can control the Zapheads if only he can get them to appreciate chain of command."

"Well, I'm civilian all the way. So, what's the plan?"

"Did you happen to see a little boy anywhere? About ten,

wild hair, maybe carrying a baby doll?"

"Afraid not."

"Well, that's my plan."

"Not much better than mine. I was going to find a bar and plug some quarters into the karaoke machine and sing 'Your Cheatin' Heart' 'til closing time."

CHAPTER TWENTY

"Turnips," Franklin said.

Jorge almost responded in Spanish, but remembered his promise. "What?"

Franklin pulled a dark clump of leafy stalks from the ground, revealing the rounded golden root. "Turnips are the perfect survival food. They grow almost year round, the roots store through the winter, and they have just about every vitamin you need."

They were in the vegetable garden at one corner of the compound. From working on the Wilcox farm, Jorge had an understanding of the shorter growing seasons of the Blue Ridge Mountains, as well as the humid, wet climate. Therefore, he admired the garden's placement, which allowed nearly a full day's sunlight while much of Franklin's camp remained concealed by trees.

"You plan well," Jorge said.

"No, I've just been around so long I've figured out a thing or two." He twisted the yellowing outer leaves from the stalk and tossed them into the goat pen, where the short-horned nanny sucked them between her jaws.

Broad leaves of autumn squash and pumpkins covered one end of the garden, and bean vines twisted along a lattice of sticks. The corn was already making ears, and bees hovered around the golden tassels. A dense orchard of short but bountiful apple and pear trees stood on the other side of the small house, nearly shading a small, rough-hewn shed. The top of the shed was covered with solar panels, and Franklin had opened the rear door to show Jorge the rows of batteries that stored the collected energy.

"Something like this takes…," Jorge searched for the right word, dragging the hoe between the rows to pile fresh soil around the turnip roots. "Vision."

"Nah," Franklin said. "Anybody could see it coming that didn't have blinders on. I was part of the Preparation Network, teaching people how to get ready, but it didn't do much good. Humans are a funny breed, Jorge. I reckon they're as funny down in Mexico as they are up here."

Jorge had given little thought to his brothers and sisters in the Baja, or his mother in their little crowded house. He wasn't sure whether he wished them a swift and merciful death or if they were even now on the run from the people that Franklin had called the "Zapheads."

"If this happened all over the world, like your man on the radio said, then I suppose it's not so funny," Jorge said, leaning on the hoe and looking out across the mountain ridges in the distance. The nearer peaks were flush with the deep green of summer's end, but the horizon was draped with wraith-like, ragged clouds.

"That's the look of cities burning," Franklin said. "Enjoy this fresh air while you can."

"Do these Zapheads burn things?"

"Tell you the truth, I don't know if that's the Zapheads or the government. I wouldn't be a bit surprised if they were ready for whatever opportunity came along. Giant asteroid hitting the earth, nuclear terrorist attack, shift of the earth's geomagnetic fields. Every ill wind blows somebody some good."

Although Jorge had little interest in any kind of politics, he didn't see what the U.S. government would gain by destroying its own territory. Not for the first time, he wondered if Franklin had spent too many years alone, with nothing but his mad dreams, paranoia, and obsessive vision.

Rosa called to them from the doorway of the house. Marina stood beside her, wrapped in a blanket. She still looked pale and her hair was moist with sweat, but she managed a feeble wave before Rosa led her back into the shade.

Jorge decided to ask the thing that had been bothering him. "Mr. Wheeler, you are clearly a man who likes to be alone and to depend on no one. If this is so, then why do you help us?"

Franklin put the turnips into a wooden basket atop some tomatoes and small purple cabbages. "I lived out there once," Franklin said, waving vaguely off the mountain. "Just about like anybody else. I had a job in industrial design making rich folks richer, found a sweet little woman and settled down. I never did trust the government, and I got in a little trouble because of things I was writing on the Internet. Whatever they say about 'the land of the free,' that's complete bullshit. You're only as free as they want you to be."

Then why isn't your own family here? Why take in mine? But Jorge thought it best to only listen, so he turned his attention back to the weeds that skirted the bed of tufted carrot greens. Besides, it seemed like Franklin was warming up for a rant.

"Government had me under surveillance," Franklin said, no longer working now, just kneeling in the dark dirt and gazing off where the past remained just out of sight. "Just because I was warning people that the shit was about to hit the fan. After 9/11, Homeland Security became just about the most powerful force in Washington, because its slimy fingers reached into every pocket and every campaign fund and every Congressional bill. The last thing any government ever wants is for the truth to get out. At different times, I was considered a white supremacist, a radical Muslim, a neo-Nazi, a Communist, even a Swedish spy—if you can imagine any reason in hell that Sweden needs our secrets."

"Were you arrested?"

"They just wanted me to go dark. Even with all these new laws that let them throw anybody in jail forever without a trial, they knew that arresting me would draw publicity, and then more people would find my websites. So in a way, me going into hiding like this was the best thing for both of us. I'm fine with being a martyr, but I want it to be for the right reason, and the right reason hadn't come along yet." Franklin swept his gnarled, calloused fingers to the world beyond. "And now, the right cause came along, but there ain't no Internet left."

Jorge remained cautious. "So you want us to help you spread the word about your survival camp? If you help us, we can help others?"

"Hell, no," Franklin said. "It's too late for all that. I'm not even helping you. I just couldn't let that little girl die."

Jorge realized the old man did have a compassionate streak beneath his wary, antisocial façade. "We are grateful and we promise to work hard while we are here, and to leave whenever you ask."

Franklin appeared not to hear. "My granddaughter, Chelsea, was Marina's age when she drowned."

Jorge had a good idea of the man's pain because of his own worries. "I am truly sorry to hear that."

"I was working on the camp even back then, using a network of dealers to get all these solar panels, wind turbines, water tanks, and such as that. I suspect the government had their eyes on me. Hell, I didn't know which of those things flying overhead were hawks and crows and which were surveillance drones. They got 'em the size of insects now…well, they *did*, I mean."

Jorge picked a lime-green caterpillar from a collard leaf

and studied it a moment before squishing it between his fingers. "Why did they let you come here if they knew?"

"Like I said, it got me out of the spotlight. I planned to bring my family up here, but by then my wife had left me and my kids and grandkids had pretty much written me off as a crazy old coot. The ones who didn't were my granddaughters, Rachel and Chelsea. Rachel, she's a real Christian, acting the way Christ taught instead of the way these idiot preacher politicians are telling people they ought to behave. You a religious man?"

Jorge had learned in the United States to always say he was a Baptist, especially in the South, but he saw little reason to lie to Franklin. "I was raised Catholic, but we haven't gone to church much lately."

"Never hurts to believe in something bigger than you. Just make sure it's a thing of the sky and not a thing of mankind. Because mankind isn't bigger than any of us. Mankind is not bigger than life. It's exactly life-sized and hates to admit it."

Jorge was trying to figure out what that meant when Franklin went back to his story, apparently used to coming out with random musings but just as quickly, discarding them. "Rachel was the only one who didn't think I was a survivalist wacko. She said God needed the world to end in order to renew itself as a better place, just like Jesus had to die on the cross in order to save everybody's soul. I guess there's some comfort in that, since all the doomsday preachers use fear as a fundraising tool. She'd even been reviving some of my old websites, putting them under different names."

"Did she get in trouble, too?" The sun was lower in the sky now, pushing shadows across the compound.

"She'd barely got started when Chelsea died." Franklin swallowed with the bitterness of the memory. "They were out at the lake, the two of them, and Rachel turned away just for a second—had to go use the bushes. And she came back to find Chelsea face down in the water."

Jorge wanted to offer condolences but decided silence was more respectful and appropriate. Customs were different in the United States, but shutting up worked in any language.

"In three feet of water. But she was a good swimmer. They did it to send a message."

"They"? Does this man really think the government would drown his granddaughter?

Franklin spat in the dirt and stood, wiping his hands and picking up the basket. "Well, that's when I came up here. Is your wife a good cook? I'm passable, but I keep it simple."

"She cooked for Mr. Wilcox on weekends."

"Well, this ain't no fancy rich-people's food, but it's clean and free of poison and you can really taste it. So, let's treat it like it's The Last Supper."

Jorge followed Franklin back to the house, wondering if they should leave far sooner than their host might wish.

CHAPTER TWENTY-ONE

"Holy crap!"

Campbell swerved his bike, narrowly missing the little kid. The front tire hit the curb and the bike flipped, pitching Campbell across the sidewalk and into the weeds along the side of the street.

Campbell had pedaled in the direction of the gunshots, figuring it was the most likely place to find Pete, and the first exit off the highway had led right past a gas station into a middle-class neighborhood. He had slowed, hoping not to get shot or attacked, but he had mentally prepared for any possibility except the one that had occurred.

His elbow throbbed and his knees were skinned, but no bones appeared to be broken. His first thought was that the kid might be a Zaphead, which would explain why he'd run out into the street toward the bike.

But the boy simply stood there, staring at Campbell, a baby doll dangling limply from one hand.

Definitely not a Zaphead, or he'd be on me while I'm down.

Campbell sat up, his shirt wet from a broken water bottle in his backpack. "Hi there," Campbell said, in his friendliest voice, as if they were crossing paths on a playground instead of in the middle of the apocalypse.

The kid said nothing, merely hugged his doll. He looked about ten, an age when most kids were carrying baseball gloves and iPods and Gameboys instead of dolls. But he'd likely seen horrors that even the most violent video games had not displayed.

"Live around here?" Campbell asked, even though the street looked as dead as all the others he'd traveled over the last few weeks.

Had it only been a few weeks since the solar flares? The world felt as if it were covered in a great layer of dust already.

The boy's head twitched just a little, which Campbell took for a negative shake. Campbell scanned the houses that bordered both sides of the street, vacant cars parked here and there along the curb and in the driveways, another neighborhood caught unaware when the catastrophe had struck. Human flesh was moldering and decaying behind those closed doors.

Campbell dug in his backpack and pulled out a granola bar. He unwrapped it and stood, holding it out to the boy. He felt like a parody of the stereotypical pervert, gaining a kid's trust with a treat. "You hungry?"

The head twitched again, eyes peering warily from beneath the bill of the Carolina Panthers ball cap.

"What do you say we get away from the street?" Campbell said. "Might be some bad guys around."

The boy's lower lip trembled. "B-bad guys?"

Ah. So you know about the Zapheads. And yet somehow you're still alive.

"Come over here, out of the street," Campbell said. "Maybe you can help me fix my bike."

The front rim was hopelessly warped, but Campbell pretended to check the bike's condition. The boy eased a few steps closer and Campbell took a bite of the granola bar, chewing deliberately.

"Dang, I forgot this was yours," Campbell said around a mouthful of honey-coated oats. "You can have the other half. I don't have cooties or anything."

The boy almost smiled. He came closer, loosening his grip on the filthy doll, which was wrapped in a makeshift bandana with a length of yarn wrapped around the waist to make a dress. Campbell nodded at it. "That doll's really rocking that outfit."

"She's not real."

"Nice of you to protect her from the bad guys," Campbell said, checking both ends of the street for movement. "You must be a superhero."

The boy shook his head more vigorously. "Just a boy."

"Me, too. Come on, let's go over here out of the street."

"Rachel made the dress," the boy said, once Campbell had led him to a covered garage that at least gave the illusion of protection. A late-90s model Cadillac was parked inside, the chrome buffed, polished and gleaming like a mirror.

"Rachel? That your sister?"

"No, she brought me here after my mom died, but then she left me. We were going to Mi'sippi to find my dad."

Jeez, what a heartless bitch. "Yeah, I lost a friend, too. I came here looking for him. His name is Pete."

"I'm Stephen."

"I like that name. If I ever had a kid, I'd name him that." Campbell peered into the Cadillac to make sure it was unoccupied. The keys were in the ignition, taunting him. "Have you seen anyone else around?"

"After Rachel left, some guy in an Army suit let me out of the shed where she hid me. Said I was Zaphead bait and I'd better start running. So, I did. I didn't stop until you almost run me over."

So, Stephen knows what a Zaphead is. I guess they grow up fast these days or not all. "This guy in the Army suit? He was one of us? I mean, not a Zaphead?"

"I think there was more of them in a big brick house where DeVontay went."

"DeVontay?"

"Rachel's friend."

"Can you show me the house?"

Stephen shook his head, squeezing the doll. "I don't want the Zapheads to get me."

"I promise I won't leave you like Rachel did." Campbell wondered if he was doing the same thing Arnoff had done to him and Pete, forcing him into servitude.

"Will you take me to Mi'sippi if I show you?"

"Sure, Stephen. Anything you say."

"Okay, then. But you have to take Miss Molly, too." Stephen held out the doll, as if testing Campbell's commitment.

"Sure, all of us. Even DeVontay if he's still there." Campbell looked around the garage for a weapon. On the bicycle, he'd felt relatively safe because he could easily escape a Zaphead, even though they seemed to be faster and better coordinated now. If he was about to travel on foot, he wanted a way to defend himself.

But the garage offered nothing in the least bit deadly. The Cadillac's owner was as meticulously ordered as the car's condition suggested. Old issues of *Car & Driver* were stuck in plastic organizers on a set of metal shelves. Electric power tools were arrayed in a line along the wooden work bench, their cords neatly coiled around the handles. Bottles of motor oil, windshield washer fluid, and antifreeze stood at one end of the shelf, as well as a gasoline can. Campbell shook the can and it sloshed.

Great. Now all I have to do is toss this on a Zaphead, light a match, and walk away. Ridding the world of Zappers, one human torch at a time.

Campbell put down the gasoline can, and then remembered what Arnoff had said about the Zapheads loving to watch stuff burn. Maybe something in their short-circuited brains loved the simplicity of destruction, or maybe it was some deeply buried desire for purification that lived in the ghosts of their human selves. Either way, he might have a way to distract the Zappers until he figured out his next move.

You guys like to play firebug, let me get it started for you.

He twisted the lid from the gas can and poured it all along the bench. The fumes of the gasoline stung his eyes and made his head swim. He flung a trail of gasoline over to the Cadillac, wondering if it would blow like in the movies.

"You ever had a weenie roast, Stephen?"

"No, but my dad likes to barbecue."

"Okay, then, think of this as one big backyard barbecue." Campbell moved a few feet away, wondering if he'd spilled any gasoline on his clothes. He didn't think he'd impress Stephen much if he managed to accidentally immolate himself.

He pulled one of the issues of *Car & Driver* from its rack. The cover featured a decked-out muscle car that looked like a '69 Chevy Camaro. Campbell ripped a few pages from the interior and pulled a lighter from his pocket. He lit the corner of the twisted, makeshift torch.

"Okay, let's roll," he said to Stephen, tossing the torch onto the wet stream of gasoline, which had now soaked into the concrete. It immediately swelled into a thick, bright flame and spread outward in both directions, but they were out of the garage before it reached the Cadillac.

Campbell led Stephen across the backyard of the house, wondering if the Cadillac's owner was taking the big sleep inside the house. Perhaps he should have checked. It wouldn't have been right to burn another man's car without asking, even though the big gas-guzzler was just another dinosaur now.

"We'll follow the street from over here, then come around to the house from the back way," Campbell said, the bonfire now crackling behind them as thick smoke roiled into the sky. "Think you'll be able to find it again?"

"Yeah," Stephen said, tugging his hand free from Campbell's. "I'm not a baby, you know."

"Well, I'm just a little scared."

"But you're a superhero."

"Yeah, but I'm in my secret identity right now."

"See that big tower? That way."

Through the trees, Campbell could see a bulbous water tower framed against the scattered iron-gray clouds. The town's name was spelled out in black letters across the circumference, but the first part was hidden, so Campbell was left to wonder where in the hell "-iston" was.

They climbed over a waist-high fence, Campbell boosting Stephen over after first transporting the baby doll. The rows of houses faced the backs of similar houses, and the gaps in the landscaping and fencing revealed yet another street, as if the neighborhood was just another homogenous suburb, with American flags, lawnmowers, and the occasional corpse lying facedown in the grass.

Campbell saw movement behind one of the sliding-glass doors and wondered if he should check for other human survivors. But then the glass shattered and a Zaphead staggered outside, a half-naked man wielding an aluminum baseball bat. Campbell pulled Stephen into the concealment of a boxwood hedge, covering the boy's mouth so he wouldn't call out. The Zaphead passed within twenty feet of them, headed toward the burning garage.

"Bad guy," Stephen whispered after the Zaphead had vanished from sight.

"Yeah."

They continued to pick their way across the yards. They came to a dead dog tied to a length of chain. Flies buzzed around the bloated body and the stench was overpowering.

"Why did Rachel leave you?" Campbell said, drawing Stephen's attention away from the grisly scene of death and the blunt reminder of what was waiting for all of them.

"She went into the Army-man house to get DeVontay."

"Why did DeVontay go in?"

"He thought there were people like us. You know, good guys."

Campbell wondered about the wisdom of finding other survivors. So far, his luck had been pretty bad, and he wondered if humans under duress could truly work together for the common good.

Nothing like a good, old-fashioned apocalypse to blow that peace, love, and understanding horseshit to the moon.

"There's the shed she put me in," Stephen said after they'd crossed another yard that featured an unkempt vegetable garden. "She promised she'd be back. But the Army men came and let me out and told me to run or die."

The door to the shed was open, and Campbell warily scanned his surroundings, wishing he had a gun.

"Somebody's been in there since I left," Stephen said. "They threw tools all over the ground."

"Maybe Rachel came back."

"Or maybe the Army men did."

They heard a shout to their left, from the direction of the street. Campbell dropped to his belly and crawled along the ground until he saw the fight. A woman in military garb was fending off a Zaphead, and two bodies were piled around their feet.

"I'd better help her," Campbell said. "You stay here."

Stephen grabbed the back of his shirt as he tried to stand. "No. She was one of the ones who told me the Zapheads were going to get me."

"But she's one of *us*."

"If you help her, she might give me to the Zapheads again."

Before Campbell could make a decision, the soldier solved the dilemma by plunging a knife deep into the Zaphead's abdomen, ripping upward in a flash of silver and gush of crimson. The soldier's high-pitched curses were likely to draw the attention of any other Zapheads in the vicinity.

The boy stared transfixed as the soldier shoved the dead Zaphead away and wiped her knife on the leg of her camouflage trousers. His face showed no real shock or surprise. Campbell wondered if this was how children reacted to warfare, after the repeated exposure ultimately gave way to numbness.

Welcome to the new normal.

"Where's that house?" Campbell asked him.

"Ruh-round the corner, I think."

"Okay, we'd better stay away from the street."

By the time they'd crawled back into the relative seclusion of the back yards, the soldier had recovered and collected her rifle. Campbell didn't want to be around when the Zapheads came out and the bullets started flying.

He was just about to start jogging when a female voice called out: "*Stephen!*"

CHAPTER TWENTY-TWO

Rachel hugged Stephen, hardly believing he was alive.

Guess I owe you for another answered prayer, Lord.

They'd ducked into the nearest house after finding the door unlocked. A sweep had revealed that it was empty, the former occupants apparently packing hastily and heading off somewhere after hearing the news of strange phenomena. Pete checked the fridge, finding only molded food and half a bottle of Sprite that had long since gone flat, while Rachel discovered a hand-operated can opener and served Stephen a cold can of chicken soup. They gathered in the darkening kitchen, Pete creating a stink with a tin of sardines that he ate with his fingers.

"You must be Rachel," said the man who had apparently rescued the boy.

"Yeah," she said. "Who are you?"

"This is my home boy, Campbell," Pete said. He punched Campbell on the arm. "Guess you can't get rid of me so easy after all. Where's Arnoff and the gang?"

"Back on the highway, looking for World War Three."

"They're in luck, then. Apparently there are rogue Marines or some shit around here. They jumped me on the highway and took me prisoner and…hell, I have no idea why."

Rachel looked past Stephen's shoulder and said, "Zaphead bait."

Campbell glared at her. "What's the big idea, abandoning this kid? Don't you have any sense?"

Rachel's grip tightened on the pruning shear and she held it up, letting Campbell see the blood on the metal tip. She forced herself to breathe evenly or anger would overwhelm her. "We got along just fine before you rode in on your white horse like a one-man cavalry."

Pete gave an uneasy laugh. "Hey, guys, we're on the same team here, right?"

Campbell shrugged and looked down at the floor. "Sorry. Guess we'll all wound a little tight right now."

"She saved me," Pete said to Campbell. "I'd be lying dead out there in the street if it wasn't for her."

Rachel ignored the praise, busy adjusting Miss Molly's outfit. She gave the doll back to Stephen, who cradled it like a football.

"Did you hurt somebody?" Stephen asked, pointing to the bloody pruning shear.

"No," she said. "Just a Zaphead."

So, you've made the final leap. Not all living creatures are equal in God's sight, and it turns out Jesus didn't die for everyone's sins.

"She's pretty wicked with that thing," Pete said, imitating her swing and giving it a home-run exaggeration.

"I'll keep that in mind next time I need to chop off somebody's head." Campbell looked through the curtains at the surrounding houses. "Is this neighborhood as dead as it looks?"

"Yeah," Rachel said. "We saw a few Zapheads when we came through." She pointed to the rising thread of smoke that hovered over the rooftops and trees. "Something's on fire."

"I played arsonist to create a distraction," Campbell said.

"Looks like you did too good of a job. The smoke is getting thick."

"Let's roll," Pete said. "There's not any beer in this place."

"Sounds good to me," Campbell said. "I'll bet we can borrow bicycles from some of these fine, upstanding citizens around here."

Rachel wasn't sure she should trust her instinct, because it was clouded with guilt. She should take Stephen and head north and find Grandpa's legendary compound on the Blue Ridge Parkway, even if it meant these guys tagging along. DeVontay was probably already dead, thrown to the Zapheads like some perverted version of the ancient Romans throwing Christians to the lions. She could picture The Captain curling his lips in a sour sneer and giving the thumb's down.

"I'm not leaving without DeVontay," Rachel said.

"He promised he'd take me to my dad," Stephen said.

"People just throw around promises like they're water," Campbell said.

"We can take care of it," Rachel said, annoyed with Campbell's holier-than-thou attitude. "You guys go on with…whatever it is you were doing."

"We're just standing around waiting for Zapheads to tear us limb from limb," Pete said. "Yep. Just killing time."

"Okay," Campbell said. "I'd hate to let that white horse go to waste. What do we do?"

Rachel wasn't sure whether she welcomed the help. Her plan had been to return to the house, wait until nightfall, and then sneak in and free DeVontay. She had to admit it wasn't much of a plan, because she wasn't sure where Stephen fit in.

"They've got guns and we don't," Rachel said.

"Damn," Pete said. "You don't think they'd actually shoot us, do you?"

"Their leader is a little unstable, to say the least. Apparently, they were holed up in a military bunker when most of the troop turned into Zapheads."

"Can't blame him for going a little nuts," Campbell said. "I think the flares affected us all more than we realize. I was talking to a scientist and —"

"Jeez, Campbell," Pete cut in. "That guy couldn't even hit

tenure track, so I wouldn't put a lot of stock in his babbling."

"How many people were with this Arnoff guy?" Rachel wondered if more survivors than she realized were around. Maybe most of them were hiding, looking out of the cracks of basement windows and waiting for the Second Coming.

"Four others," Campbell said. "They may be headed this way, but I don't think I'd wait on them."

"Well, we can't just sit here and wait for the Zapheads to mutate into whatever it is they're becoming."

"Or for *us* to change," Campbell said.

"I don't like the sound of that," Pete said.

"Change into what?" Stephen asked. Rachel wanted to cover his ears. And his eyes. And to spare his nose the scent of burning houses and rotted flesh.

"So," Pete said, "full frontal assault in a suicide mission. I'm game. Hell, we're going to buy it one way or another."

"I've got an idea, but it's a little risky," Campbell said.

"I hope it involves heavy drinking," Pete said. "I'm starting to sober up and I don't like reality."

Rachel stroked her fingers through Stephen's hair. It was thick like Chelsea's, with little curls. She wasn't going to lose anyone else in this life if she could help it.

"Okay," Rachel said. "Let's hear it."

"Well, it's pretty easy to start a fire," Campbell said. "Right, Stephen?"

The boy nodded. "And the Zapheads like it."

"And the Zapheads like it. So, we create a diversion like they do in the war movies, then when everybody's running around confused, we go in and get your friend."

"What if we scorch DeVontay in the process?" Rachel asked.

"I didn't say it was a *good* plan. You got anything better?"

Rachel studied Campbell's eyes behind his thick, black-rimmed spectacles. His pupils were large with excitement, rimmed with a gray-blue the color of Puget Sound in the winter. His hair was mussed and dirty, his chin a little too small for his brow, and his shoulders suggested he lifted more cellphones than weights. He was the kind of guy to whom she wouldn't give a second glance in a coffee shop or bookstore, but out here, in After, he gained an awkward masculinity and nobility.

Or maybe he was changing from what he had been before, a victim of the sun's subtle workings.

Maybe YOU'RE the one who is changing.

No. She was pretty sure she was still a good Christian. That little display of violence against the Zaphead had been justified. Hadn't God of the Old Testament been a vindictive warmonger before Jesus brought peace into the world? If you turned the other cheek in this sad new world, you were liable to get it bitten off.

"I guess we can't wait for more white knights to ride over the hill," Rachel finally said. "If this is what the Army becomes when the puppet strings break, maybe my grandfather was right."

"Right about what?" Campbell asked.

"One of his sayings is, 'When the walls fall down, all we have left is the enemy within.'"

Pete shook his head. "That's some heavy shit. I hope he's not out there walking around with a hatchet."

"I'm pretty sure he's one of the ones who survived, assuming he didn't transform," Rachel said. "He was planning for this."

"Planning for this?" Campbell said. "Even the scientists were caught with their pants down. They pretty much figured we had a good five billion years before the sun became a red gas giant and gobbled us up."

Pete bent over, stuck out his rear, and let out a loud, flapping fart. "There's a gas giant for you," he said.

Stephen snickered, and even though Rachel didn't approve of the sophomoric humor, she was relieved that the boy seemed to be recovering from the latest trauma.

"Okay," Campbell said. "Sun's going down. We're better off doing this right when it gets dark."

"Follow me," Rachel said, taking Stephen's hand. She checked through the front window to make sure all was clear, although she intended to use the back door.

Oh, sweet Lord. Are you serious?

"Guys," she said. "I think you need to see this."

They crowded around behind her, Pete's fishy breath fouling the air. Outside, the sunset was dusky and smoky, a hint of autumn in the surrounding maples and oaks. Faint ribbons of aurora borealis wended across the atmosphere like giant lime-green specters. Night shadows crept along the yards and across the windows of the houses, giving them a sinister aspect that suggested terrible secrets inside. But it was the activity in the street that drew their attention.

Two people were tending to one of the fallen Zapheads. Rachel couldn't be sure, but she believed the corpse was the one she had struck with her pruning shear.

"Soldiers," Pete said. "What the hell do they want with a dead Zaphead? I can't see them wasting time giving one a proper burial."

"It's not soldiers," Rachel said. Even in the poor light, she could see that one of the figures was wearing a light-colored T-shirt, not camouflage, and what looked like khaki cargo shorts and sandals. The other wore what looked like a bathrobe, the belt dangling, and the mop of hair above it could have belonged to either gender. The two stooped down and lifted the corpse to a sitting position.

"Oh, hell, they're not going to *eat* him, are they? Don't tell me these glittery-eyed bastards are turning into zombies?"

"Shhh." Rachel cast him a hard look and nodded at Stephen, whose eyes widened as his grip on the doll tightened.

"He's just kidding," Campbell said to the boy. "He's read too many comic books."

"I like comic books," Stephen said. "Spiderman is my favorite."

"Cool," Pete said, trying to cover his goof. "I had some issues in my backpack, but I lost it when the soldiers jumped me."

"You're in luck," Campbell said, motioning toward his own backpack on the couch. "I figured you'd want them if I ever caught up with you. I rescued them for you."

Pete caught on that they were trying to distract Stephen from what might be a gruesome discovery. He patted Stephen on the shoulder and said, "First appearance of the Green Goblin, little man. And in near-mint condition."

"Not so near-mint anymore," Campbell said. "But you can read it with the flashlight. Just keep the beam hooded so nobody can see it from the street."

"Sweet!" Stephen said, just like any normal boy would, not one who had endured the wholesale destruction of his race and seen the world change into a hostile wasteland. Rachel's heart clenched just a tiny bit, but she wouldn't allow any tears of sympathy. She'd cried herself out after Chelsea's death, and any future breakdowns would have to tap an entirely new and undiscovered reservoir.

Rachel and Campbell put their noses to the window, shoulders touching, their breath fogging the glass. The two figures attending the Zaphead now lifted it and held it sagging limply between them, much like a couple of sailors might drag home a drunken mate.

"You think they're going to bury it?" Rachel asked.

"It would be the first time that I've seen. But I have to admit, I've spent more time running and hiding from them than watching them."

"They're moving like humans. Good balance and posture, their motions focused on something besides destroying."

"Yeah. But if they're survivors, what do they want with a dead Zaphead?"

Rachel could think of a few possibilities, including Pete's imaginative leap of cannibalism, but that didn't make sense, because there was still plenty of food around. Scientific experimentation was unlikely, given the utter breakdown of all academic systems, and she couldn't come up with any use for a dead body otherwise. "Maybe they're cleaning the streets."

"You mean to make it look like there are no Zapheads around? Gunning for some type of community award or something?"

"No, to lure more Zapheads. Maybe they've got some vigilante thing going on."

Pete carelessly swept the flashlight beam across the room as he turned a page, reading aloud to Stephen. Rachel scolded him, afraid the light would attract the people outside like curious, single-minded moths.

Instead, the pair on the street kept dragging the corpse, heading east toward the fire that Campbell had started. The spreading conflagration threw a reddish cast to the sunset, the smoke roiling against the purple-streaked sky like a tableau in the tempest of hell. The person in the bathrobe lost her grip on the corpse, and the robe parted to reveal mottled flesh.

"I think they're Zapheads," Rachel said.

"Doesn't make sense," Campbell said. "Zapheads are

violent, mindless killing machines."

"Maybe we simplified them so we could pretend we understand them." Rachel didn't like that answer, but was it any worse than the reality of the last few weeks?

The man in the T-shirt turned and looked directly at Rachel, or at least she felt that way. Even from thirty yards, the hooded aspect of his eyes told her it was a Zaphead. He was of average height, wearing a crew cut and topsiders, and he could have been a guy washing his driveway with a garden hose, a beer in his hand while waiting for the afternoon's football games to kick off.

Rachel ducked a little, pulling Campbell down while calling out, "Keep low, guys, they're looking this way."

They crouched in the gloaming for a long minute, with the only sound the distant crackle of the bonfire. Rachel expected a knock on the door, or maybe for a body to fling itself against the window. She wished she hadn't left her pruning shears in the kitchen.

She grew tired of the tension and parted the corner of the curtain just enough to see the two Zapheads carry their fallen comrade on down the street. Rachel was surprised to think such a thing, but they had escorted their dead companion with a tenderness that was in direct contrast to all the violence she'd witnessed from them.

"I should follow them," Campbell said. "See what's going on."

"No," Rachel said. "How can that help us? Right now, we need to save DeVontay and get out of here before your fire scorches us alive."

"We can all be superheroes!" Stephen said, apparently becoming so engrossed in the comic book that he'd blurred the line between fantasy and reality. Rachel almost envied him.

"Sure, kid," Pete said. "A super-duper ray gun will do the trick."

As if to punctuate Pete's words, a brittle *crack* resounded from outside, drawing Rachel's attention. At first she thought it was the popping of wood from the heat of the fire, but the Zaphead in the white T-shirt was sprawled in the street on top of the corpse he'd been helping to carry. A dark stain spread across the back of his shirt.

Gunfire.

Another short rang out. The last Zaphead ducked and peered into the smoky murkiness, then fled out of the street into a side yard.

"Bet it's The Captain and his goon squad," Rachel said.

"Or maybe Arnoff's group," Campbell said.

Pete joined them at the window. "Sweet. Let's team up."

"At this point," Campbell said, "I can't tell the Zappers from the humans. And I'm not about to get shot to find out."

"He's right," Rachel said to Pete. "But you guys do what you want. I'm going to get DeVontay." She called to Stephen in the darkness of the living room. "Get your stuff, honey, and meet me at the back door."

CHAPTER TWENTY-THREE

At first glance, the ranch house appeared to be abandoned.

Rachel parted the waxy leaves of the rhododendron that bordered one edge of the yard. The windows were dark, although the glimmer of the distant bonfire reflected in the windows. Campbell's act of arson had spread, rimming the twilight sky in the east with an angry red-orange. Flames leaped and flickered above the treetops, casting striations of light across the land. The air stank of smoke, and breathing was difficult, but Rachel couldn't help thinking of all the cremated corpses whose fine ash now floated into her lungs.

"Dang, Campbell," Pete said, crouched behind her on the property adjoining the ranch house's yard. "That's some bonfire you built. You're doing your part to wipe the slate clean, huh?"

"Maybe these guys have already left," he said.

"No," Rachel said. "I don't think they're all that interested in survival. They're more interested in the war."

"The war against who?" Campbell said. "I think we've all pretty much lost this one."

"You don't understand soldiers. Better to go out in a blaze of glory than get your butt kicked."

Stephen squeezed her hand, the little guy curled into a ball beneath the foliage of the shrubbery. "Don't go in there."

"I can't leave without DeVontay. If I'm not back in fifteen minutes, these guys will take you to your dad. Right?"

"Uh...sure," Pete said. "We're headed that way anyway."

"Okay, then." Rachel said. "I'll start the fire on the end near the garage. That will give everybody a chance to escape before it gets out of hand."

"Got any accelerant?" Campbell asked.

"I saw a charcoal grill in the back yard before it got dark. There was a can of starter fluid beside it."

"Another weenie roast," Stephen said.

Rachel chuckled, although the sound of reassurance was more like choking on a chicken bone. "Need some paper, though."

After a moment, one in which something large popped and exploded inside the distant conflagration with the *whoosh* of an airliner at liftoff, Pete said, "Damn it. Well, so much for the investment potential." He unzipped his bag and shoved a stack of comics in her hand. "Bye, Spidey. It's been real."

"It's for a good cause," Campbell said.

"Sacrifice is for suckers," Pete said, "but this better get me some serious brownie points in heaven."

"I'll put in a good word," Rachel said, hoping she didn't sound too sanctimonious. She'd been praying fervently in the past hour but had kept it to herself.

Well, yourself and God. Because you're not in this thing alone.

She checked to make sure her lighter was still in her pocket, then tensed to push her way through the rhododendron. "I'm going with you," Campbell said.

"We're more likely to be spotted that way," she said. "Besides, you need to look after Stephen."

She felt a strong hand gripping her forearm. She turned and saw wildfire rippling in Campbell's eyeglasses, and behind that, his gleaming, earnest eyes. "If you go in there, I have to go with you," he said.

Anger burned inside her, as hot as any fire. "This isn't the time for some stupid post-apocalypse man-code. In case you haven't noticed, the codes are pretty much erased. So don't pull your macho bullshit, because I've made it this far without you."

Stephen drew in a shuddering gasp, and Rachel immediately regretted her outburst. She stroked Stephen's hair and whispered. "It's okay, honey. I'll get DeVontay and be right back. I promise."

Pete let out a snort of disbelief but Campbell stayed silent. Rachel clutched the small stack of comic books in one hand, her pruning shear held in the other. The ludicrous nature of her position struck her. If she'd seen somebody outfitted like this in a viral YouTube video, she'd have dubbed the viral star a demented supergeek, doomed to a life of cat memes and celibacy.

Just call me Joan of Arc. Hopefully, without the "burned at the stake" part.

A shiver of stray light, perhaps made by a flashlight beam, tracked across the inside of the ranch house. At the same time, a gust of wind pushed the distant fire into a swollen mass of heat, illuminating twisted columns of smoke that boiled up into the heavens.

Rachel thought she heard someone's voice through the shattered picture window. The corpse had been removed from the sill, although a dark heap lay in the shadows of the flowerbed near the edge of the porch.

"Okay, wish me luck," Rachel said, bracing to sprint along the perimeter of the lawn. Given the darkness, she was pretty sure she wouldn't be spotted, but she didn't trust Captain America's little A-Team. They might just be a little trigger-happy now that one of their number had been killed by the Zapheads.

"You don't need luck," Pete said. "You need a shot of booze."

"Good luck," Campbell said, giving her arm a squeeze of encouragement. "If anything happens, we'll create a distraction so you can escape."

"Mancode?" she asked.

"Nah," he replied. "Just good, old-fashioned outsmarting-the-bad-guys strategy."

"Wait," Stephen said. "I thought those…Z things, the Zapheads…were the bad guys."

"And *your* job is to take care of Miss Molly," Rachel said to him. "Okay, I'll meet you back here with DeVontay, if everything goes according to plan."

"Nothing ever goes according to plan," Campbell said. "Or this wouldn't be After."

"Yeah," she muttered under her breath, and then she launched herself from the shrubs and ran, crouching and keeping an eye on the house, her broken pruning shears held before her like a jousting lance.

The strange glow on the horizon swelled into a perpetual sunset, and Rachel was afraid she was too exposed to make it to the end of the house without being seen. However, she quickly cut across the yard and soon dropped to her knees at the end of the house from which she'd escaped. Above her was the black rectangle of the access from which she'd made her escape—the lack of windows on this side of the house gave her confidence.

The charcoal grill smelled of old grease and soot, with ashes piled around its rusted legs. But the can of starter fluid was nearly full, and she sprayed it against the wooden siding, the heavy petroleum scent pushing the scorched aroma from her nostrils. After soaking the wood, she leaned her weapon against the house and fumbled the lighter from her pocket.

In the distance, she heard more pops and crackles of the approaching conflagration, and again, she wondered why The Captain hadn't moved his unit from the area. And, she wondered if DeVontay was still inside.

He will be.

Because you NEED him to be.

And she wondered how much of her need was fueled by guilt over Chelsea. She wasn't sure of her motivations, but it was easier to believe she was noble and righteous. But Pete's words came back to her: *"Sacrifice is for suckers."*

She wasn't losing. Not this time.

Rachel sparked the lighter to life and flapped open one of the comic books, fanning the pages. She touched the fire to one corner and a finger of flame crawled up the edge of the paper, the ink giving off lurid colors. She pushed the torch over to the moistened boards and the fire took an enthusiastic drink of the fuel and leaped across the siding.

Rachel was so transfixed by the mesmerizing flame and the way it seemed to hover just over the fuel that she briefly forgot her surroundings. Suddenly, she heard a shout from the street and instantly ducked behind the old charcoal grill, hoping its bulk would conceal her.

Is that Stephen and the guys? What would they be doing in the street?

Then came the *pak pak pak* of semiautomatic gunfire. A bullet skinned off the wooden siding ten feet above her head. But she didn't think she was the target.

She lifted her head just enough to see the silhouette of a human figure running down the street. The hail of bullets peppered the trees as the figure vanished between two cars parked in a driveway. She wasn't sure whether it had been a Zaphead or someone running from the shooters, but cracked laughter came from the unseen end of the street.

"Goddamn, did you see that sonofabitch runnin' like it had ants crawling up its zap-hole?" yelled a man with a rural accent.

"Save your ammo, Donnie," said another voice, lower, calmer, and more authoritative.

It didn't sound like The Captain, although the arrogant tone of command was similar. By now, the flames had licked along the end of the house, spreading beyond the petroleum-soaked blotch. A thin ribbon of smoke wended into the sky to merge with the gauze of haze overhead.

Rachel crawled around the corner of the house, slapping her pruning shears ahead of her. The screen door hung open, sagging a little on its hinges. Even though she might be visible from the street, she wondered whether she should sneak in the broken window. Depending upon how many of The Captain's goons were on duty, she doubted she could fight her way to the back room where she'd been held captive with DeVontay.

She decided it might be better to wait until the fire penetrated the house and forced them to flee. They'd likely not waste the time freeing DeVontay.

Assuming he's even alive.

Well, she could either dwell on the reality of her situation or fall back on her faith. Her faith was always there, wrapping her in its saccharine web, protecting her and restraining her. Jesus, in His darkest hour on the cross, asked why God had forsaken Him, and God didn't answer. She didn't expect an answer now, either.

She had nearly decided the house was indeed unoccupied and was about to sneak to the back door when a muffled explosion roared from the open window. Someone was firing a gun from inside the house.

Shouts—human shouts—in the street were followed by return gunfire.

Oh my Lord, they're shooting at each other. The last living humans are trying to kill each other.

Perhaps she shouldn't be surprised. After all, killing was what humans did.

The fire licked up the side of the wall, reaching the eaves and the roof shingles. Black smoke boiled into the sky as wood cracked and popped from the heat. The back door burst open and Captain America ran out, his face sweating and shiny in the reddish glow of the fire-lit night. Two soldiers followed on his heels, all three running for the rear of the property. Rachel was relieved to see they were heading away from where Stephen, Pete, and Campbell were hiding. Another soldier, this one the woman who had fought off the Zaphead in the street, hobbled out of the house and ran after them in the dark.

"Bruenig," she called. "Johnson. Navarro. Wait up."

She'd barely reached the back hedge when her shoulder erupted in a spout of dark fluid. The gunshot sounded a split-second later, still reverberated between the houses as she sprawled on the scruffy lawn, moaning and leaking.

"Damn," Campbell called from the concealment of the rhododendron. Then, louder, he shouted, "Arnoff! Hold your fire!"

Rachel realized the group firing on the soldiers must have been Campbell's and Pete's traveling companions. She kept low and scrambled toward the back door. Before, there had been more soldiers, but perhaps The Captain had sent them on reconnaissance, or maybe they'd been killed by Zapheads.

Or maybe they were stacked inside the house, executed by their crazy commander, victims of bunker fever.

She didn't have time to waste. "I'm going in," she called over to Campbell, and then she burst through the back door, her pruning shears held at the ready. The interior of the house was murky, the smoke hanging thin and stale, and the faintest light oozing through the windows.

"DeVontay!" she called, keeping low and heading for the hallway, banging her shin against a piece of furniture in the dark. Around her, the shell of the house whispered and hissed with the spreading flames. She didn't have much time.

The hallway was almost completely black, but Rachel recalled the straight shot to the back bedroom where she and DeVontay had been held captive. She slammed her shoulder against the closed door, and then twisted the knob, wishing she'd thought to bring a flashlight.

She sensed movement in the room, so perhaps they hadn't bound DeVontay to the bed again. That was good, because she needed every second. Fire crawled over the roof, consuming the asphalt shingles with a greasy roar of pure joy.

Rachel shouted his name again, competing with the hunger of the fire. The flames had reached the windows and backlit the house, sending shimmering bands of deep red behind her. A shape hung before her, a black, man-shaped shadow against the glow.

"DeVontay, come on," she screamed, rushing forward and reaching for him.

The hand snatched her wrist and yanked her forward, the stench of fetid breath cutting through the acrid smoke.

"Rachel?" DeVontay called from somewhere outside.

CHAPTER TWENTY-FOUR

"They're blowing the hell out of everything that moves," Pete said.

Campbell covered Stephen's ears against the popcorn staccato of gunfire and the growling blaze. The darkness had given way to a half-light.

"I knew Donnie was going to crack sooner or later," he said. "I was hoping to be miles away when it happened."

"She's been in there too long," Pete said. "The whole damned house is about to fall in."

Stephen gave a squeal of dismay at the news. Campbell wished he could elbow Pete in the gut to shut him up, but Pete was retreating deeper into the shrubbery, as if the vegetation could ward off stray bullets. Campbell saw a man on the roof of a nearby house, aiming a rifle into the street. He couldn't be sure, but he guessed it was one of the camouflaged soldiers.

"Yee-haw," Donnie whooped in his unmistakable Southern drawl.

The soldier fired a couple of rounds in the direction of Donnie's voice, triggering a volley in response. The soldier froze, outlined against the hellish horizon for a moment, then he flung out his arms and dropped his rifle. He collapsed and rolled down the slanted roof, disappearing from sight.

"So much for being on the same team," Pete said. "We better get out of here."

"We told Rachel we'd wait."

"Raaaay-chel," Stephen wailed.

"Shh," Campbell said. "We'll get her." He turned to the darkness behind him. "Pete?"

But Pete was gone, vanished in the shadows between the houses. Campbell cursed under his breath. He didn't dare leave Stephen alone, not after all the trauma he'd endured. But he couldn't just sit there while people died, either—there weren't all that many left to spare.

"Come on, Stevie Boy," he said, grabbing the child's arm and dragging him forward.

They burst from the rhododendron hedge, exposed in the flickering light of the burning house. It spat and sputtered like a volcano, sucking oxygen from the wooden shell to feed the wild orange-red fury on the roof. No one could last long in such an inferno.

Campbell pulled Stephen along behind him as he ran toward the house. He saw a man run into the open back door just as Stephen called, "DeVontay!"

"Is that your friend?" Campbell asked.

Stephen nodded, tucking his doll under his chin and squeezing hard. Campbell figured DeVontay had a better chance of reaching Rachel than he did. But he was spared any dilemma or guilt when a familiar face stepped into the glow of the fire.

"Well, well, well," Arnoff said. "Guess your scouting mission went all to hell."

Arnoff's hunting jacket was blotched with something wet and dark. His rifle pointed up, the butt riding the inside of one elbow, and his eyes were bright with a strange fever.

"I found Pete," Campbell said.

"Us against them," Arnoff said, staring at the boy. "Are you one of us, or one of them?"

Campbell nudged the boy behind him, using himself as a shield against Arnoff's apparent madness. "I found some other survivors, too."

"Some survivors shoot back."

"They…they're military. They're doing a Zaphead clean-up."

"Well, they're doing a crappy job of it," Arnoff said. "We must have seen four dozen Zappers back there at the big fire. They were drawn like moths. Me and Donnie took a bunch down, but some of them snuck off into dark."

"Where's Pamela and the professor?"

Arnoff hooked a casual thumb behind him. "Back there somewhere. They'll be along shortly."

Behind Arnoff, Campbell saw DeVontay drag Rachel from the house, smoke boiling out after them as a portion of the roof folded in like sodden cardboard. But they weren't alone. Something clung to Rachel, limbs entwined around her as DeVontay flailed at it.

"Ruh-ray-ray!" Stephen stuttered.

Arnoff turned in the direction of the boy's gaze, watching the struggle fifty feet away. Without a word, he raised his weapon and peered down the barrel. Campbell leaped toward him, bellowing in rage, but the gun ripped out a percussive clap of noise and yellow light flashed from the tip of the barrel.

The three figures rolled off the porch into the landscaping. Campbell dashed across the lawn, forgetting Stephen in his panic. Someone rose up from beside the steps, shadow melding with the low trees and flowers. Arnoff fired again and the figure was flung backward by the force of the bullet.

"Hold your fire, goddamn it," Campbell yelled, expecting a bullet in the back for his trouble.

Arnoff chuckled loudly, the sound a perfect harmony to the madly swelling fire. Another form crawled from the landscaping, and Campbell recognized Rachel's long, dark hair. His heart gave a leap of relief, and he was sickened by his own longing and selfish need.

"You okay?" he asked, kneeling in the dewy weeds and pulling her toward him.

She looked at him with bloodshot, bleary eyes, coughing and wheezing. "Stephen?" she managed to gasp.

"Right over there," Campbell said, pointing to where the boy stood near Arnoff.

DeVontay stood up beside the porch, wiping his torn sleeve against his face. His dark skin glistened with sweat. "Careful who you shooting at," he said to Arnoff.

"Don't worry none. I know a Zaphead when I see one."

"We all look alike in the dark."

"No comment," Arnoff said, scanning the nearby rooftops. Stephen ran across the scraggly lawn as Campbell helped Rachel to her feet, and the boy dropped his doll in the enthusiasm of giving her a hug. DeVontay joined them and put a protective arm over Rachel's shoulder, sending a flare of jealousy burning across Campbell's chest.

"You came back for me," DeVontay said to her.

"Told you I would," she said. "Are you a doubting Thomas?"

"I'm a doubting DeVontay," he said. "I've been let down before."

Campbell glanced down at the Zaphead, which had a dark red dot in the center of its forehead where the bullet had struck. In repose, the rounded face looked like that of a math teacher's or a financial advisor's, fortyish, pale, a plump fold of fat under the chin. The corpse reminded Campbell of Uncle Frederick from D.C., a lobbyist who told political jokes that were neither funny nor insightful and who always seemed to end up with the last piece of fried chicken at family reunions. This Zaphead might once have been somebody's uncle.

Campbell turned to Arnoff. "Are you sure this guy was a Zaphead?"

Arnoff shrugged. "Odds were better than fifty-fifty."

Rachel and DeVontay gave Campbell a dubious look, but he answered, "We've made it this far, so stick with the winners."

They moved away from the house as the flames engulfed the core, waves of dry heat wafting across Campbell's skin. The fire had tried to spread across the lawn, but the dew had stifled it, so it contented itself with the wood, plastics, and fabrics already in its possession.

Campbell looked around the edge of the fire's light. "Pete?"

"Your friend ran off again?" Arnoff said. "Maybe he's not much a friend after all."

"It wasn't his fault he got taken as a prisoner of war," Campbell responded.

"We'd best get away from this house before the Zapheads come out to party," Arnoff said.

Rachel pulled Stephen to her side. "We're grateful for your help, sir, but we have other plans."

Arnoff propped the butt of his rifle against his hip and angled it outward at forty-five degrees. "Little lady, I don't know what you've been smoking these last few weeks, but like Campbell here said, better stick with the winners."

"Sorry, man," DeVontay said. "We promised the boy we'd get to Mi'sippi. And maybe our chances are better if we ain't trucking around with some trigger-happy cowboy."

Before Campbell could move between the two men, Arnoff took an aggressive step forward. "Watch it, boy," Arnoff said. "You're starting to look a lot like a Zaphead in this bad light. Somebody might make a little mistake."

"Come on, Arnoff," Campbell said, about to put a hand on the man's shoulder before deciding against it. Arnoff tensed like a cobra, and his dark eyes seemed cold and reptilian.

"Let's find Donnie and the others."

Arnoff scowled and then spat in the grass. "At least one of you has got a little sense."

Campbell wasn't sure of his loyalties anymore. Pete was his buddy, and they'd been through plenty together, but Pete was likely to get them both killed. Arnoff, Donnie, and the others had firepower on their side, as well as an established social structure that provided the illusion of civilization. Rachel, DeVontay, and Stephen seemed more like a family unit than a pack of mutual survivors.

Rachel's face, although streaked with black soot, shone with a benevolent radiance as bright as the fires that surrounded them. Campbell knew most of it was projection, his own hope that he'd find something more in After than just the next breath. He needed a reason to live. And she was the first female he'd encountered that was anywhere close to his age.

Somebody's got to breed, right?

"Watch out for the soldiers," Rachel said. "They're well-trained, heavily armed, and mildly psychotic."

She limped toward the street, DeVontay supporting her, Stephen trailing just behind them. The house crumbled into a pile of charred lumber, hissing from its blue heart, a mild mockery of the malevolence delivered by the distant sun.

"Maybe we should give them a gun," Campbell said to Arnoff.

"Don't go trying to save the world," Arnoff said. "There's no future in it."

"Well, what's the plan, then? Walk around shooting Zapheads until you run out of ammo?"

Arnoff checked the chamber of the Marlin, pulling a few cartridges from a vest pocket and sliding them into the tube. "Going from house to house, you'd probably find enough ammo to kill every Zapper on the planet, a hundred times over. Thank God for the Second Amendment."

"I'm not sure the Bill of Rights applies anymore," Campbell said.

"Maybe not. I can just see a bunch of Zapheads sitting on the Supreme Court right now. Wouldn't be able to tell much of a difference, if you ask me." Arnoff scanned the rooftops and the perimeter of the surrounding yards. Now that the fire had banked itself and burned low, the neighborhood had fallen quiet again, although the holocaust to the east was spreading.

They heard Donnie in the distance, giving his redneck rebel yell followed by a series of semiautomatic rounds. Arnoff grinned. "Hunting season," he said, heading in the direction of the volley.

"I'll catch up in a minute," Campbell said. "After I find Pete."

Arnoff didn't even turn around. "Compassion was a game for the old days, son. Brownie points don't add up to shit in the afterburn."

Campbell clenched his fists in rage. He could hear the echo of his overbearing dad's, *"Get with the program!"* in those words. Was it any wonder that Campbell always shrank from responsibility and rejected authority? Assholes had always run the world and set the rules. Maybe it wasn't so bad that their power had been wiped away by a few massive spasms of the sun.

Campbell left the dying red glow of the house fire and entered the shrubbery where he'd last seen Pete, digging in his backpack for his flashlight.

CHAPTER TWENTY-FIVE

"Got any Slim Jims?" Rachel asked DeVontay.

He grinned, his teeth and eyes the only part of his face visible in the gloom. "I knew you'd come around to good eatin'."

They'd spent the night in a strip motel, walking just far enough to be reasonably sure the expanding blaze wouldn't reach them before dawn. The motel's small windows were set high in the wall, situated to allow neither easy access nor sunlight. The check-in counter had been abandoned, although the cars parked outside many of the rooms gave the illusion that it was business as usual at the Parkview Travel Plaza.

Although dawn was still probably an hour away, Rachel felt a little better from her brief sleep. DeVontay had dozed with his back against the door, his pistol resting between his legs on the dusty carpet. Stephen had climbed up on the lone twin bed with Rachel and had fallen asleep instantly, and was still snoring like a buzz saw.

Rachel stroked a tendril of hair away from his soft cheek. "Poor little guy. He's had a rough time of it."

DeVontay passed her some Slim Jims and a bottle of water from his backpack, as well as a pack of cheese crackers. She'd always had a pet peeve about eating in bed. She considered it a sign of sloth and personal failing. Now, in retrospect, her admittedly uptight view of morality seemed foolish.

She wondered what other views might change in the days and weeks ahead. She bowed her head and said, "Dear Lord, thank you for the food we are about to receive for the nourishment of our bodies, that we may have strength in Your service. Amen."

The prayer was so automatic she hadn't realized she'd said it aloud until DeVontay added, "Amen." After a moment, he said, "You're really a holy roller, ain't you?"

"No rolling going on here," she said, tearing into one of the salted meat snacks with her teeth. "I just need all the help I can get."

"That's cool. My momma was in the church choir. She was Mennonite. I had to go when I was little, but I never got into it. Too many rules for my blood."

"Doesn't all this…this *After*…make you want to find peace in the Lord?"

"Well, depends on how you look at it. Maybe God is going to save us, or maybe God caused all this in the first place."

"My faith hasn't wavered," Rachel said, a little too forcefully. Pride was a sin, but failing to testify was a different kind of arrogance. Or maybe she was just trying to convince herself.

"Okay, fine," DeVontay said, pulling more snacks from his backpack and ripping into the cellophane. "Do you think this is the Revelations coming true? The seven-horned beast and all that shit?"

"I don't take the Book of Revelations literally," she said. "I don't think the final battle is going to take place in the Holy Land, or that the Antichrist is walking among us."

"But there's something in there about the world ending in fire from the sky, right?"

"After the seventh seal is opened, a great star falls from heaven and a third of the sea turns to blood. But there are also earthquakes, locusts, and foul waters. I don't see any of that, do you?"

"So, it's possible this isn't really the end of the world? Just a warm-up act."

She couldn't tell if he was teasing her or not. The first

blush of dawn took some of the darkness from the window, and Rachel became aware of the shabby furniture in the room. The bed linens seemed clean enough, though, and she was in no position to complain. The toilet didn't stink, so at least those particular waters hadn't been fouled by the great whore of Babylon.

She patted Stephen's arm, which was curled around Miss Molly. "All I know is it's not over as long as there's a single human left," she said. "We're here to care for each other as best we can, do the next right thing, and stay in service to the Lord's will for us. We don't have to understand it. Our job is to just keep showing up."

"So, you don't see all this as a showdown of Good versus Evil?"

"Are the Zapheads evil just because they have destructive natures? Maybe they're serving the Lord's will just as we are."

"Everything happens for a reason, huh? Sounds like the excuse people use for some sucky choice they made."

"And God gives us free will, so we have the chance to choose goodness and grace and salvation."

DeVontay stood, clutching the pistol, and peeked out of the high window. Satisfied, he turned back to her, his face now plainly visible in the dawn. He seemed angry, his skin stretched taut over his jawbones, his forehead furrowed. "Except, we didn't get no choice, did we? We wake up one day and we're in hell."

"No," she said. "We're alive." She touched Stephen's shoulder. "We still have something to live for."

"Oh, yeah? Come take a look at this."

Careful not to rouse Stephen, whose snores had quieted, she slipped out of bed and joined DeVontay at the window. Outside, she could see the surroundings that had been hidden the night before. They were in a mixed-use commercial area, a few apartment buildings separated by retail and light industrial uses—a plumbing supply shop, a fenced lot with stacks of wooden beams and piles of sawdust, and a thrift shop with toddler clothes in the window.

But it was the activity in the street that drew her attention. People—*Zapheads*—were walking up the street. Although they appeared nearly unaware of each other, all of them at least fifty feet apart, they were headed in the same direction. They moved with none of the uncoordinated sluggishness of a few days before, nor did they seem particularly intent on destroying anything.

"Weird," she said. The scene was rendered even more surreal by their utter silence. If not for their transfixed, unblinking eyes, she would have thought they were fellow survivors. Even now, she wondered if maybe Zapheads and survivors were sharing the same street in relative harmony, perhaps coming to accept one another.

"Creepy as hell. Where they going?"

Rachel looked at the angle of the shadows that stretched from the sides of the buildings and the few cars in the street. "They're heading east. Back toward the big fire."

"So, maybe they're not in hell, just *heading* for it."

"It seems like there are more of them."

"These sons of bitches ain't coming back from the dead, are they?"

Rachel almost made a joke, but DeVontay clearly was simmering on the verge of exploding. "Whatever instinct is driving them, it's brought them out in the open. Maybe a lot of them were inside before."

"Inside killing people, maybe. Don't forget what they done."

"Well, maybe they've changed."

"Yeah, right. Praise the Lord, they saw the light. Maybe

they're not even mindless killers anymore. Let's run outside and start singing *Dancin' in the Street* and see what happens."

DeVontay had raised his voice so much that Stephen let out a plaintive, confused cry. "Mommy?"

Rachel shot DeVontay a venomous glare and hurried to the bed. She swept the boy up in her arms and held him tightly, the sheet swaddling his shoulders. Rocking back and forth, she whispered, "Shhh, honey. It's okay."

DeVontay began stuffing his things into his backpack as if preparing to leave. Stephen finally became aware of his surroundings. "Whu-where are we?"

"North of Charlotte," she said.

He wiped at his eyes with a grimy fist. "Is that close to Mi'sippi?"

"Closer than yesterday," she said.

"I think we better wait it out," DeVontay said, again monitoring the street through the beige curtains.

"It's not any safer traveling at night," Rachel said. "They don't seem to sleep."

"They don't eat nothing, either. You'd think they'd wear down after a while."

Rachel didn't like having this conversation in front of Stephen, but she didn't see any way around it. "Well, let's face it. We just don't know anything. Right after the Big Zap, they were killing every living thing in sight, random destruction, acting mindlessly. Now they're moving with more purpose, like they're getting settled into their new lives."

DeVontay pulled one of the curtains wide. "You call that shit *'life'*? It's like somebody opened up their heads like a jack-o'-lantern and stuffed them full of poisoned cotton candy."

"Cotton candy?" Stephen said, standing up on the bed and trying to see out the window.

Rachel pulled him back down into the bed and gave him a

pack of crackers. "You better keep your strength up. We've got a long walk ahead."

"Why is walking better than staying right here?" DeVontay said. "We can hole up, make a run to a store now and then, wait this thing out."

"We have no idea what we'd be waiting for. You think the Army's going to roll in and save us? We've already seen how that plays out."

"Then we ought to find those guys from last night— Campbell and them—and band together so we have a better chance of fighting them off."

"The Zapheads outnumber us. I don't think we've gotten a good idea of their population. They've gone from random, individual acts of violence, where you might only see one or two at a time, to a more open, communal behavior."

"This ain't psychology class. This is war. Plus, you don't even know what those things are thinking about. They might as well be puppets hanging on invisible strings."

"I like puppets," Stephen said with enthusiasm, spraying cracker crumbs from his mouth. Then, his face darkened. "But I don't like Zapheads."

Rachel again glared at DeVontay, who ignored her anger. "But Zapheads may not be our only problem. Look at The Captain and his storm troopers. What if they're not an isolated case? What if there are pockets of military forces out there, armed to the teeth and making their own rules? They're as likely to slaughter us as the Zapheads are."

"That's an even better reason to stay here, then. Those idiots might be shooting everything that moves."

"No," Rachel said, not knowing how to put it in a way that wouldn't frighten Stephen even more. But perhaps the fantasy of reaching his father was enough to sustain him for now. "The fires are spreading. Imagine all those toxins in Charlotte.

When that city burns, the smoke is going to be a killer."

"So, our choices are choking to death, getting shot, or getting our brains bashed in by Zapheads," DeVontay said.

"The one thing we can't do is just sit here and pray," Rachel said.

"Oh, is the holy roller losing faith?"

"Faith without works is dead," Rachel responded, hating herself for reducing a complex passage from the Book of James into a catch phrase. "That means fighting the good fight."

"Like chopping up Zapheads with that sling blade?"

"I plead self-defense," she said.

Stephen scooted off the bed, tossing his cracker wrapper on the floor.

"Stephen?" Rachel said. "Did you forget something?"

"No. I got Miss Molly right here," he said, turning the doll to face her.

She scowled and looked down at the wrapper. "Trash goes in the trash can."

As Stephen bent to pick up the wrapper, DeVontay said to her, "You make the apocalypse so much fun."

"Okay," Rachel said. "Time to go."

"Go where?" DeVontay said, sitting on the bed.

"Mi'sippi!" Stephen said.

"Stevie, you're a little too eager to go out there," DeVontay said to him. "Lots of stray bullets flying around."

"We'll be better off once we get away from the city," Rachel said. "Fewer people, fewer Zapheads, fewer fires."

"Back to nature, huh?"

Rachel was serving as sentinel at the window. The streets outside the motel were quiet. She hadn't seen any Zapheads for the last hour or so. Distant bursts of gunfire had erupted intermittently, but Rachel didn't believe that Captain America and his troops were on this side of town. For the one thing, the hunting wasn't as good.

"We're heading for Mount Rogers." Rachel smiled at Stephen. "It's on the way."

"What's up there?" DeVontay asked.

"Somebody who was ready for this."

"What, you got ESP all of a sudden?" DeVontay asked. "The sun heated you up some new superpowers?"

"My grandfather has a compound there. He's what you might call a 'survivalist wacko.' He got interested in self-reliant living back during Y2K fever, when some people thought the computers would go berserk and throw civilization back to the Stone Age."

DeVontay scowled. "Well, we all saw how that one turned out."

"Yes, but Grandpa Wheeler figured civilization had gotten too complex, that modern systems would inevitably break down for one reason or another. Like a motor that had too many moving parts and not enough oil. He also believes the world's governments were serving the will of the very wealthy. At some point we'd have to learn to live outside the structure."

"He got that right." DeVontay nudged Stephen. "Get your stuff together, Little Man. We got some walking to do."

Rachel stuffed her supplies in the backpack, rediscovering the bottle of suicide pills the pharmacist had given her. Why hadn't she already gotten rid of them?

DeVontay pulled out his pistol, opened the door a crack, and surveyed the street. "This is as good a time as any. Unless you want to make the bed first?"

CHAPTER TWENTY-SIX

Jorge dreamed of great dragons, their green scales glittering in the sun as they soared over a burning land. Dozens of them poured their flames upon the earth from above. Their gaping, lipless mouths spat sparks and steam, and their brittle cries were like thick sheets of glass sliding across gritty metal.

He awoke in a sweat, not knowing where he was. The dragons faded from his mind's eye, but the shrieks continued.

He fumbled one hand across the thin blankets until he found Rosa's warm body, and then rolled to where Marina still slept on the cot. He checked her forehead, pleased to find it relatively cool.

The front door to the cabin burst open, letting dawn rush in. Franklin Wheeler was silhouetted in the opening, a shotgun in one hand, the other tugging up his filthy flannel underwear.

"Goddamn ya, leave my chickens alone," the old man yelled.

Jorge rose from the makeshift bedding and hurried outside. Franklin stood in the yard, raising the shotgun to the sky as squawking hens raced for the cover of the garden and trees. As Franklin aimed, Jorge squinted against the morning sun and saw a hawk, its wings spread wide in a display of aerodynamic majesty. Its breast was mottled, the tail feathers red, the sharp beak pointing into the morning breeze.

The shotgun belched out a thunderclap, pellets spraying the tops of trees. The hawk lurched and faltered, a few feathers floating away from its body. The wings curled in against the breast and the bird of prey dropped like a wet rock into the forest beyond the compound.

"Got the bastard," Franklin said, pumping the shotgun and ejecting a smoking red plastic shell to the dirt.

"A red-tail hawk," Jorge said. Red-tails were common in the mountain forests, territorial and intelligent, and their keen vision served them up small rodents and birds. Mr. Wilcox's property had harbored several mating couples, and Jorge had occasionally seen one of the hawks swoop down and claim a jackrabbit from the Christmas tree fields.

"Is everything okay?" Rosa called from the doorway, Marina wrapped in a blanket and standing behind her.

"Just killing a predator," Franklin said, not realizing his words could have a double meaning.

"Is okay," Jorge said, waving them back into the house.

The hens were still unsettled, although most of them had found clefts in the weeds where they crouched, clucking and fluttering their wings. One, however, lay in a lump by a metal watering tub, one yellow leg poked awkwardly in the air.

Franklin shouldered the weapon and walked over to the dead bird. "I'm glad it's a white one. I got three just like it, so I didn't bother giving them names."

The chicken's head had been torn from its body, ruby-red giblets hanging from the opening. Jorge looked around but he didn't see the head. The hawk hadn't been carrying it, so it must have been planning to eat the bird on the spot until its meal had been interrupted. The flies had already found the corpse.

"You mind getting the shovel?" Franklin asked, scanning the sky as if expecting another hawk to make a dessert run.

"Why?" Jorge asked in return.

"To bury it. Put it in the garden and the nutrients go back to the soil."

"But it's in good shape," Jorge said. "*Es sabroso*. Tasty."

Franklin shook his head. "I run a no-kill operation here. The chickens give me eggs in trade for their room and board."

"It's dead anyway," Jorge said. "You didn't kill it."

Franklin's face curdled as he looked at the hen. He shook his head. "I don't know if I could eat it. Almost like eating one of the family."

"Rosa will cook it very nice," Jorge said, knowing his English grammar was slightly off but hoping Franklin wouldn't notice.

"I...I don't think I could pluck it and clean it," Franklin said.

"You give me a sharp knife, the job is done."

Franklin nodded. "Guess there's not much use letting it go to waste. Like you said, dead is dead."

Jorge's admiration for the man had taken a downward slide. All the defenses and food storage and solar-energy panels meant nothing if Franklin wasn't prepared to make use of every resource. But Jorge also felt a surge of pride. He and his family had something to contribute here. They could be part of this society and culture, as small as it was.

As Franklin went into the house, Jorge called to him, "Please tell Rosa to start a pot of water boiling."

Jorge lifted the hen, which was surprisingly light, given its bulk. Birds were deceptive in size because of their feathers and hollow bones. This hen could feed the four of them for at least two meals, assuming Franklin's springhouse did a proper job of cooling. Besides, the most unpleasant part of the task—chopping off the head and taking the life—had already been delivered as a gift courtesy of Mother Nature.

By the time Franklin returned, now dressed in blue jeans and a wool sweater, Jorge had already plucked most of the larger feathers from the wings. He took the knife and dissected the carcass, splitting down the breastbone to the tail and letting the internal organs spill. He carefully collected the heart and liver, both of which were still warm. The gizzard was packed with crushed grain and a few tiny bits of gray gravel.

"Well, will you look at that," Franklin said, apparently overcoming his squeamishness. "I guess you might call that her last supper."

"The rocks help grind the food for them," Jorge said. He knew most Americans had no hands-on relationship with the meat they consumed. Mr. Wilcox had been the same way. Meat was something that came in clear plastic wrap from the store, or else was seared and slapped between pieces of bread at McDonald's. Their meat was a stranger to them.

Jorge used the tip of the knife to scrape the lungs away from the insides of the ribcage. After he severed the drumsticks just below the knee joints, he peeled away the skin as if removing a tight glove. Normally, he would dip the fowl in boiling water and pluck the feathers, but he figured a skinless bird would be a lean treat and more easily allow Franklin to forget it had once been a pet.

"Are you a man who doesn't like killing?" Jorge asked Franklin, dangling the naked chicken so that any offal and juice could drain.

"I reckon I could kill if I had to," Franklin answered. "Like that hawk there. Normally, I'd never shoot one. But when you come and mess with what's mine, that's when I fight back."

Jorge told Franklin about the men he'd fought back at the Wilcox farm, and how the men had changed into something threatening and alien.

"No, they ain't men no more," Franklin said. "I heard on the shortwave radio they're calling them 'Zapheads.'"

"Well, if they come here, you might have to kill them."

"If they come here, then they're breaking the one law of

this here compound," Franklin said, sweeping an arm to indicate the garden, the animal pens, and the outbuildings. "And that law is to live and let live, respect the fences, and mind your own business."

"It is good to be self-reliant," Jorge said, proud he'd learned such a word in his studies with Rosa. "But there's another law that applies."

"Huh," Franklin grunted. "What's that?"

"We're all in this together." He held up the chicken. "And let us hope this isn't our last supper."

CHAPTER TWENTY-SEVEN

Two…three…four…

Campbell counted the Zapheads on the streets surrounding the church. After a fruitless search for Pete the night before, he'd broken into a Baptist church, found the stairs to the steeple, and locked himself in. From the ground, the eastern horizon had appeared to be lit by a single bonfire that had spread. But from a vantage point fifty feet in the air, Campbell had seen at least a dozen large fires, dotting the black landscape many miles into the distance.

Now, in the glare of daylight, the fires were largely hidden, although a thick gauze of haze lay over the world. A black circle of ash marked the house that Rachel had set afire last night. He'd traveled maybe a quarter of a mile in the darkness, but it had felt like a marathon of slogging through molasses. He was exhausted.

The church was at the edge of town, the short square streets lined with houses that gave way to roads that curved gently into wooded areas. The streets were remarkably free of corpses, leaving Campbell to wonder if someone had been on morgue duty. Cars and trucks were scattered across the asphalt, although the traffic here must have been light when the solar flares erupted. On the street outside the church was a school bus, its wheels on the sidewalk. Campbell was grateful the windows were darkened by the angle of the sun, so that he couldn't see inside.

The Zapheads moved between the vehicles with as much indifference as water flowing around stones. Although they didn't acknowledge one another in any way, they seemed aware of each other's presence. The creepiest thing was, they were all heading east, back toward the largest of the fires.

Movement on a side street drew his attention away from the ambling, vacant-brained creatures. A figure burst out of the garage bay of a service station, head lowered, dragging his backpack behind him so that it bounced on the sidewalk. Campbell recognized the black T-shirt.

He stood and cupped his hands into a megaphone of flesh. "Pete!"

Pete didn't look up, but the Zapheads froze in their tracks and tilted their heads up to the church steeple.

Holy shit.

Campbell ducked below the ledge of the steeple, wondering how well Zapheads could see. But after a moment, he realized he would lose Pete again, so he raised his head until he could peer over and track Pete's route. Pete was farther up the sidewalk, passing a row of shops with broken windows, and making a mad dash before abruptly turning into a brick building that sported a green awning and a protruding wooden sign that Campbell couldn't read.

Should be easy enough to find, assuming that he holds the fort.

But Campbell had a more pressing concern. The Zapheads had begun making their way toward the church, cutting across unkempt lawns and filthy parking lots.

A couple more emerged from nearby houses, the half-dozen effectively surrounding the church. They appeared to act in concert, although none of them grunted or signaled. It was their silence that was most disturbing—as if they were tapped into some massive hive mind that gave them instructions from afar.

Campbell mulled his options. As much as he loathed Arnoff, he wished the trigger-happy cowboy was up there with him, playing sniper and, one by one, picking off the Zapheads. He'd even take the soldiers, who probably didn't care if innocent humans were caught in the crossfire as long as the "enemy" was wiped out. But concepts like innocence had no place in this new reality.

And, he had no weapon.

The nearest Zaphead was a man in a polyester business suit, the sleeves and cuffs a darker gray than the rest of the fabric. He still wore a necktie, although the knot was loosened halfway down his shirt. He wore eyeglasses that sat askew on his face, disturbing the rounded Asian symmetry of his face. His jet-black hair spiked out like greasy wires.

He was small-framed, so Campbell could knock him out of the way if necessary. But the Zaphead about fifty feet behind the Asian didn't look so easy to handle. This one wore a mechanic's coveralls, dark blotches spattered across the khaki cloth. Campbell couldn't tell if the stains were oil or blood, and he didn't want to look too closely. The mechanic was a few inches north of six feet, barrel-chested, and moving with the malevolent grace of an angry rhino.

The two Zapheads to his left were female, both middle-aged, full-boned, and thick-hipped. If it came down to it, Campbell would take his chances on the one in the yellow cardigan sweater. She looked a little more bookish, like a schoolteacher who'd been headed to the kitchen for a cup of tea when the thermonuclear madness of the sun had other ideas.

Closing in on the rear of the church was a skinny African-American guy in police blues and sunglasses. Although he had a gun strapped down in its side holster, he ignored it in favor of his thick black nightstick, which he swung from his hand like a batter determined to drive in the winning run in the bottom of the ninth. Campbell hoped his own skull wasn't slated to become the baseball.

The final Zaphead—at least among the ones he could

see—was a young boy of perhaps fourteen, his forearms covered in tattoos, blond streaks now growing through the blue dye of his hair. Campbell could easily imagine him on his skateboard, weaving through traffic and flipping a bird at the cop. Now they were like the best of buddies, happy campers on the winning team.

Except, none of them looked happy. Their body language said they had a mission, a virus to eradicate from their midst.

In case he lived long enough to follow Pete, Campbell took one last survey of the surroundings, scooped up his backpack and dashed down the dark, narrow stairs. At the landing, he considered locking the front door and holing up, but he was pretty sure the Zapheads could wait him out. After all, he only had a day's supply of food, and he wasn't sure they even needed food or water.

Besides, if they really wanted in, they could shatter any of the large, stained-glass windows that featured stylized images of Christ with children, lambs, or serious-eyed men in robes. But he didn't want to leave via the front door, because four of the Zapheads were closest. He hurried down the aisles of the nave, toward the altar, hoping to find a side exit.

"Where the hell do I go?" he implored of the large, brass-coated cross fastened on the wall above the altar.

"Seek and you shall find," thundered a voice, so resonant and clear that Campbell thought it was a broadcast recording.

Finally cracking. God's talking back.

Then Campbell rounded the front row and saw a man sitting in the pew, hunched forward and clasping a hymnal. The man was balding, his white shirt sleeves rolled to the elbow, his dark leather shoes spotted with gray.

"How long...who...?" Campbell couldn't believe the man was just sitting there while civilization crumbled outside. But, he had to admit, the construction of the church hushed most sounds from outside and was probably as peaceful a place as any to die, outside of a well-stocked survival bunker.

"They're coming." Campbell wondered if the man even knew about the Zapheads. His sunken eyes and vacant, rapt smile gave the impression of a man whose cares were few.

Then his eyes lit with a fierce passion. "But the day of the Lord will come like a thief, and then the heavens will pass away with a roar, and the heavenly bodies will be burned up and dissolved, and the Earth and the works that are done on it will be exposed."

"Uh… some people out there are coming to kill us." He wasn't sure if "people" was the right word, but he didn't have time for a brief history of the end of the world. He cast about for a weapon of any kind.

"The Book of Peter," the man said. "Do you know Peter?"

"Yeah. He's holed up a couple blocks away. Come with me. We have a better chance with the two of us."

The man waved to the empty rows behind him. "I can't leave my flock."

"You the preacher?" Campbell thought he heard something scraping against the church door.

"I am a servant."

Campbell's frustration mounted. He didn't have time to deal with a madman. But he still clung to old notions of camaraderie and civility, even if it meant those values were baggage. "Well, you better serve yourself right now. Or you're going to be dead."

"And the dead in Christ will rise first."

Campbell gave up. There was banging at the main door, the noise made even more disturbing by its steady rhythm and insistence.

Almost like they're not enraged, just stopping by for a visit to check on the neighbors.

The altar was about a foot higher than the nave floor, and was flanked by two tall brass candlesticks that matched the cross. United States and North Carolina flags stood on thick wooden poles on either side of the cross in an incongruous mash-up of church and state that was particular to Southern Baptist churches. A darkened set of stairs led down on one side of the altar. Despite the high windows, the light was so weak that Campbell didn't think he'd fare better by wandering deeper into the bowels of the church.

Campbell jumped onto the platform and grabbed the state flag, attracted by the sharp wooden point on top of the pole. It was about seven feet tall, and as he removed it from its heavy base, he realized that it would be far too cumbersome to ward off an attacker. He gripped one of the tall brass candle holders, knocking the stubby candle from it as he gave it a test swing. It was about three feet in length and had a satisfying heft.

"That's property of the Lord," the preacher said, rising from the pew and dropping his hymnal.

"I'll give it back when I'm done." Campbell made one last attempt to get the preacher to come with him, holding the candlestick aloft. "Side door, make a run for it—I got your back."

The preacher turned toward the main entrance, where the pounding of many hands continued. "All are welcome in the house of God."

The preacher clasped his hands and bowed in reverence as he started his slow trek up the aisle. He murmured some sort of poetic prayer, but Campbell didn't wait around to see how the message played to his newfound congregation. Instead, he descended the stairs into darkness.

On the lower floor, a few small utility windows illuminated a narrow hall that broke off into several meeting rooms. Campbell hoped he hadn't backed himself into a corner. He felt confident that he could fight his way past one or two Zapheads, but he didn't have any delusions about playing gladiator against a crowd of them.

He tried a door to his left. It opened onto a dim room that had probably been used for Sunday School classes. The stench hit him like a sheet of ice. Bodies were stacked in various positions on the floor, arranged in the shape of a cross. As Campbell backed out of the room with his nose buried in the crook of his elbow, he wondered if the preacher had laid out some sort of demented holy tribute in a burst of apocalyptic fever.

Out in the hall, he heard the preacher's voice soaring into a rhapsodic welcome.

Why haven't the Zappers killed him yet?

Turning a bend, he spotted a fire exit. As he kicked the release bar, gripping the heavy candlestick, sunlight poured around him, and he was cravenly grateful that the preacher had offered himself as a decoy.

CHAPTER TWENTY-EIGHT

They kept to the shadowed side of the street, moving fast. Rachel led the way, hoping she was headed north. DeVontay seemed to be even less of a Boy Scout than she was, so he didn't question her judgment. Or maybe he was keeping his eyes in the side alleys, worried less about the destination than the journey.

They'd gone at least ten blocks without seeing any signs of life—if such a word was even appropriate under the circumstances. Birds flapped in the eaves of the buildings and the canopy of trees, and Rachel heard a hound dog baying in the distance once, but mostly, the town was just a still life of abandoned cars and silent storefronts. The stench of death emanated from inside many of the buildings, so they didn't bother with a door-to-door search for survivors. Calling out for them was risky as well, since the noise might attract Zapheads.

The streets were remarkably free of corpses, given the density of the population, but once they came upon a shrunken man with a stringy white beard, leaning against a brick wall with his arms tucked under his knees. In the old days, he might have passed for a homeless man, rags tied around his ankles.

"Hey, Pops?" DeVontay whispered, afraid to touch him.

The man didn't move so they kept going. Stephen's expression didn't change, which saddened Rachel. A boy shouldn't be hardened to the point of numbness. His days should be filled with bubble gum, comic books and video games instead of death.

The street signs were just as ordinary as ever, a mute

testament to places gone by: Hayward Street, Depot Street, Old Bristol Turnpike. They passed a bridal shop, the front window filled with headless and armless mannequins, impossibly anorexic, displaying flowing white dresses. Rachel's breath caught at the sight. She'd never be a bride now, not like that.

"Yuck," Stephen said, bored by the window shopping. He walked to the edge of the street and bent to play with the trash that had collected in the rain gutter.

DeVontay pressed close behind her. "That man back there...you notice something funny?"

"Just another somebody that didn't make it," she said.

"He's fresh. Not dark and bloated."

Rachel glanced at Stephen, appreciating the relatively healthy glow of his skin compared to the putrefaction all around them. "Just because you survive the solar flares doesn't mean you don't have to die someday."

"But he wasn't beat up, from what I could see. Just curled up like he was waiting for it."

Rachel again thought of the pills the pharmacist had given her. Not everyone had a spiritual or moral aversion to suicide. For some, suicide might look like an elevator to the Pearly Gates.

"There are lots of ways to die," she said. "He was old. Maybe he had a heart attack. Or couldn't get his medicine."

"Don't nobody die from natural causes anymore."

"Okay, then. Maybe he had a bullet hole in his back. Shot by the military."

"No puddle of blood around him."

Annoyed, Rachel checked the reflection in the storefront glass and saw Stephen walking into the street. She called to him, but he kept going, dragging Miss Molly by the hair as if he'd forgotten he was carrying a doll. DeVontay took off running after him, and Rachel broke free of her paralysis and followed.

When they caught up with Stephen, they were able to see the town square, a fifty-foot courthouse with a cracked concrete façade and a dome top surrounded by oak trees whose leaves were darkening with autumn. The courthouse lawn was a wide public commons crisscrossed with walkways, punctuated with a bronze statue of some Revolutionary War hero gone green with patina and pigeon poop. The idyllic small-town postcard was marred by wrought-iron benches that bore a tableau of corpses. More corpses were slumped on the courthouse steps, which was as crowded as if district court was holding a brief recess to allow a smoke break for the accused.

"Lots of them," Stephen said, enthralled and not at all horrified.

There had to be a few dozen, including some children, although they didn't seem to be grouped as family units. Indeed, at first, Rachel thought they might have been arranged that way, like a photo shoot for a modern *auteur* of the grotesque.

"More fresh ones," DeVontay said, and Rachel realized what had been disturbing her more than the sheer number of dead: they, like the old man leaning against the brick wall, were not yet in advanced stages of decomposition.

"Do you think...?" She didn't want to continue while Stephen was within earshot, but DeVontay filled in the blanks for her.

"Yeah," he said. "These are Zapheads. They're dying."

Rachel wasn't sure whether she should be cheered by the news. The Zapheads had been trying to kill her for weeks, sure. But they'd just been following their instincts. And if all Zapheads died, then the world would become that much lonelier. Even more devoid of what had once walked the Earth as a collective humanity.

They followed Stephen to the closest bench, where a girl of about six lay curled on her side. Her pink dress was mussed and her stockings torn, but otherwise, she might have been sleeping.

"She was put there like that," DeVontay said. "She didn't die in that position."

Stephen knelt and spoke to her. "Hey, are you okay?"

Rachel stood behind Stephen and put a hand on each of his shoulders. "She's with the Lord now, Stephen."

Stephen looked around the commons. "Which one of them is the Lord?"

"The one up in heaven," Rachel said, although she looked around to make sure Jesus Christ wasn't among them at that very minute. After all, if He was planning a return trip to Earth, then Taylorsville, North Carolina, was just a good a spot as any.

Of course, she was also aware that such thoughts could well be the beginning of madness. The great visionaries and prophets of the Old Testament were on the borderline of textbook schizophrenia, with their burning bushes, wheels of fire in the sky, and voices telling them to kill their own children.

"This is creepy as hell," DeVontay said. "You think these are Zapheads?"

"They understand," she said, keeping her voice down. If any of them were merely sleeping, she didn't want to wake them.

"Understand what? Did you get into some happy juice somewhere? Popped into the liquor store while I wasn't looking?"

"They understand that the world has changed," she said.

"They're aware."

"You talking about these same Zapheads that have been trying to kills us for the last two weeks?"

"They're taking care of their dead," she said. "It's the last shred and act of humanity, to honor the dead." She had the sudden horrifying thought that perhaps these were all victims of a mass suicide, that a group of Zapheads realized something had gone wrong in their heads and they'd chugged the cyanide Kool-Aid, rather than surrender to their baser natures, their killer instincts.

Such an action would have taken higher-order functioning, communication, and socialization, none of which were traits that the Zapheads had displayed so far.

But what do you really know about them? You've been too busy running and hiding—and surviving—to really pay attention.

"They don't look so scary now," Stephen said.

"Their troubles are over." Rachel almost added, *They're the lucky ones*, but the journey wasn't over yet. If there was one thing she still believed, it was that God had put her here for a reason.

Even if God was now the architect of greatest mass murder in history, she still believed. *Still.*

"Let's get out of here before somebody comes to add to the pile," DeVontay said.

"Come on, Stephen," Rachel said.

"Just a second." The boy went over the bench where the little girl was sleeping. Without touching her, he gently laid Miss Molly in the crook of her arm. Stephen practically skipped back over to Rachel's side, taking her hand.

"Now she won't get lonely," he said, smiling up at her.

Rachel thought of her sister decomposing inside a fiberglass casket in a Seattle cemetery. Beside her pale corpse, Rachel had placed under one stiff, cool arm her sister's stuffed panda, Farley, a copy of her favorite book, *The Princess Bride*, and a photograph of the Earth taken by the Hubble telescope. Rachel had prayed her sister wasn't lonely, either. In whatever After she now knew.

DeVontay led them back to the street, the pistol still dangling near his hip. A few gunshots popped in the distance, and the breeze carried the acrid brusque of smoke, but otherwise, the place was as peaceful as any small-town Sunday afternoon.

As they passed the bridal shop again, Rachel thought she saw movement inside. She didn't say anything, but she didn't look too closely, either.

CHAPTER TWENTY-NINE

As Campbell burst into the sunlight, he raised the heavy candlestick, expecting a fight.

Instead, he found that the side door opened onto a little cemetery, with unkempt grass, faded plastic bouquets of flowers, and low marble markers in uneven rows. The graveyard was bounded by a fence about two feet high, designed more as a boundary than to actually keep out vandals and stray dogs. Making sure no Zapheads were on that side of the church, he oriented himself with the view he'd mapped out while in the belfry.

A copse of maple trees offered enough concealment to get him to the street. But he was stunned to see no Zapheads around the church.

Are they all inside?

He imagined the Zapheads closing in on the deranged reverend, reaching for him even as he delivered the Word in an attempt to reach their hearts and save their souls from the eternal flames of hell.

But he was grateful for the martyr act, because it allowed him to slip between an Irish-themed restaurant and an antique store, angling down a side alley flanked with overflowing trash cans, propane tanks, and heating units. A body was splayed out atop a busted garbage bag as if it had fallen from above. Campbell didn't look too closely, but the exposed hands and face were dark and swollen with rot.

Now two blocks from the church, he exited warily onto the street, which was Hardin Boulevard, according to the sign. He recognized the angle of the architecture, with the skyline featuring one five-story building featuring an old-fashioned clock with rusty metal hands standing tall against the smoky horizon. The other buildings on the block were two-story, cars and trucks parked along both sides of the street and only a few vehicles slanted at angles across the median strip.

Looks pretty dead.

Campbell decided to just sprint up the street rather than sticking to the shadows. If he was spotted, he'd have enough lead time to make a decision out in the open rather than risk being jumped from one of the doorways. Besides that, the big brass candlestick was feeling better and better in his hands.

The bar where Pete had entered stood on the corner, with metal tables under an awning. A red vinyl banner ran down the edge of the upper story, sporting the name Fat Freddy's, with "Pub & Grill" in smaller letters beneath it. Campbell and Pete had passed more than a few Friday nights in such establishments, eating wings and eyeing girls, but mostly drinking whatever cheap domestic beer was on tap.

Campbell wondered if all the Zapheads in the vicinity had been drawn to the church. He'd seen them responding to noise, violence, and fire, but the church had offered none of those attractions. Just when Campbell had become used to—certainly not comfortable or at ease with, but *used to*—things as they now stood, the rules changed.

Not that Campbell had ever made much sense of the world even before it had figuratively tilted on its axis. Grade school had been an indoctrination of sorts—"Go here when the bell rings, do this and this and this"—but Campbell had been bewildered by the anxiety of sitting in a room with twenty-five other kids. High school had been just as surreal, mostly because he'd seen those roles that adults were forced to adopt, and he didn't see any role he'd be able to successfully fake. Because he was pretty sure everyone was pulling a mask, all characters straight out of Central Casting:

the chisel-faced military recruiting officer, the tow-truck driver with the Popeye forearms, the gum-chewing waitress at the Waffle House, the I.T. nerd with the Batman fixation.

So, a world populated by Zapheads wasn't really too much of a leap, was it?

Regardless, he was grateful that none of them were around. If the church offered what they needed, that was just fine with him, and God bless.

Campbell dashed between a Mitsubishi boiling with blue bottle flies and a Honda sedan with all four doors flung open and spilling the stench of corpses. He vaulted over a motorcycle lying on its side, nearly losing his balance, then came to Fat Freddy's entrance. He peered through the oval glass set in the wooden door but couldn't see much. He pushed his way in, squeezing the candlestick.

"Bro! Just in time for Happy Hour!" Pete's voice came from the darkness somewhere near the back of the establishment.

As Campbell's eyes adjusted, he made out the dim rows of tables, some of them occupied by dead people fallen face first into their moldering food. A few candles flickered, reflected in the bar mirror along with rows and rows of gleaming bottles. Campbell wiped his nose against the rot, still not accustomed to the sweetly corrupt odor.

But the smell of candle wax and alcohol were strong as well, creating a lurid mixture. Pete stood behind the bar, a half-full bottle of brown liquor before him, along with a water glass. At first, Campbell thought that Pete had somehow found some drinking buddies, because four other people sat at the bar, perched on high wooden stools with glasses in front of them.

"Pete, who are these guys?" Campbell's heart turned into a frozen stone in his chest.

Pete merely grinned, tossed back a couple of ounces of whiskey, and slammed the glass back down with a brittle *thunk*. "Drinks on the house," he said, slurring his words just a little.

Campbell navigated the tables, holding the candlestick before him as if it was a cattle prod and he might need to jolt some of these corpses out of the way. "Coast is clear, man. We can get out of town with no hassle."

Pete waved to the row of bottles, his grinning eyes flashing in the candlelight. "Leave? I died and went to heaven. Beer's warm, and there's not any ice, but can't complain. Nosirree."

Campbell glanced at the bodies leaning against the bar. They were in stilted, swollen poses, the stools jammed under them to keep them erect. One, a biker wearing a sleeveless jeans jacket and a watchman's cap, had maggots roiling in his eye sockets.

"Pete," Campbell said warily. "Why don't you just grab a bottle and come with me? You can drink it on the road."

"No way," he responded, sloshing some whiskey into the biker's full glass so that the liquid ran along the length of the bar. The glasses in front of the other corpses were full as well.

"You…" Campbell didn't know how to process the tableau. His best friend had lost it, finally cracked under the strain. And Campbell felt a chill deeper than fear: the deep, icy well of loneliness into which he was dropping.

"Party's just started!" Pete bellowed to his patrons before tossing down another few ounces of straight whiskey. Pete wiped his mouth and beamed, the candles making his face look sinister and red, like a demon in a B horror movie.

Campbell ignored the stench of the desecrated corpses, which Pete had obviously dragged from the dining tables to create his impromptu drinking session. He leaned against the bar as Pete slammed a glass down on the wood.

"What'll ya have, pardner?" Pete said. Then his face took on a sodden solemnity. "You know what really gets to me about all this? I just can't wrap head my around a world without celebrities. Lady Gaga, Jay-Z, Lindsay Lohan. I mean, inquiring minds want to *know*."

"In Lindsay Lohan's case, I don't think it would make much difference."

"LeBron James. Depp, man. A world without the Deppster."

"You're drunk," Campbell said, preferring that diagnosis to the prospect of madness.

"Seriously. Did they turn into Zapheads? Is there a Brad Pitt Zaphead out there somewhere be-bopping along with a little soul patch?"

"Don't dwell on it. Deal with what's in front of you."

Pete looked at his glass and grinned. But he quickly turned maudlin again and groaned with dramatic flair. "Taylor Swift. Not Taylor? She's so cute and sweet and I got a Jodie Foster-level crush on her."

"You can't just sit here and wait for them to find you," Campbell said, eyeing the front door. He wondered if any Zapheads were deeper in the building, maybe down in the basement or in the bathrooms. Pete didn't have a weapon of any kind, and his backpack was tossed carelessly by the cash register.

"The more, the merrier," Pete said, waving at the impressive array of bottles. "We got plenty for everybody. Zappers, survivors, and"—Pete gave a benevolent sweep of his non-drinking arm to indicate the corpses—"the stinking silent majority."

Pete started to take another big gulp from his glass but Campbell caught his wrist, sloshing liquor onto both their arms. "Remember you told me to let you know if you ever hit bottom with your drinking?"

"I was probably drunk when I said that," Pete said, bloodshot eyes narrowing. "You can't hold people to stuff they say when they're drunk. Otherwise, I'd have been married six times already."

Pete laughed at his own miserable joke, but the sound was swallowed by the still, dusty space. Any mirth and merriment that might have soaked into the walls had long since evaporated, although the smell of booze, corrupted food, and bloated corpses did plenty to crowd the air.

Glass shattered somewhere near the front door, and Campbell swung around with the candlestick raised. "They found us."

Pete didn't seem to care. He drank straight from the bottle of Knob Creek, then wiped some of the liquor under his nose like a mortician applying menthol before digging in on the day shift.

"Get down," Campbell said, snuffing the nearest candle. He crouched in the dark, discomfortingly near the legs of one of Pete's dead clientele.

The front door swung open, flooding light into the bar. A figure was framed in silhouette, and Campbell wondered if Zapheads could see in the dark. Not that it mattered. Pete stood near the other candle, his face bright in the yellow circle of the flame.

Campbell tensed, waiting for the Zaphead to attack. Instead, the silhouette said, "Thought you might be in here."

Arnoff!

CHAPTER THIRTY

From the camouflaged platform built into the branches of an oak tree, Jorge had a nearly panoramic view of the surrounding ridges and valleys. "Wheelerville," as Franklin Wheeler called his tiny compound, wasn't the highest point in the Blue Ridge Mountains, but it stood apart from the towering canopy of Mount Rogers and smaller mountains that bore craggy granite faces topped with pine stubble. A hawk flew over the gray belt of haze that wreathed the valley, and Jorge wondered if it was the same one that killed the chicken.

In the distance, the threads of smoke from the cities blended into a charcoal smudge on the horizon. The air carried only the faintest tinge of the acrid odor, though, as if the mountains scrubbed the prevailing wind clean as it pushed from the northwest. He didn't know anyone in those cities, but he felt a loss, nonetheless. Marina might have gone to college there, or he and Rosa might have found some better type of work.

Tightening the focus on the binoculars, he swept his view to the parkway that threaded through the trees below. The same abandoned vehicles dotted the road, some of them plowing into the grassy shoulders as their drivers had died instantly. One wooden guardrail was uprooted and splintered where a truck had barreled through and gone off the edge. A camper lay on its side, coolers, mattresses and a rotted corpse spilled from its rear.

He was about to climb down when he saw movement on the road.

Probably a deer. With nothing to scare them, they can reclaim the land.

He sighted through the binoculars and saw a woman running up the slope of the road. She wasn't moving very fast, and her cheeks were streaked with filth, hair tangled. She looked exhausted, like a horse that had been ridden across a desert. She carried a cloth bundle clasped to her chest.

She doesn't move like one of them.

"Franklin?" he called.

Franklin came out of the house, where he'd been fidgeting with the radio. After lunch, Franklin said he "needed some bad news," so he went to his desk while Rosa cleaned the dishes from the meal. Franklin squinted against the sun as he looked up at Jorge. "What's up, besides you?"

"Someone on the road," Jorge said. "A woman."

"Hell fire," Franklin said, scurrying to the tree and scaling the makeshift wooden handholds that were nailed to the tree. He moved with a swift grace that belied his age, scurrying up like an old mountain goat. He took the binoculars from Jorge and Jorge pointed out the direction.

"Huh," Franklin said. "Looks like she's alone."

"She isn't a…what do you call it?"

"Nah, she's not a Zaphead. Just a scared woman." He gave the binoculars back to Jorge and turned to climb back down.

"Shouldn't we go get her?"

Franklin looked around the compound. "I set up Wheelerville for a dozen people to survive whatever came our way, short of nuclear holocaust. And you punched three of the tickets when you wandered through the woods with a sick girl. I'm expecting more company, and I don't think we've got room to spare."

"You can't just leave her out there."

Franklin squinted. "What are you? Some kind of Communist? That what they teach you south of the border?"

"She's young and alone—"

"She's survived this long, so she's not made out of cardboard. I ain't in the business of saving the world."

Jorge tried to make sense of the contradiction. Franklin had helped his family, yet now was denying someone else in need. Jorge gazed through the binoculars, tracking the woman's progress. Her jeans were worn at the knees, her brown hooded sweatshirt matted and grimy. She twisted her head, wild blonde hair whipping out as she glanced over her shoulder.

Something's after her?

Jorge swiveled the binoculars down the road, where the pavement disappeared amid the shadow of massive trees. Three of them burst from the woods, and Jorge had no doubt of their intentions.

"Them!" Jorge said, pointing. "Those Z things. Chasing her."

Franklin snatched the binoculars away and peered through them for a moment. "Damn. She might be carrying a baby."

Then he lowered them and started scrambling down the tree. Halfway down, he looked up at Jorge and said, "You wanted to play hero, here's your chance."

By the time Jorge reached the ground, Franklin had already grabbed a rifle and backpack, tossing Jorge a belt that held his machete. Rosa called to them from the door of the house. "What is happening?"

"Lock the gate behind us," Franklin ordered, with a calmness that contradicted his haste. "There's a gun on the wall if you need it. We ought to be back in twenty minutes."

"Jorge?" Rosa said, eyes wide.

"Lock the gate," he said. "Keep Marina inside."

Jorge followed Franklin out of the compound, ignoring Rosa's calls. Soon, they were winding down a forest path that

Jorge never would have noticed, much less been willing to navigate. Franklin trotted with a sure-footed gait, and Jorge had difficulty keeping up, even though he was three decades younger. He measured time not in minutes, but in the huge granite slabs that jutted from the ground, the rotted stumps and silvery creeks they hurdled, and the streaks of golden sunlight that broke through the branches to dapple the ground.

Jorge had become disoriented, losing any sense of the locations of both the compound and the road. He focused on Franklin's back, the odors of mud, rotten leaves, and pine sap assailing him with each gasp of air. Then the trail widened and became a stretch of scrubby meadow, a couple of abandoned cars visible beyond a low stone fence.

"Keep low," Franklin said, motioning down with one hand while steadying his rifle with the other.

"How much farther?" Jorge said, sliding his machete from its sheath.

Franklin crouched and lifted the butt of the rifle to his shoulder, sighting down the barrel. "About a million miles."

Then Jorge parted the scrub with his blade and saw the RV. The woman was about thirty feet from it, her pace slower than before, mouth parted as she sucked for air. Her bundle was tucked against her chest, one arm squeezing it even as she reached out for the door on the side of the RV.

Behind her, the Zapheads were gaining ground, maybe fifty feet to close the distance. She made it to the door and tugged on the handle, but it didn't yield. Jorge realized he and his family might have been in the same position if they'd pursued his plan to camp in it.

The three Zapheads Jorge had seen from the lookout in the compound had been joined by two others. They could have been parishioners of one of the little churches that dotted the mountains, or customers of a barbecue restaurant, or the office staff at Marina's school. Their clothes were filthy, and three of them were female. The one closest to the RV was a teenaged boy in a sleeveless T-shirt, knees pumping as he moved in for the kill.

The rifle roared and the teenager's chest blossomed with red spray. He pitched forward and tumbled twice on the pavement and laid still, legs tangled beneath his body, one arm poking upward at an awkward angle.

The other Zapheads froze, looking in the direction of the sudden noise. Jorge wasn't sure they were visible, but the woman hadn't hesitated. She hammered on the door of the RV, shrieking in a broken voice. "Let me in! Let me in!"

As the kneeling Franklin leveled the rifle for another shot, the brush parted beside them. A dark face stared out, eyes wide, mouth gaping to reveal yellowing teeth.

"¿Hola?" Jorge said, startled, thinking it was one of Franklin's friends. Then he remembered that Franklin had no friends.

The woman pushed through the scrub pines and high weeds, moving fast. Franklin, getting ready to fire again, must not have noticed her. She was barely three steps from him. Jorge lifted his machete, hesitating.

What if it's not one of them?

She spat a rasping hiss, lifting her right arm. Her hand clutched a jagged, mossy stone. Jorge shouted a warning.

Franklin turned, knocking the rifle barrel against her. She was heavy and solid, the metal *thwacking* off her flank. She swatted the gun away with ease and she lifted the rock again. Its weight caused her arm to tremble.

"Cut her down,' Franklin said, his voice even.

"I…" Jorge looked at her, wondering if she had kids.

"It's not human," Franklin said. *"Cut her!"*

The rock descended and Franklin raised one forearm to block the blow. Jorge jumped forward and slung the machete at her wrist. The swing was high and the blade skidded off the stone with a metallic ping. One of her fingers popped into the air, streaming blood. She didn't utter a sound.

She jammed the stone toward Franklin's head. Franklin rolled away and Jorge gripped the machete handle with both hands and gave a roundhouse swing.

The blade bit into the back of the woman's neck and the stone flew from her grasp, grazing Franklin's cheek and thudding off his shoulder. Sickened, Jorge pulled the machete free of her flesh. The wound yawned open, showing white tendons and a chalky stitch of skull bone.

She emitted a red *urk* and collapsed. Franklin pawed at her, shoving at her round body, and Jorge realized the rifle was under her. He glanced back at the RV.

The woman was climbing a little access ladder on the back of the vehicle, struggling to keep her balance with one arm wrapped around her bundle. The four remaining Zapheads gathered around the RV, swatting at the air below her feet as if confused by the ladder.

"Go get her," Franklin said, shoving at the dead Zaphead. "She *is* human. So is the baby."

Jorge broke into a run, sweat beading his skin. He held the machete before him like Antonio Banderas as Zorro, although he hated Banderas because Rosa had called the actor "*muy* sexy." Blood from the blade blew back against his cheek. A high-pitched, electric keening sang in his eardrums.

He leaped over the low stone wall, which was little more than a decorative border. The woman was now atop the RV, sitting and pushing herself backwards with her feet. A Zaphead dressed like a fisherman, right down to the knee-high rubber wading boots, put an experimental hand on the ladder, as if trying to divine its magic.

The nearest Zaphead turned when Jorge reached the shoulder of the road, and Jorge almost dropped his machete. He recognized the woman. She was the cashier at the farm supply store, a buxom, chain-smoking woman who always wore a field-green John Deere jacket. She had no jacket now, nor a shirt, and her breasts swung like sodden melons in the cups of her dirty bra.

Whenever Jorge bought a load of cracked corn, hay, or fertilizer for the Wilcox place, she'd averted her eyes as he filled out the bill of sale, careful to never make contact with the skin of his fingers. Now she had no problem looking at him: her eyes were like electric-blue drill bits boring into his skull.

"¿Señora?" He faltered but kept stumbling forward, hoping she would say something familiar so he wouldn't have to cut her. Anything would do, even her side-of-the-mouth, "Back yer truck to the dock and the boys'll load 'er."

But all she could do was hiss, and Jorge realized that was the source of his ringing ears. The others were hissing, too, like the chirrup of crickets in an endless night. But still, Jorge couldn't strike her. She was a racist, one who almost certainly wished his kind would never cross the border, but she was a human being.

Wasn't she?

But before he could decide, the top of her head exploded in a thunderclap of gunfire. Her head flew back, her breasts wobbled, and her knees folded as she collapsed on the pavement.

"Move, you jackass!" Franklin hollered. "They're Zapheads, for Christ's sake."

The other Zapheads turned in his direction, although the fisherman had finally figured out how to lift his leg and place it on the bottom rung.

Four to go.

But Jorge realized he didn't have to kill them. They weren't acting aggressively, not like the ones back at the Wilcox place. Instead, they were eyeing him with wary interest, much like they had the ladder: as if he was something new and beyond their understanding. He didn't want to risk it, though, so he chopped low and nicked a hefty wedge out of the calf of a young man in shorts and sandals. The man collapsed, the hiss from the back of his throat rising in pitch and volume.

Pain. So they feel it, despite what Franklin says.

The fisherman had scaled a few more rungs, but the two remaining Zapheads backed away, their eyes glittering like wet diamonds.

"Don't shoot!" Jorge shouted at Franklin, partly because he wasn't sure they were a danger and partly because he didn't fully trust the old man's aim.

The fisherman continued his climb, moving faster as he figured out the rungs. He was nearly to the top of the RV, where the woman sat in the middle of the roof, hunched as if protecting her baby.

"Hold on," Jorge said to her, but she didn't respond. Jorge ran to the rear of the RV and began climbing after him. Jorge gave one machete chop at the man's rubber heel, but it lifted free just before the blade careened off metal.

The fisherman stood in his tan vest, head lifted as if sniffing the breeze. He put one hand on a small satellite dish to steady himself, then wriggled it back and forth. The steel bar holding the dish gave a grating squeak and tore free. The man lifted the dish like a weapon and turned to face Jorge, who was still three rungs down the ladder.

A shot rang out, whining over Jorge's head. The Zaphead

lifted the dish and Jorge thought about dropping to the ground. But he didn't think he could climb it again before the mutated fisherman killed the woman and her baby.

Instead, Jorge launched himself forward and rolled. The fisherman paused, the dish still held high, as if he also hesitated to kill. Jorge swung out one of his workman's boots into the man's kneecap. The leg folded but didn't collapse.

The Zaphead hissed in pain, or perhaps rage, and swatted the dish downward as if Jorge were an oversize fly. Jorge raised his machete—*just like Banderas would*, he thought—and blocked the blow, although the impact drove the back edge of the blade precariously near his face.

On his back, Jorge raised both legs and drove the bottoms of his boots into the Zaphead's stomach. A chuff of air was driven from the man's abdomen as the kick lifted him off the RV's roof and sent him, arms flailing, over the edge. The body struck pavement below with a soggy splat, while the dish clattered a few feet down the road.

Jorge didn't bother to check the damage. Instead, he went to the young woman, whose face contorted between expressions of fear and gratitude. A tear ran down one grimy cheek. Up close, she looked even younger, maybe seventeen.

This could be Marina in a few years, he thought, even though this woman had reddish-gold hair instead of Marina's dark Latina features.

"Come," he said, holding out one hand. "We have a safe place."

She stared at the gore-clotted machete blade. Jorge looked down at it and wiped it on the leg of his pants. "Only when necessary," he said.

"Get and come on," Franklin shouted from the bushes. "Else, I'm going to have to start killing these others."

Jorge looked down the road. Two more Zapheads had

emerged from the forest, although they didn't move with any sort of speed or menace. Jorge was struck yet again with the notion that they appeared more curious than anything, as if they'd been dropped into an unwelcoming world without a road map.

That, I can understand, mis amigos.

"Come," Jorge said, more gently this time. "My wife will help care for your child."

She relaxed a little and peeled back a fold of her bundle. Jorge saw just the tiniest stretch of pink skin before she closed it again and tried to stand. She nearly lost her balance, and Jorge steadied her. The two Zapheads at the rear of the RV had backed away another 10 feet, staring up as if watching a scene on the stage of some theater of the absurd.

"Don't shoot," Jorge shouted at Franklin, who now stood by the stone fence, the rifled aimed at the nearest Zaphead. "I don't think they will hurt us."

"Then what was Captain Ahab up there doing? Playing badminton?"

"They're confused."

"Well, hell, they ain't the only one."

Jorge went down the ladder first, offering to carry the baby, but the woman violently shook her head. So Jorge climbed down and stood guard while she made a cautious, awkward descent.

"Go," Jorge said to the Zapheads, motioning with his machete. "*Salir.*"

They merely stood with their intensely glittering gazes, although the two new Zapheads kept approaching. When the young mother reached the pavement, Jorge guided her toward Franklin and the trail back to the compound.

"Took you long enough," Franklin said.

"That is how we do it south of the border, old man," Jorge

said.

"Well, don't be taking no *siestas* until we make sure these things don't follow us, *sí*?"

It wasn't until they were halfway up the mountain that Jorge felt his stomach unclench, and he knelt and vomited in the leaves while Franklin stood sentinel.

He didn't feel very much like Antonio Banderas now.

CHAPTER THIRTY-ONE

"Sure could use a GPS," DeVontay said.

He squinted up at the sun, which was sinking toward the western horizon. They had left the little town behind, although its smoke still stained the air. Beyond it, the higher columns of diffuse gray marked the progress of Charlotte into the atmosphere. The clouds were like clumps of dirty wool riding high, uncertain currents.

Rachel sat in the shade of a sycamore, studying the street behind them. The images of the bodies strewn across the courthouse lawn still haunted her. Everywhere she looked, she hallucinated corpses into the shadows and crevices, arranged in horribly artful arrays.

Keep it together, Ray Ray. Stephen needs you.

The boy had grown more animated with every mile they'd walked. Leaving his doll with the dead girl had served to purge some of his melancholy. Rachel wondered if his current ease was even more worrisome than his near-catatonia. But there was no psychological handbook for diagnosing the emotional conditions of After. This was all new ground.

"That way," Rachel said, pointing vaguely northwest. They had entered a rural area and houses were fewer and farther between, so they were less likely to encounter Zapheads. They'd been following a gravel road for the last five miles or so, encountering only a few abandoned vehicles. Rachel didn't want to think about the bodies that might have been in them and whether they'd been removed and used as art.

"You sure?" DeVontay studied the ragged map in his hands. "I-77 runs north, and it's back over that way."

"We don't want to follow the interstate," Rachel said. "We need to stay away from population centers."

"Where we will find food?"

"House to house," Rachel said.

"Where will we sleep?"

"House to house."

Stephen, who was digging in the ground with a stick, looked up. "Does that mean we can have any house we want?"

"Sure," she said. "Our pick of the neighborhood. As long as no one is living there, I don't think they'd mind if we used it."

"I want a house with a swimming pool." He swung his stick at a moth that was fluttering in a wobbly pattern around him.

"Don't kill it," she said.

"Why not?" he said with a pout, although he lowered his stick.

"Because life is sacred."

"Then how come everybody's dead?"

Rachel wanted to give an automatic answer, but all the options felt hollow: *Because God willed it so? Because the universe is a powerful bitch? Because they were not worthy?*

Instead, she settled on the lame response that made her feel painfully like an adult. "Because."

DeVontay headed up the road, wiping the dust from his forehead with a kerchief, and then wrapping it around his head like Jimi Hendrix. "I bet that house up there has a pool," he said. "Or maybe a fish pond."

The two-story white farmhouse had a tin roof that glinted in the dying sun. The yard was fenced, and the surrounding property was broken into several pastures. A tractor was parked outside a red barn, and two spotted Jersey cows picked at the grass, ignoring them. The surrounding land sloped up to forest. A dusty Ford pickup sat in the driveway near the porch. Rachel could see a rifle in a rack through the rear window.

"I wanna fish!" Stephen said, running to catch up with DeVontay. Rachel shouldered her pack and followed them. The house offered good visibility and looked pretty secure, assuming a family of Zapheads wasn't gathered around the kitchen table...

"Hello?" DeVontay called, cupping his hands. Only the wind answered.

DeVontay was checking out the truck by the time Rachel caught up. "Empty," he said, although he gave Rachel a look that suggested it wasn't.

"Stephen, come look at this," Rachel said. She went to the apple tree in the side yard and pulled a branch low so Stephen could pluck a few of the ruby-red Macintosh apples. When she looked back, DeVontay was rummaging in the truck, emerging with the rifle in his hands before slamming the door shut.

"I'm checking out the house," he said. "Wait there until I get back."

Rachel led Stephen to the little garden that had been overtaken by weeds. The tomatoes were mostly rotten and the cucumbers had yellowed, but the mustard and collard greens were dark and healthy-looking. "Help me pick some," she said, kneeling in the dirt. She stuck a turnip green in her mouth and chewed, savoring its vibrant bitterness.

"Gross," Stephen said.

"You want to be strong like Spiderman, don't you?"

"Your teeth are green." The boy glanced at the barn. "What's in there?"

"Hay," she said. "Now, let's pick. It will be good to have

some fresh vitamins after all that canned food."

"Hay tastes better than this," he said, heading for the barn.

"Don't go in there alone," she said, lifting the lower front of her shirt to form a sack for the greens. She collected fistfuls of greens, waiting for Stephen to return. She was so intent on her harvest that she didn't realize for a moment that he'd kept going.

He was almost to the barn. "Stephen!" she called.

The boy stood at the barn's heavy wooden entrance, which was suspended by metal wheels on a steel track. The door opening was about two feet wide, and thick darkness waited beyond it. Rachel couldn't imagine the boy would go in there, not after all the horrors he'd endured.

The boy took one look back, but he didn't seem to notice Rachel. He cocked his head as if hearing distant music, and then slipped inside the barn. Rachel dropped the greens and hurried after him, the weariness and tension of the past days hitting her in a wave and weakening her legs. A blister on her big toe screamed in red electricity, but she pushed herself, thinking of her sister.

She called him again. The word was like a thunderclap in the quiet pastoral setting, birds falling silent in the nearby forest. She reached the door and the dark air inside was almost a solid thing, rich with the dust of hay and manure, and obsidian block framed by rough wooden planks and chicken wire. Rachel didn't want to touch that miserable darkness, much less enter it, but Stephen was inside.

She'd promised to take care of him.

She stepped inside, calling his name, listening to the ticking of the hot tin roof. She derided herself for growing overconfident. She should have taken the pistol from DeVontay after he'd found the rifle. But the peace of the farm valley had lulled her into a false complacency, allowing her to forget that this was After and the rules had changed with one massive belch of the sun.

Stumbling in the darkness, Rachel fought an urge to wait for DeVontay. She was pretty sure no Zapheads were lurking in the barn, or they would have reacted to her voice. Still, the deep shadows carried the weight of menace, like the held breath of a stalker. Something wasn't right here.

As her eyes adjusted to the shafts of light leaking through the cracks and windows, she was able to make out support posts and stalls, with tufts of yellow hay littering the dirt floor. On the center beam, three shapes dangled from ropes like old sacks of feed. Stephen stood silently, peering up at them.

"Oh my Lord," Rachel said, limping to the boy's side. She tried to pull him away, then cover his eyes, but he wriggled free.

"What happened?" Stephen asked.

The bodies were of a man and two young boys, obviously brothers. Their black tongues protruded from their gaping mouths and their eyes bulged. Although flies swarmed around them, they apparently had been dead no more than a day or two.

"This isn't good, Stephen."

"Did they kill themselves?" Stephen's voice was cold and vacant again, as if his post-traumatic autism had seized control.

Rachel thought it was likely the man hanged his own children before killing himself. It didn't look like the work of Zapheads. But she didn't know which answer would give Stephen the most comfort. Perhaps there was no comfort to be found in death.

Perhaps.

Or maybe the man had taken stock of After and made a decision based on love and mercy. Despite the resources of the farm, the man may have seen no future that didn't end in a violent death. Maybe this was the man's way of protecting his family from Zapheads, killing his wife in the truck and then ushering his offspring to an eternal peace instead of facing another day of living hell.

Perhaps this had been the ultimate act of faith.

"I don't know what happened," Rachel said, and in this, at least she avoided a lie.

"I want my mother," Stephen said.

Rachel hugged him. "I know you do, honey."

"And my dolly."

"I know. Why don't we go into the farmhouse? I'll bet these boys had some toys, and I bet they wouldn't mind if you played with them."

"They're dead," he said. He sneezed from the dust, then sniffled.

Rachel's eyes were hot with tears, but she wouldn't allow herself to sob. "Let's go, honey."

This time, Stephen allowed himself to be led from the corrupt air of the barn and back into the sunshine. Rachel glanced up at the high, uncertain clouds.

How could you do this, God? What possible plan do You have for all this?

But she couldn't trust her own faith at the moment, because she was afraid it was slipping away. The one certainty of her life, the power that had given her comfort amid all the sorrow and hardship and added joy to every pleasure, was now as ephemeral as the distant smoke. And without it, who *was* she?

DeVontay was waiting on the porch when they reached the house, the rifle angled over one shoulder. "All clear," he said, almost giddy with relief. "Even some canned food and a gas stove, so we can have us a home-cooked meal."

Then he noticed their faces and glanced around warily. "What's up?"

Rachel gave a wave back toward the barn. "We can stay in their house. They don't need it anymore."

"Oh. Well, come on in and let's eat." He held the door open for them, and Rachel could read the question in his eyes: *Was it Zapheads?*

"I think we're safe here," Rachel said. Despite her subdued anxiety, she found herself eager to escape in exploring the kitchen. "Why don't you find a place for Stephen while I cook some dinner?"

She couldn't shake the image of the limp, hanging bodies from her mind, nor the widening gap in the center of her abandoned heart.

CHAPTER THIRTY-TWO

"Saw you running down the street and figured you'd lead me to your buddies," Arnoff said.

"What buddies?" Campbell didn't like the way Arnoff had his semiautomatic rifle cocked on his hip, a macho posture that would have been cartoonish under other circumstances.

"Your Army buddies."

"Wouldn't mess with 'em," Pete said, pouring himself another drink without offering Arnoff one.

"I don't want to mess," Arnoff said. "I want to join up. Enlist in Team Human."

"I get the impression they're not looking for recruits," Campbell said. He glanced at the tavern door, hoping Arnoff had cleared the street before following him inside. If the Zapheads were gathering into groups, even a semiautomatic might not be enough.

"Their commander will listen to reason," Arnoff said. "Donnie and the professor can shoot a little, and Pam...hell, she can cook or something, or keep the men happy. Safety in numbers."

"I'm telling you," Pete said, his drunkenness taking a belligerent turn. "He's stars and stripes forever. And he doesn't need numbers like us."

Arnoff glanced around the dim room as if noticing the corpses for the first time. "What do you know about it?"

Campbell moved away from the bar, expecting Arnoff to stop him, but the man was more interested in what Pete had to say. Pete muttered something incoherent, but Campbell made out a personal invitation for Arnoff to commit a depraved and self-inflicted sexual act.

He glanced through a grimy window, at the silent cars and still bodies, at a baby carriage tipped on its side near a fire hydrant. A pigeon with a broken wing skipped along the sidewalk, the only sign of life.

"You were with them," Arnoff said. "They grabbed you on the highway."

"They wanted me for Zaphead bait," Pete answered. "Just like you did."

"We all have a part in the plan," Arnoff said. "Some parts are bigger than others."

"What's your plan, then?" Campbell asked. "Assuming The Captain lets you join the A-Team? You're going to start a genocide sweep? Gun down all the Zapheads? And kill anybody else that's not your type while you're at it?"

"Hold on with the Commie talk. This is about survival of the human race. Survival of the fittest. I don't know what them things are, or why they want to bash our brains in, but I don't need the professor to know when something needs killing."

"They're changing," Campbell said, trying to formulate ideas he'd only just begun considering. "I don't think they're attacking us…us *normal* people…just because they want us out of the way. I think they're as scared and confused as we are."

"To hell with your Commie talk." Arnoff waved his arm at the dead bodies, the gray, dreary bar that once had teemed with music and laughter and the communal clink of glass. "They're a danger to not just our life, but to our way of life. If we want all this back, we've got to win today. Then we can fight for tomorrow."

"I'm done fighting," Pete said. "I'm ready to drink instead. But you'd be happy with The Captain and his happy little troop. They're heading for a base up north."

"A base?"

Pete took a sip from his glass, enjoying Arnoff's anxiety. "Yeah. Said there was a secret military base up there, underground, total doomsday prep. Built for nuclear war, he said, but outfitted for pretty much anything. And I guess the Big Zap counts as 'anything.'"

"How far north?"

"Off to see the wizard," Pete said, voice slurring. Even for someone with Pete's tolerance levels, the prodigious amounts of whiskey were taking their toll. "Wonderful Wizard of Ozzzzz."

Arnoff swung the barrel of his rifle forward and shattered Pete's bottle. The strong, sweet odor of the whiskey briefly overwhelmed the fermenting of the dead.

Pete snarled and reached from behind the bar to swipe at Arnoff. "You goddamned animal."

"How far north?" Arnoff repeated. Even in the bad light, his eyes and teeth gleamed with a fierce menace that briefly sobered Pete.

Pete gave a weak wave of surrender and disgust. "To the Blue Ridge Parkway."

"I need more than that. The parkway's nearly five hundred miles long."

"Milepost 291, he called it. Don't know what that means."

"You better not be shitting me, or I'll track you down and leave you hanging on a lamppost so the Zappers can eat your liver."

Pete snorted in disgust and reached for another bottle in the row behind him. Campbell watched the tableau in the dusty bar mirror and was startled by the person standing to the left of Arnoff. Campbell tilted his head to the side to be sure the reflection belonged to him. Gaunt and stubbled cheeks, windswept hanks of greasy hair, deep purple wedges under each eye.

I don't know about zombies, but we're becoming the living dead.

Arnoff rested his rifle against a bar stool and fished a map and flashlight from his pocket. He wiped away the pool of liquor with one elbow, and then spread the map on the pitted wooden surface. Campbell couldn't help bending over and looking when Arnoff switched on the light.

"What town is that near?" Arnoff asked Pete.

"Who do I look like, Ranger Rick? I heard him mention 'Boone.'"

Arnoff ran a stubby forefinger along the map of North Carolina, outward from the red circles he'd drawn to mark their current location and his route since leaving Charlotte. "About a hundred miles. Should be able to get there in a week to ten days of hard walking."

Pete laughed again. He no longer bothered with a glass, sipping straight from the bottle of Knob Creek and wincing at the taste. Campbell studied the map, noting the small towns that dotted the highway to Boone. Arnoff scowled at him and folded the map with crisp efficiency.

Taking up his rifle, he headed for the door. "You guys coming, or you going to wait here for the Zappers?"

Campbell shouldered his pack and followed. Pete, however, didn't move from his position behind the bar. He stared past them as if lost in a Happy Hour from long ago, where the beer flowed and the Stones kicked from the speakers and the neon lights winked their green and red seductions.

"Come on, Pete," Campbell said, waiting at the door. Arnoff, after making sure the street was clear, headed across.

"You're getting to be as much of a bossy asshole as Arnoff," Pete said, although he came around the bar, nearly tripping on a dead biker whose leather vest was splotched with the excrescence of death.

Arnoff was already down the block, about to turn the corner. Campbell was afraid the man would leave them behind. And as bad as the Arnoff option was, Campbell imagined it would be far worse to spend another night alone in a church steeple. He dodged between vehicles, ducking low in case any Zapheads were around.

When Campbell reached the corner, Arnoff was barely in sight. The man had forgotten all about them.

Campbell turned and motioned for Pete to hurry. Pete had just exited the bar and squinted against the glare of sunset. He dragged his backpack with one hand, and the other gripped a quart bottle of liquor by the neck. As he staggered forward, slumped and skulking and jerky, Campbell fought a wave of irritation.

What a loser. He looks just like a Zaphead, the way he's—

The distant volley echoed off the canyons of the building facades. Pete's head lifted, mouth open in shock. The sudden blossom of crimson on his shirt spread across his chest. Then his legs folded and he dropped, the liquor bottle smashing on the sidewalk.

Campbell ran toward him, keeping low. "Hold your fire!" he screamed, not sure it would do any good.

The soldiers clearly didn't care. Anyone not in uniform was a target. The Captain's words came back to him: *"We're the government. You're either with us or against us."*

Campbell expected the next bullet to pierce his own flesh, and he almost welcomed it. But all was silent as he knelt in the dead town beside Pete, whose blood mixed with the tequila in a sick and final concoction. Campbell knelt, muttering to his dead friend, as dusk fell around him.

It was After.

And he was alone.

CHAPTER THIRTY-THREE

Jorge helped Franklin barricade the compound after their return. The sun was sinking, sending long fingers of shadows across the leaves and grass. The surrounding mountains were striated in bands of black and reddish brown, the thick haze wreathing the horizon. The first flickers of aurora borealis were visible in the far northern sky, lime green and magenta tufts hanging like a shaman's psychedelic vision.

"Think they will come for us?" Jorge asked Franklin.

"Hard to figure. They weren't acting right."

"They weren't attacking. But they were attracted to the woman."

"Maybe they wanted her baby."

Jorge thought of Marina and what he would do if Zapheads took her. The near-hysterical woman was inside, being comforted by Rosa. Her baby was safe, and Jorge vowed to help Franklin defend the compound to the death. This was their homeland now.

Franklin ran a hoe handle through a metal spool of barbed wire as Jorge slipped on a pair of thick leather gloves. He climbed a short ladder and pulled a strand of the wire across the top of the wooden gate as Franklin clipped the wire with cutters. He wound it among the planks in big, loose loops so that anyone who tried to climb the gate would become entangled in the barbs.

Franklin had placed a series of spotlights in the trees on the perimeter of the compound. He'd told Jorge they wouldn't burn long off the battery system due to their high wattage, but the light was an additional security measure if they needed it.

"You were prepared for defense, not just survival?" Jorge

asked as they gathered the tools.

"A lot more going on up here than just me," Franklin said as they headed for the faint reddish glow from inside the cabin.

Jorge found himself looking forward to sitting around the cozy, candlelit interior with more people to care for. He'd agreed to take the first watch tonight, even though Franklin had declared his alarm systems up to the task. "What do you mean?"

"The parkway. That's one hell of a road. Government pitched it as a scenic route for the tourists, but it was built to hold up to heavy truck traffic. *Real* heavy traffic."

"I don't understand."

"I'm not the only one who thought this was a good place to hole up. Some in the Preparedness Network believed there's a secret military bunker up here. Makes sense. You've got a road built to withstand aerial bombing in an area with no real industrial value."

"Is that why you brought me and my family to your compound, and why you're willing to bring others?"

Franklin stopped just outside the cabin. From inside came the low murmur of women talking.

"A real survivalist knows it's not just about surviving," Franklin said, squinting up at the aurora that was almost bright enough to read a book by, if not for the muting effects of the haze. "It's about *living*. Just having food, supplies, and ammunition won't do you any good in the long run, because what kind of life is that? You hide in a bunker for twenty years, all alone?"

Jorge hadn't considered survival as anything beyond the next breath. Each day since the solar storms had been a challenge, but he had to admit that he felt more vibrant and his senses –all his senses—were keener and more vivid than they had been since childhood. Perhaps the prospect of losing the world had imbued it with a deeper mystery and richness.

"It's about community," Franklin continued. "Getting along and building something better from the ruins."

"You said others would be coming."

"I hope so, son."

Jorge didn't know how to respond to the term of familiarity. Thus, he ignored it. "We better see how the woman and her baby are."

Franklin set the tools beside the cabin door, although he kept his rifle slung over his shoulder. They entered to cheerful warmth, with a small fire crackling in the woodstove and several candles ringing the room. Jorge smiled at Marina. She seemed to have grown up in the past week, fully healthy, and now was on the verge of womanhood herself. But Marina didn't smile back. Her face was grave, lines creasing her forehead and the sides of her mouth.

She and Rosa were flanking the woman, who was nursing her baby.

The woman looked up. "Thank you," she said, beaming with a mother's wistful glow. "Thank you for saving us. For saving *him*."

She pulled the child away from her breast and turned it toward them. Franklin sucked in a hard chuff of air. Jorge's chest grew icy and numb.

The child was perfectly formed, its little hands balled into fists, a tuft of wispy hair on the large skull. It was a beautiful little boy.

Except the eyes.

They sparkled with a strange, unnatural glitter, reflecting the candlelight like broken mirrors.

Jorge had seen those eyes before. On the men who had tried to kill him, and on the parkway down by the RV.

The child was a Zaphead.

CHAPTER THIRTY-FOUR

Stephen coughed again, sending a trickle of unease through Rachel. What if the boy got sick? *Really* sick?

DeVontay had dragged a couple of extra mattresses into a top-floor bedroom that had belonged to one of the dead boys. Then he'd gone outside to look for a shovel, saying he wanted to give the family a proper burial in exchange for their hospitality. Stephen didn't fall for it, and Rachel wondered if DeVontay would simply stack the bodies in one of the barn stalls like so much cordwood.

Stephen was bundled under blankets in the dead boy's bed, staring at the ceiling. Rachel had found an oil lamp, and its soft, bobbing glow send spooky shadows along the ceiling.

"Will the boy's ghost come back?" Stephen asked. "Will he be mad that I played with his train set?"

Rachel brushed Stephen's uneven bangs from his forehead, casually testing his temperature. "Of course not. He's up in heaven, playing with brand-new toys."

"Is his family there?"

"I'm sure they are, honey."

"Does he have a doggie?"

"It wouldn't be heaven without a dog, would it?" Rachel glanced at the window and the darkness that settled over the forest. DeVontay had left the pistol with her and promised tomorrow they would take some target practice with the rifle.

They'd silently agreed they would stay at the farmhouse for the time being. Rachel was excited about the prospects of the garden and the meals she could prepare, and DeVontay said the place could be easily defended if necessary. "Good lines of sight," he'd said, as if that didn't mean having plenty of time to shoot anyone who tried to approach.

"I miss Mommy," Stephen said, staring at the shadows that flickered and danced on the white ceiling. "I hope she's in heaven, too."

"It wouldn't be heaven without a mommy, either," Rachel said. She smiled. Stephen coughed again, and something in his chest rattled.

Just the barn dust.

"Tomorrow, we'll gather some apples," she said. "And maybe play in the creek. I saw a little boat in the closet. Think that will be fun?"

Stephen nodded and coughed again.

Rachel thought of the three bodies hanging in the barn. She wondered if the farmer had hung his pigs there, skinned and salted for curing.

How long had After preyed on the farmer's mind? How many times did he tell his children everything would be okay? How hard had it been to shoot his wife after she'd changed?

Stephen coughed again, twice.

What courage it must have taken. The farmer must have truly believed a better life, a better world, awaited them. Faith into action, love into purpose.

She rummaged in her backpack and found it. "How are you feeling now, Stephen?"

He rubbed his eyes. "Sleepy. And tired."

She was tired, too.

She would tell him to think of his mother, waiting for him. Or would that scare him? What if he pictured his mother the way she'd been in the hotel, lying on the bed with the flies roiling around her mouth? What if that stench carried with him to the next After?

She recalled the pharmacist's instructions. First, the antiemetic to prevent him from throwing up. And then, the

Nembutal.

A glass of clean, filtered water from the creek sat on the desk beside the bed. Given his small size, three pills would probably be enough.

She bowed her head and closed her eyes. *Dear Lord, is this merciful?*

For the first time in her life, she felt the question was issuing forth into the deep vacuum of endless, empty space. A phone call with nothing on the other end of the line.

She had never been so frightened.

"Here, honey, I have something to make that cough go away," she said, somehow managing to keep the tremor out of her voice, although her fingers shook as she twisted open the pill bottle.

"Where's DeVontay?" he asked.

"He'll be here in a minute. Take this, honey."

She gave him the antiemetic, which he swallowed with a grimace. "Yuck. That's gross."

"Drink this." She handed him the glass of water and he drank.

She was about to give him three of the pills when she looked into his face, hoping to see some sign of peace and acceptance. Instead, she saw Chelsea's funeral face, the pale and powdered baby-doll skin with eyes forever closed.

She tightened her fist around the pills and then flung them toward the corner of the bedroom, where they rolled across the hardwood floor.

"You're right," she said. "Medicine's yucky."

Downstairs, the door slammed, and DeVontay called up the stairs.

"How long do I get to sleep in the boy's bed?" Stephen asked, drowsy now.

"For a few days," she said. "Then we're heading to the

mountains where it's safe."

"I thought we were going to Mi'sippi."

"We'll get there," she said. "We've still got a long way to go."

THE END

Scott Nicholson is the international bestselling author of more than 20 books. He lives in the Blue Ridge Mountains of North Carolina, where he tends an organic garden, strums guitar, and practices armchair Taoism.
Visit him at www.AuthorScottNicholson.com or email hauntedcomputerbooks@gmail.com.

<u>OTHER BOOKS BY SCOTT NICHOLSON</u>

Solom #1: The Scarecrow
Solom #2: The Narrow Gate
Solom #3: The Preacher
Liquid Fear
Chronic Fear
After #1: The Shock
After #2: The Echo
After #3: Milepost 291
Disintegration
The Red Church
Drummer Boy
McFall
The Harvest
Speed Dating with the Dead
The Skull Ring
The Home
Creative Spirit
October Girls
Scattered Ashes
Monster's Ink
Thank You for the Flowers
They Hunger
Bad Blood (Spider #1)
Cursed (with J.R. Rain)
Dirt
Grave Conditions

38057874R00166

Made in the USA
Lexington, KY
20 December 2014